FIG TREE JOHN

FIG TREE JOHN

By Edwin Corle

LIVERIGHT NEW YORK

2.987654321
SBN: 87140-518-0 (cloth)
      87140-046-4 (paper)
Library of Congress Catalog Card Number: 79-148665

MANUFACTURED IN THE UNITED STATES OF AMERICA

To

M. D. C.

CONTENTS

Fig Tree John is not only one of our greatest novels about the predicament of the American Indian, it is also one of the best studies of the white man's weaknesses as perceived by the red man. Hence Edwin Corle's little classic is far more "relevant" for us today than when it first appeared in the 1930s. For now the white man, somewhat humbled by his own follies, is almost willing to learn something from other ways of life, almost ready to see himself as the "ofay-watchers" have always seen him.

Agocho—the Apache brave who is the main character in *Fig Tree John*—is shocked by the white man's low regard for the terrain he lives on, by his reckless efforts to bend Nature to his immediate needs, by his willingness to make love in ugly, "unnatural" structures. Datilye, Apache wise man, regards the whites as doomed—and not even aware of it—because each one is "trying to get more than the others" and cannot "see beyond his own covetous desire and learn that this very desire is making him do everything wrong." And N'Chai Chidn, or Juanitio, or Johnny—his three names symbolize the cultural collisions Corle is concerned with—winces at the white man's obscene need to verbalize every experience. The Indian characters, by contrast with their white "superiors," strive for communion with themselves, for inner balance, and they feel much more at home in the Cosmos.

These Indian criticisms of white culture, accurately reflected in Corle's fiction, foreshadow our own blackest self-diagnoses. Today our psychologists moan that the average (white) man hasn't heard from himself in a long time. Our scientists suspect we have really fouled our nest beyond cleansing. Our artists portray us as disconnected from our deepest sources of vitality. Our rationalistic approach has at last come up with some shibboleths and slogans—like Environment, Ecology, Earth Day, Body Language, Language of Silence—for what the Indian always knew, totally and plainly, to be the only way of life, practised Every Day.

These observations digested, we appreciate Edwin Corle as the kind of writer Marshall McLuhan has in mind when he describes the artist as a prophet. "Art as radar acts as 'an early alarm system,' enabling us to discover social and and psychic targets in lots of time to prepare to cope with them. . . . Knowledge of this simple fact is now needed for human survival." When Corle first identified our targets, we did indeed still have lots of time. Even so, in the 1930s John Collier, President Franklin D. Roosevelt's Commissioner of Indian Affairs, saw only a slim chance (he called it *The Long Hope*) that the white man would ever learn what the Indian has to teach: how to survive in harmony with inner and outer Nature.

Of course, Edwin Corle has not written a major novel simply by catching the right ideas by the tail in their cubhood. Fortunately, his themes manifest themselves in superbly sustained narration; in swift, credible characterization; in sensuous respect for techniques; in language cut to the bone and of necessity fleshed out by the reader's responses; in symbolism and irony so intrinsic as to reach us subliminally.

•

Possessed of what we call "artistic temperament," Edwin Corle had this advantage over most white men (an advantage every Indian would regard as his birth-right): he felt impelled to discover his own nature, to be true to it, to comprehend (but not violate) the relation between man and his environment.

One day in 1920, then fourteen and en route from his native New Jersey to the West Coast, Edwin Corle* looked through a Pullman car window out across the Salton Sea. This large body of dead water had been created in the year of Corle's birth when the Colorado River broke channel, raged over into southern California, and covered hundreds of square miles of below-sea-level desert. As we shall see, the Salton Sea took on profound personal and cosmic significance for Corle. He went to high school in Hollywood, studied English composition under an inspiring teacher, Professor Herbert F. Allen, and in his graduate work at Yale, served an apprenticeship in playwriting under the renowned Professor George Pierce Baker. After a period of travel, he returned to the Southwest because (as Lawrence Clark Powell puts it) away from his homeland "a Southwesterner sickens for his dry and wrinkled land where 'sky determines.'" Corle earned his living as a radio writer doing occasional play-doctoring stints at MGM and RKO studios.

In his spare time, he would drive through the San Gor-

*Pronounced "KORL"

gonio Pass, down around the Salton Sea, through scrub growth and rolling sand hills, into the Imperial Valley. From each trip he returned with rich materials for stories about Mojave Desert people. His "Amethyst" was accepted by *Atlantic Monthly* in 1932, and the following year Liveright published *Mojave, a Book of Stories*. Corle was well represented in Edward J. O'Brien's *Best Short Stories of 1934*, and his short tales were soon appearing regularly in commercial magazines like *New Yorker, Harper's, Esquire*, as well as in "little mags" like *Prairie Schooner*, and quarterlies like *Yale Review*.

Corle was obsessed with one desert personality—Fig Tree John—who would not fold himself neatly into the tight structure of a short story. So the twenty-eight-year-old writer felt impelled to try the novel form. He had first seen the name Fig Tree John on a road sign near the west shore of the Salton Sea, pointing toward a turbid waterhole where Fig Tree had lived in exile from his people. After learning that Fig Tree and his wife were dead, and their son and his wife gone away, Corle roamed the desert from Yuma to Mecca seeking information about Fig Tree, the man and myth. Edward Carr, a rancher whose land adjoined Fig Tree's claim, felt certain that Fig Tree was not from any California tribe but rather from the Apache peoples. This tied in with Corle's information that Fig Tree assumed the right to share his son's wife: this was an Apache custom. Corle now visited Apache reservations in Arizona and New Mexico, concluding his research in the Southwest Museum in Los Angeles under the active guidance of a distinguished ethnologist, Frederick Webb Hodge. (Later Hodge inscribed a copy of his *History of Hawikuk:* "To Edwin Corle who knows the soul of the

Indian. . . .") Corle decided that his own re-creation of Fig Tree John would be a White River Apache (in his own tongue called Agocho) from central Arizona, home of the wildest Athapascan people, including that master of sweeping guerilla warfare, Geronimo.

Corle's research justified his determination to use Fig Tree John as a symbol of Southwestern Indian culture, described by Powell as "religious and ritualistic, uncompromising, moral, and doomed to extinction at the hands of the white race which it could not comprehend and which in turn was too materially busy and nervously impatient to try to understand [the red race]." After his personal observations, interviewing, research, and themes had all fused into a cogent story line, Corle produced the finished manuscript in one sustained twelve-week burst of creativity ending just before Christmas 1934.

Oliver LaFarge, already famous as author of another classic Indian novel, *Laughing Boy*, was one of the first to acclaim *Fig Tree John* when it appeared in September 1935. Writing for *Saturday Review*, LaFarge noted that Corle had taken "two of the great possible themes—the functioning of the intellect in savagery and the adjustment of the Indian to a white world—salted them with action, spiced them with a sound love element, set them against a peculiar . . . background which throws them into sharp relief, and made the whole into a sensitive and delightful story." *Fig Tree John* was well-received in a British edition the following year; a portion of it was featured in Joseph Jackson's 1944 anthology of Western writing, *Continent's End;* an abridged paperback version appeared in 1952 under the dubious title of *Apache Devil.* And a special limited edition, with spirited illustrations by Don Perceval and a colorful "regionalist" foreword by Powell, was issued in 1955, one year before Edwin Corle—by then author of fifteen books, married, father of a ten-year-old girl—suddenly died in his prime.

It was Corle's novels and stories—along with LaFarge's various writings and Collier's *The Long Hope*—that taught my generation how to respect the Indian's life-style, especially his way of enfolding himself in Nature, something we were consequently better able to appreciate when we camped in places like Mesa Verde:

> *Into the cracks in the tableland*
> *They tucked their pueblos, small adjustments*
> *In the cliffline, nests of clay and stick,*
> *Below the scorched mesa, embracing*
> *The sandstone damp with sea memory,*
> *They molded their cool cells for the drape*
> *Of loosened limb, for the shape of love.*
>
> *They sketched their rooms in free hand: floors lift*
> *Like strata, walls surprise like outcrops,*
> *Bricks touched like spilled rocks that drifted*
> *Into status. Here they rarely dreamed*
> *Nightmares of the right angle, or schemed*
> *The tautest distance between two points,*
> *Or heard the pressures of perfect cubes.* *

•

Considering Corle's artistic strengths, I especially admire the way he structures *Fig Tree John*. Its form, con-

*Walter James Miller, "Cliff Dwellers at Mesa Verde," *Western Humanities Review*, Winter 1959. © 1959 by University of Utah.

tent, function are virtually identical. At first glance, *Fig Tree John* seems to be entirely dramatic in form, but actually it proves to be highly musical in its architectonics.

The tale is dramatic in structure insofar as Corle begins near the crisis, and then opens the floodgates of the past so that the current sweeps us forward again to the climax. That opening scene, seething with quiet, is the perfect starting point. We see the now almost legendary Apache brave as he appears to a white neighbor in 1928: withdrawn, bitter, half-alive, squatting in a junkheap of whitemen's artifacts, but able to strike like lightning out of his lethargy and to return at once to reverie. The Apache is expecting the return of his son. Their stormy life together presumably is the theme of the Apache's motionless meditation; his rumination takes him back to 1906 (the opening of the long middle section of the novel) when once on this very spot, he enjoyed a profound, pulsing unity with all Nature. But his son, born here, loved here, has defiantly mingled with the whites, a defiance the exhausted old man now believes he has crushed. Young Johnny's return home brings the story to its tragicomic resolution; in the third section, Johnny chugs his axe-battered, hoodless Ford out onto the white man's highway to join his Mexican wife about to deliver his child.

So much for the formal lessons, the neat *in medias res* structure, so well learned in Professor Baker's class. Far more interesting are those structural devices I call musical, which Corle developed for himself. In some scenes, Corle blends physical action with awesome inner search, like a composer using a lively treble theme over a slow bass undertow. Again, Corle renders many scenes, apparently random-tandem in nature, as statements of a basic motif. Agocho, waiting for a storekeeper in a white town, experiences a casual, momentary sexual interest in a white woman. This adumbrates first his son's total attraction to a white girl, and later Agocho's own ambivalent attraction toward the same woman.

Usually Corle restates a motif with ironic overtones. Agocho regrets he cannot include, in his son's lonely puberty rites, the ritual of the running-chase after Apache virgins. But when young Johnny asserts his love for Maria, it is unwittingly consummated in Apache fashion as Johnny chases her over the desert sands. Sometimes Corle achieves his musical balances with quiet variations, as when Johnny, no longer regarding himself as Apache, performs an Apache burial just as his father had taught him. More often Corle strikes a balance through extreme contrast: for example, between Agocho's successful rescue of a white man from death in the desert and Agocho's fruitless pursuit of white murderers over the same sands. Musical patterns in Corle help explain why such an apparently bare-as-bones narrative can keep its tight grip on the reader's imagination.

Like many novelists learning their trade in the naturalist tradition, Corle almost entirely eschews the formal figure of speech, preferring instead the stock, basic symbol. Agocho feels strong affinity with the Colorado River, with its placid surface and passionate depths; he regards with fond reverence the brownish-purple fruit of the fig-tree, which, transplanted to new terrain, finds new roots and flourishes with graceful fecundity. "Fig Tree John," as a grateful white man senses Agocho should be dubbed, can be struck by tenderness or rage or an anguished blend of both at the sight of a white dress (Corle used this color symbolism five years before Richard Wright published *Native Son*). And Agocho feels a deep, unarticulated delight in removing from the white man's lawn a sun-dial, that meticulous measure of the white man's mechanical, outer time. Corle is exploring this aspect of the Indian character many years before Erich Fromm is to tell us how urgent it is that we relearn *The Forgotten Language*.

•

Corle is never blind to the weaknesses and faults of Apache life. For one thing, we easily infer that for the woman, in Fig Tree's time at least, it was better to be born white than red. Maria exerts greater control over her own life with Johnny than his mother Kai-a could exert in her relationship with Agocho. Conversely, Johnny probably will enjoy a greater challenge from his white wife than Agocho could have expected from his red woman; for Agocho's male-supremacism makes him a lonely creature in his own *kowa*, while Johnny can hope for intimacy in his domestic situation.

True to our definitions of tragedy, the Indian's greatest weaknesses stemmed directly from his virtues. His preference for blending himself into—while still preserving— Nature made him vulnerable to a technology blandly willing to squander, violate, and pollute. His spiritual traditions—which taught him that in communing with himself he was in touch with ultimate reality, and that his own dignity was part of the cosmic pattern—rendered him helpless before a people more concerned with power than with potence. Agocho's simple ethics, his patient waiting for signs, insights, and certainties, obviously served him well in a homogeneous culture but cannot cope with the swift complexity of a clash of cultures.

Portraying both cultures at their best and their worst, Corle makes no judgments at all. Like James Fenimore Cooper, Oliver LaFarge, and John Collier, Edwin Corle simply makes us regret that these two great peoples never meshed their talents while both of them were still in their prime. How many such chances do we have?

WALTER JAMES MILLER

Professor of English
New York University

PART I
1928

FIG TREE JOHN

1928

THE white man turned from the sandy beach of the inland body of dead water, crossed an alkali patch where nothing could grow, and struck off into the greasewood. The Salton Sea was immediately hidden from his view, for as soon as he was free of the alkali soil the greasewood bushes and the mesquite grew in abundance, and the mesquite was slightly higher than his head. He threaded his way through the bushes, trying to follow a vague trail and constantly losing it.

Every few minutes he would stop and look about. The ground sloped slightly upward away from the beach and he kept following the rising ground. Once he stopped and called, "Fig Tree."

There was no answer. The white man moved on. He knew that he was near his destination but that he had chosen the most difficult way of finding it. He owned a date ranch about a mile to the north and he had walked from his place down the beach of the Salton Sea to find a water hole belonging to his neighbor, Fig Tree John. It would have been much easier to drive down the highway that ran parallel to the beach about a mile in from the sea. Then he could easily have taken the sandy trail from the highway through the greasewood and mesquite and arrived at Fig Tree's with no trouble at all.

3

The water hole was between the highway and the Salton Sea, but was only a few hundred yards in from the beach, and the white man had thought he could locate it without much trouble by taking the beach route, but instead, he found himself wandering around in the greasewood like a tenderfoot.

He stood still again and called, "Fig Tree!" but got no answer. Then he called, "Johnny Mack!" and still no answer.

It was all a waste of time and more trouble than it was worth. He stood perfectly still and faced the west, looking very carefully at the Santa Rosa Mountains on the horizon. He considered the peaks for a moment and then decided that the fault was his. He had not gone far enough down the beach before turning off into the brush. To rectify this, and to save the trouble of returning to the beach again, he struck off to the southeast through the greasewood maze.

Another two hundred yards brought him to the edge of a small clearing exactly as he had estimated by taking his bearings from the mountain peaks. And even before he saw the clearing he knew that he was on the right track. For mingled with the pungent creosote odor of the greasewood came that stronger indefinable smell of Indian. He pushed through the bushes and looked across the thirty yards of open ground.

There was the water hole in the middle of the clearing, and around it several drooping cottonwood trees and beyond them a dozen fig trees. There was a shack beside the cottonwoods and all about it was a litter of trash—boards, boxes, papers and indefinable refuse. Near the shack was a small hut, or kowa, and before the hut, in the sun, sat Fig Tree John. A gray mongrel dog appeared from somewhere and came scampering toward the white man. It gave a few lazy yelps and then contented itself with sniffing at his heels, darting away when he paused, and then returning and sniffing again.

The white man called, "Hello, Fig Tree," but the Indian continued to sit still and paid him no attention. The white man moved across the clearing toward the still figure, watching him carefully as he approached.

"Fig Tree," he called again, and he grinned slightly because to him there was something ironic in the still figure sitting in the sun. Fig Tree John was a name with legend behind it. Romantic imaginations had built up stories and traditions about him—a White River Apache, a great chief, the smartest Indian in the Colorado desert, a killer of five white men, a dangerous hombre, another Geronimo—all had been said of Fig Tree John and probably none of it was true except that he was an Apache, and the white man wasn't sure that he was a White River Apache; he might have been a San Carlos or a Mescalero. Fig Tree himself had never been explicit.

This decrepit figure sitting in the sun, nearly deaf, nearly blind, unable to read or write, unaware of the coming of strangers, was anything but the great red warrior that legend persisted in making him. He was more of a pitiable old man than a fascinating figure of pioneer days, and the white man smiled at him as he squatted in the sun in a state of coma rather than consciousness.

When the white man was about ten feet away he saw that Fig Tree's lips were moving. He was talking to himself, mumbling some unintelligible jargon with a stupid concentration that made him unaware of the presence of friend or foe. The white man had the impression that he had been squatting there for a long time talking meaningless words to himself in his seventh age of man.

The scene surprised the white man. He hadn't realized that Fig Tree was that far gone. But now that he stood quietly before the Indian and looked at him appraisingly he appeared smaller than when the white man had seen him last. He seemed to be shrinking with age. Fig Tree had never been a tall man, but still, the figure that the white man recalled had had a vigorous stalwart body that had been capable of great feats of brute strength, and now his jacket of coyote hide and his dirty khaki pants looked too large for him, and the muscles of his face were sagging so that there were many lines and wrinkles.

Although the white man stood still and watched and did not move a muscle, his presence slowly made itself known to Fig Tree's consciousness. The Indian stopped mumbling, looked at the shadow of the white man on the ground before him, followed it to the white man's feet, and then looked up at his body.

"Hello, Fig Tree, I came to see you," said the white man in a loud voice. "You don't get up my way any more so I took the trouble to come down here. I've got a letter for Johnny Mack."

The Indian looked at the white man and seemed not to recognize him. His expression did not change and the white man wondered if Fig Tree had lost his reason. It had been almost a year since they had seen each other but he and Fig Tree had been neighbors for ten years, and while they were never good friends they were always on speaking terms. Fig Tree's black eyes looked up at the white man steadily without any reaction as if they were looking at empty space. Then, very slowly, he lowered his head and stirred slightly.

"Johnny Mack not here," he said.

"Isn't he living down here?"

Fig Tree said nothing.

"Do you want this letter? The post mark says Banning. Johnny Mack must have a friend up in Banning." Fig Tree looked up and reached out a brown hand toward the envelope that the white man held before him.

"Johnny Mack come here," said Fig Tree. "Johnny Mack *stay here.*"

He accentuated the "stay here" and the tone of his voice was belligerent.

"That's what I thought," said the white man, bending over to speak close to Fig Tree's ear. "Tell him I might give him a job for a couple of weeks. Pretty soon time to pollenize the dates. Job for Johnny Mack."

"Johnny Mack not here," said Fig Tree.

"That's all right. Tell him I want to see him—give him a job."

Fig Tree took the letter and looked at it. The address on the envelope read:

MR. JOHNNY MACK
CARE FIG TREE JOHN
CARE MR. PAUL
MECCA, CALIFORNIA
PLEAS FORRWARD

Fig Tree scanned these directions, turned the writing upside down and scanned it some more, and then looked at the back of the envelope. Finding nothing there, he placed it beside him and continued to sit in the sun.

The white man looked from Fig Tree to the little shack and its untidy setting, at the muddy water hole, and at the dozen fig trees laden with unripe figs. The only sound was the hum of hundreds of flies constantly circling in the air, lighting on everything, and then circling again. The white man was debating whether to return by way of the highway or to take the shorter route through the greasewood and return by the beach of the Salton Sea. The gray mongrel sniffed at his feet and got in his way when he tried to move.

Fig Tree, still sitting, reached over and picked up a stone as large as an orange, and with a sudden movement, startling in contrast to his lethargy, he hurled the stone with terrific force at the dog, emitting an unearthly yell as he did so.

The white man was startled and he turned suddenly. The stone hit the dog in the ribs. It gave a yelp of pain and raced around the side of the shack out of sight. Fig Tree, pulled off balance by the effort of hurling the stone from a seated position, righted himself and resumed his comatose state.

The white man looked at him. It seemed impossible that there was any activity left in the old boy, but his arm was good and his aim was perfect. The thing had been done with lightning-like accuracy. The white man laughed.

"Fig Tree, you're a funny old devil, do you know that?"

"Johnny Mack come here when sun go down," said Fig Tree. "Give him letter."

"That's right," said the white man, looking at Fig Tree and smiling broadly. He really liked this unaccountable old sphinx and he squatted down beside him in spite of the odor and the heat and the flies, intending to visit for a few minutes before tramping back to his ranch. After all, he hadn't seen Fig Tree for a long time, and while they had quarreled once or twice and had had difficulties over land boundaries in the early days, he felt a kind of neighborly affection for the old man.

"Don't forget. Tell Johnny Mack I've got a job for him. Savvy, Fig Tree?"

Fig Tree grunted. It appeared to be much more of an effort than hurling a rock at a dog.

"I don't suppose there's any use askin' you what Johnny's doing down here, is there?"

"No," said Fig Tree.

"Doesn't he want to work any more?"

"No," said Fig Tree.

"Well, you tell Johnny what I told you, anyway," said the white man. "I can use Johnny again. He works pretty good for me."

"See much money?" asked Fig Tree who was beginning to feel a little more cordial and who now was willing to acknowledge the white man's presence by asking a question and looking in his direction.

"Nope. It's not very good."

"Huh," said Fig Tree.

"How are your figs these days?"

"Figs pretty damned nice soon. Nice hot," said Fig

Tree, making a slight wave of his hand toward the sun.

The white man leaned back against a box and looked around at the junk scattered about Fig Tree's shack. There were some bottles, an automobile radiator cap, two lanterns—one of them broken—a bucket, a pick, some old newspapers stained yellow by the sun, a metate, and under some sticks of wood part of what had once been a metal sun-dial. The white man reached over and pushed the sticks away and pulled the sun-dial over beside him.

"Well, for God's sake," he said.

He held the sun-dial in his lap, and he gave Fig Tree a long accusatory look. Fig Tree ignored it.

"Well, I'll be damned," said the white man. "Why you old bastard. It's been over a year."

He held the sun-dial in his hands and examined it carefully. The graduated metal plane was easily readable, but the top of the style was broken off, making the instrument useless.

"Fig Tree, where did you get this?"

"No savvy," said Fig Tree.

"No savvy, eh? Well I savvy well enough. I savvy damned well enough. You stole it out of Mrs. Paul's cactus garden after it had been there a week, and you savvy that damned well."

Fig Tree gave no response.

"I don't know what in hell comes over you, Fig Tree. There's a lot of things that have disappeared off my place and I know who picks 'em up, too. Now I asked you if you saw that sun-dial when it disappeared a year ago and you said 'No,' didn't you?"

Fig Tree looked at the broken sun-dial and then he looked at the white man.

"Got tobacco?" he asked.

"Tobacco, hell! I ought to give you a good kick in the pants. I paid ten dollars for that damned thing for Sarah's garden. What the hell good has it been to you?"

Fig Tree looked away, dismissing the whole business.

"Well it's no good now," said the white man. "Rusted and busted. I won't even take it home, because if I do, Sarah will be so damned mad at you that neither you or Johnny Mack better show up on the ranch again."

He tossed it to one side and scrambled to his feet. Fig Tree didn't answer or even look at the white man.

"Now Fig Tree, get this in your head. If you or Johnny Mack ever take anything off my place again I'm going to put you in jail. And if I don't see you for another year, that's just fine. Now you give Johnny Mack his letter and tell him to come to work to-morrow—savvy all that, Fig Tree?"

Fig Tree looked at the white man. The wrinkles about his mouth might have broken into a smile or a sneer, but they did neither. The white man felt that those black eyes narrowed, almost imperceptibly, to a look that was at once challenging and defiant. Fig Tree stared at him with eyes that asked no quarter and offered none. He made no move at all. The white man stared back at Fig Tree, but presently he grinned and turned away.

"I can't waste the whole day with you," he said. "So long, you old bastard."

He walked across the clearing, found a trail through the greasewood that led to the beach of the Salton Sea

and disappeared from Fig Tree's world. As he tramped
through the brush he smiled at the memory, of the old
devil. Thief, liar, warrior, loafer—he was all of them. But
the old patriarch was slipping fast. Old age had him now
and it wouldn't be long before Fig Tree John would be
entirely a tradition of the Colorado desert. Still, there
was hell in the old boy yet. He didn't like that bawling
out he got. That was plain to see. He might have done
something about that in the old days. Those eyes of his.
But, shoo—he's just an Indian.

The white man came out on the beach of the inland
sea. He turned northward and began his mile hike up to
his own ranch. But all the way there his mind kept returning to that brown figure, squatting in the sun, thinking, mumbling, waiting. Waiting for what? Waiting to
die, that's all. Fig Tree's practically dead now. It won't
be long for him. You're done for, Fig Tree. Done for,
and everybody will be damn glad of it if the truth were
known. You can go see your wife again. You can claim
all of heaven and hell this time. And maybe you'll be
able to get away with it there. Fence jumper. Yes, everybody'll be glad of it. Johnny Mack, and Maria and everybody. Wonder what was in that letter of Johnny Mack's.
Too bad you can't read, Fig Tree, you old coot. Well
it won't make any difference to you now. Not a bit.
Not the least bit.

Presently the white man came to his own property. He
turned in from the beach, skirted the salt-brush, and
walked into the grove of date palms, heading toward
the ranch house.

PART II
1906-1928

1906-1928

Chapter I

TWO Indians rode into Yuma from the east. Although the man and his squaw and their horses were dusty, the journey had not been a hard one. They had been following the valley of the Gila River all day and at sunset they reached the point where it joined the Colorado.

The town of Yuma lay before them and they rode stolidly into it, displaying no interest in the white civilization, in stores, signs, or saloons, or any of the people in the streets. Eight days before they had seen Phoenix which was much larger with many people and at first sight really impressive. Yuma was just another white man's town and they were all more or less alike.

They passed through the main street, for in 1906 there was only one, and drew up their horses near the east bank of the Colorado River. Across the river was California, a name which neither of them had ever heard.

Other Indians were camped there, mostly Yumans, but a few Apache-Mojaves, often called Yavapais. The two strangers dismounted and prepared to make camp. All of their possessions were carried on the two horses, and the woman set about unpacking the animals while the man looked at the Indians already in camp and decided that they were of friendly tribes but not blood brothers. An elderly Yuman came over and spoke to him and they managed to carry on a conversation. The

15

stranger told the Yuman that he was called Agocho Koh
Tli-chu, which means Red Fire Bird, and that he and
his wife were Apaches, riding west from the White River
country which had been their home.

"Agocho—but white men call me John," he said.

The Yuman told Agocho that he was a friend to
White River Apaches and that he and his squaw were
welcome to camp on Yuman land. Agocho explained
that they would build no kowa because they were traveling toward the setting sun each day. Apaches, when they
travel, and they are a nomadic tribe, seldom stay in one
place long enough to build any kind of a wickiup. They
merely clear a small space of ground, spread some arm-
fuls of grass over it if there is any grass, and throw a few
blankets on top of that and that is home for a night.
The Yuman looked at Agocho's young wife with a critical eye and remarked that it would be necessary for her
to stay in one place before many days.

The contour of her body bespoke some six months'
pregnancy, but her condition retarded none of her
preparations for camp. She removed the blankets that
covered the pack and then lifted off the burden basket
containing food and cooking implements. Next she removed the water bottles, and then, from across the
saddle seat, the cumbersome rawhide carryall that contained family supplies and extra clothing. She was about
twenty years old and was her husband's youngest and
favorite wife. Agocho was probably forty-three or forty-
four, and while he clung to the polygamous privileges
of his tribe he never traveled with more than one wife,
and in the last year he had come to like this girl so
much that he rarely saw his two older women. He never

called her by her given name, Bi-Tli-Kai Nalin, which
means White Deer's Daughter and is too long, but always
shortened it to Kai-a, which has no meaning, but is
more practical.

Agocho and the Yuman were soon joined by a Yavapai, and the three of them squatted on the ground and
talked while Kai-a continued preparations for the evening meal. They spoke of food, of the soil, of dances and
ceremonies. Occasionally the Yavapai joked. Agocho
showed them his rifle which he had had only a few
weeks. He was proud to demonstrate its fine points and
they were impressed. The three of them were completely
free and at ease with one another and the aloofness
and silence that they maintained in the presence of
white people was entirely melted away.

Neither of the Indians asked Agocho why he was
traveling, why he had left his own country, where he
was going, or how long he intended to stay. He didn't
volunteer any of this information but he did ask about
the country to the west, across the Colorado River. And
he learned that there were many miles of desert with a
few springs of doubtful water and a population of jackrabbits, rattlesnakes, and coyotes. Beyond this desert,
but so far away a man could not see it, was a range of
mountains, and beyond that a country that was said to
be full of white men and many cities, though neither the
Yuman nor the Yavapai had ever been there to see for
themselves and possibly it was all a big lie.

Then the Yavapai, who was a young man, told of a
big joke on the white men. The Yuman knew of it already, but it was a tale that always pleased him and he
enjoyed it again.

According to the Yavapai, some white men had tried to grow things in the middle of that very desert that lay to the west. They had gone to the unbelievable trouble of digging ditches and diverting the water from the Colorado River so that it would flow into the desert land instead of into the sea. Of course nobody but a white man would ever attempt such a preposterous scheme, but like all of their kind, when once they started something like that they kept working away at it day after day until they got what they wanted, no matter if it took a year or two or three.

So what did they do but send the waters of the Colorado into their ditches and try to make it go where it wasn't supposed to go at all. And if an Apache doesn't know it, any Yuman or any Mojave can tell him that interfering with the river is bad medicine. The River Spirit often gets in a temper and he is best let alone. But these stupid white men never thought of that at all. They caught the River Spirit by surprise and they turned him into the desert before he knew it. They were smart enough in their way because the desert land is lower than the river, and once they got it through their canals to the desert, it flowed that way of its own accord.

But of course the River Spirit was terribly angry and he went the white men one better. They wanted him to go into the desert instead of his own way, so he showed them a thing or two they wouldn't forget.

When the Yavapai got that far with the tale he stopped and laughed, and the Yuman laughed with him. Naturally Agocho wanted to hear the river's revenge. So the Yavapai, with great glee, told him how the Colorado went mad and burst its banks, and burst the white men's ditches and flowed into the desert with such force that it flooded the white men's ranches and ruined the crops and wrecked the roads and threatened to destroy the railroad that ran across the desert.

"They wanted the river and they got it!" said the Yavapai.

"They got all of him where they don't want him!" said the Yuman.

Then all three of them laughed at the foolish white men who had received their just punishment for interfering with a Great Spirit.

The Yuman then took up the story and elaborated on the details. He explained that so much water had run into the desert that it had all collected at its lowest part and formed a huge inland sea, so big that the very length of it was a full day's journey for a strong horse. And to make things as bad as possible the River Spirit made this huge body of water bitter and salty and useless. If the white men tried to put machines to work to pump it back to their ditches it would kill everything green and make trees die. And if they tried to drink it, it made them sick. No fish would live in it and no animals came near it. It was a big curse, and a warning from the River Spirit that any time he wanted to he could make a bigger curse. The white men didn't know what to do about it and a lot of them went out and looked at it but all they did was talk a great deal and try to protect the railroad tracks from being washed out as the sea gradually became larger. But the water was there and they couldn't get it out, for not even the white men were smart enough or had charms enough to make the water turn around and run back up hill. Their predicament was very amusing, indeed.

But recently the river had decided that they had been punished enough, and it began to fall. And when it did, the white men went to work to repair their ditches and build up the embankment of the river. They offered the Yuman Indians many jobs of helping control the river by building levees and canals and ditches and reservoirs, but not one Indian would have anything to do with it. The white men thought the Indians were lazy, and they employed other white men and Mexicans, but the Indians were too wise to get mixed up in something like that.

Agocho wanted to know if the big inland sea disappeared as soon as the river became peaceful again. The Yuman explained that it had not, and it had stayed right where it was and never dried up a bit because the waste water from the irrigation ditches continued to feed it. And of course it will never dry up because the River Spirit wants it there just to remind the white men of what he can do. And if they ever find any way to drain it off or get rid of it, why naturally the river will rise up and pour a terrific deluge in there again and make a sea twice as large as it did the first time.

The story of the wise river and the foolish white men interested Agocho very much. He had never heard anything like it and he looked out over the calm, placid Colorado with great fondness. It was a perfectly harmless looking rather sluggish stream, heavy with silt. But now underneath he knew that it had a violent temper and he had great respect for it. As the rays of the setting sun hit the water they changed its muddy color to a blood red.

"Apatieh tu-ndli," he said to the others, by which he meant that the river had the temperamental characteristics of the Apache tribes. The Yuman and the Yavapai said nothing.

Presently Kai-a had supper ready, and her husband came over to the small fire and sat beside it. All during the meal Agocho thought of the trick that the river had played upon the white men. He wanted Kai-a to enjoy it and he thought of telling her the whole story. But then he thought better of it for he knew it would not amuse her as it had him. After all she was a woman without much humor, and she was carrying a child, and she had never seen very much of white men anyway. So Agocho went on with his dinner of the pulp of mescal stalks, and honey from the yucca, and a strong tea made from the dried inner bark of piñon.

When he had eaten enough of this he went over to a large wickiup belonging to the Yavapai who had told him the story. It was dark by now and they sat about a fire before the little shelter. Neither of the men had any tobacco, but the Yavapai brought out a water container which he offered to Agocho. Agocho took a sip and he was pleasantly surprised to find that the container held tizwin instead of water. Tizwin is an intoxicant not unlike beer, but much stronger. Apaches usually drink a great deal of it at a time, for if it stands for more than twelve hours it is unpalatable, and they would rather drink it than waste it.

For over an hour they sat drinking and talking until the liquor was gone. By that time they were both a little drunk, just pleasantly mellow, and of course very great friends. The Yavapai was calling Agocho by name and Agocho called him Long Ears, which was not his name at all, but was the name of Agocho's best friend back in the White River country. Then Agocho wanted to know more about the runaway river, and the Yavapai told him how to make the journey westward across the desert to see the great body of bad water that the river had put there to distress the white men.

"They call him Salton Sea," explained Long Ears.

When Agocho returned to his own camp Kai-a was asleep in the blankets and the fire had died away to a couple of glowing embers. Agocho was a little clumsy in crawling in between the blankets. Kai-a woke up and the odor told her that he had been drinking.

"You smell," she said.

Agocho didn't mind. He chuckled a little to himself as he wrapped the blankets around him.

"At sunrise we shall go see it," he told Kai-a in Apache.

"Go see what?" she asked, sleepily.

"Big lake that made the white men mad," he said.

"Where is it?" asked Kai-a.

"In the middle of the desert," said Agocho. "It's a big lot of water that ran away with the white men's ditches and spoiled all their work. River did it."

None of this made sense to Kai-a.

"Tizwin did it," she said. "You drank a river of tizwin. That's all."

And she turned slightly away from her husband and went back to sleep.

Agocho was still laughing to himself. At last he fell

into a troubled sleep, and all night he had dreams of huge avalanches of water sweeping the white men and all their property in a turmoil before them while a great crowd of Apaches watched and drank and laughed. It was a very happy time.

Chapter II

KAI-A was up before dawn. She moved around the camp, started a fire, and prepared breakfast.

Agocho stirred, sat up, dug the sleep out of his eyes, and then stood up. He took a number of deep breaths through his mouth to cleanse it of the stale taste of tiz-win. He was thirsty, and he took the sumac water bot-tles down to the river. He waded out into the stream, washed himself, drank several draughts of the river water, and refilled the bottles. The eastern sky was getting bright and the one or two remaining stars near the western horizon had all but disappeared. Agocho felt much refreshed and happy as he returned to camp. His two horses had roamed down to the tule weeds at the river's edge and he led them back with him.

Breakfast was ready but Kai-a was not in sight. Agocho sat down and presently she returned, carrying several sprays and branches in one hand and a brownish-purple fruit in the other.

"Figs," she said with a smile.

One of the Yavapai squaws had given her the fruit and the branches and had told her that it was a very practical food which could be used in many ways. If she would plant the branches and sprays in the ground they would grow with no trouble at all and she would have all the figs she wanted. Kai-a soaked the branches

24

in water and then wrapped them in a wet blanket to keep until she had a place to plant them.

They sampled some of the figs for breakfast and they were very pleased with them. As the sun rose Kai-a began to pack things into the burden basket and in a short space of time they were ready to move on.

There was no foot bridge across the Colorado at that time, only a railroad bridge and a flat-boat for a ferry. But this didn't concern Agocho at all. He rode his horse down to the river bank and Kai-a followed on hers. Agocho looked at the river carefully, watching the currents and the ripples as they broke over the numerous sand bars. The river was low in early November and fording it was easy. He decided upon his course and walked his horse into the stream. Kai-a nudged her mount with her knees and it followed.

The current was swifter than Agocho had estimated and the main channel was deeper than it looked. But there was nothing really hazardous about it. By making the horses swim about forty feet of the main channel they reached a sand bar on the other side where the water was hardly deeper than the horses' knees. They followed that sand bar to the opposite bank and the problem of crossing the Colorado was over.

Agocho turned and looked back. He could still see a few of the Yuman wickiups and some wisps of smoke curling up into the sky. The rising sun fell full upon him and made him feel that he was bursting with pent-up energy and good humor. He spoke to Kai-a and told her that the day was a good one, and when the day is a good day the world is a good world. She agreed with him. Then he looked back and yelled, "Ee-yah!" at the river and the world at large. He was acting like a seventeen-year-old boy instead of a man in his forties but he was happy and ecstatic and he didn't care. Then they turned their horses, scrambled up the embankment, and threaded their way through the scrub growth and the cottonwoods. And gradually, as they left the river behind them, the chaparral got thinner until they were riding in the rolling sand hills of southeastern California.

All morning they rode side by side across the hot desert. When the sun was directly overhead and the day was at its hottest they rested for two hours at the edge of a mesquite patch. Then they went on, keeping always a western course until the cooler hours of the late afternoon. At sunset they stopped and camped for the night. The next day was a repetition of the same thing, a slow torturous ride through empty desert country with no sign of human beings until dusk brought them to the first of the white men's ranches reclaimed from the desert by irrigation. They crossed one of the main irrigation canals and then the ranches became closer together. Frequently they saw white men at work in the fields or on the roads. Agocho decided they had traveled enough for that day and they stopped for the night beside an irrigation ditch and some tamarisk trees.

This was the country that the white men were making fertile by tampering with the Colorado River, and the general appearance of it disappointed Agocho. He had hoped to see more havoc—ruined ranches, crops washed away, white men excited, and calamity everywhere. Instead of that, the white men seemed to have everything their own way. There was nothing like the disaster that he had been expecting to see. Doubt assailed him, and he wondered if all that the Yuman and the Yavapai had told him were lies.

Perhaps that river had never run wild. Perhaps there never had been any deluge and there was no great inland sea to mock the white men. The Yuman and the Yavapai might have been joking and making a fool of a stranger whose ears were bigger than his brains. Agocho was indignant and he discussed the story with Kai-a, who, as he had assumed, was not as interested in it as she might have been.

She did not understand it at all, and she said that tiz-win tells many tales and this was only one of them. And as far as she cared, the white men could make a river run to the moon if they wanted to and she wouldn't turn her head to look at it. As if this thing in her belly weren't enough for anybody to think about instead of worrying over the loose tongue of a drunken Yavapai, who, if he had any sense, wouldn't have been talking such foolishness in the first place.

Agocho decided not to talk to her about it again, and when she continued incessantly to belittle the story, he finally became irritated and told her to shut up.

He was still a little annoyed by the whole business, but he had started this journey to the inland sea, and if such a thing did exist, he was going to find it. He reconsidered the directions that the Yavapai had told him and he knew that he must begin traveling toward the northwest from this time on.

So the next morning they started off again, and followed the trails and roads that the white men had made in a country rapidly changing its character from desert waste to ranches of cotton, alfalfa, and melons. This kind

of thing made Kai-a very irritable, and Agocho had to
confess to himself that the journey was indeed a dull
one. They saw a couple of very new and ugly little towns,
but they ignored them.

Then, even more suddenly than it had begun, the
country changed again and instantly they were in the
raw desert. Without knowing it, Agocho had passed
beyond the irrigating range of the last canal.

There was no trail in this country and their progress
was considerably retarded. But shortly before sunset
they rode up the side of a small hummock looking for a
spring that two or three cottonwood trees told them
must be somewhere nearby. Agocho had no trouble in
finding the spring. It was quite simple. But from the top
of that hill stretching off to the north and west, as far
as he could see, was a large body of water. He called to
Kai-a who was lagging behind, and when she came up
he explained with a casual triumph that there was the
great dead sea that the River Spirit had put in the
desert to irritate the white men, just as the Yuman and
the Yavapai had told him.

That night they camped beside the spring, and the
next morning, they followed a dry wash down to the
water edge of the Salton Sea. It measured completely
up to Agocho's expectations. The water wasn't fit to
drink. Animals apparently shunned it. Fish couldn't live
in it, it was absolutely useless to the white men, and of
course nobody dared think of trying to get rid of it,
even if there had been any way to do it. It was a perfect
example of the working of the River Spirit, and Agocho
had an overwhelming regard for his power. Just to see

this miracle was well worth the journey, and he did not doubt but that the Spirit was just waiting for the white men to commit some further outrage and he would flood them out of their ranches again.

Agocho felt himself bound to make some expression of homage to this power. He had no sacred medicine with him, however, no wheels or sticks or drums. So he gathered some sticks of sagebrush and arranged them in the sign of his clan, and offered them and all they stood for to the Great River Spirit, so just, so understanding, and so omnipotent.

That day they walked their horses along the shore, following the beach line, moving very slowly, simply enjoying this work of the all-powerful as people before a shrine. Several times Agocho stopped and repeated the design of the sticks so that the Spirit would understand that he, and his whole clan, and all the clans that make up the Apaches, had paid their homage and respect to this very obvious manifestation of the Gods.

Kai-a was completely humble. She had been wrong, as often she had been in the past. Here was something that very few people were privileged to see and understand. Her doubts as to the veracity of the Yuman and the Yavapai made her ashamed of herself. Perhaps they had drunk tizwin, but certainly they couldn't have been drunk on it. Agocho had been wise to appreciate their story, and she was just a squaw whose business it was to bear children and not to have an opinion about something that only wise men understood.

Agocho was so pleased with the success of the journey that he didn't notice that Kai-a's horse was continually lagging behind his and that it was getting to be more and more of an effort for Kai-a to spur him on.

Presently, as he waited for her to catch up with him, he saw that her face was tense. The trip had been hard on her and she was in danger of becoming ill and perhaps making ill the child that she carried. Why risk danger? They were in no great hurry to reach any destination. It didn't matter when they returned to the White River country of Arizona. Since they had been riding so steadily it would probably be wise to rest for a few days, and give Kai-a a chance to regain her full strength.

Kai-a herself was glad of the chance to stop. She had never had a child before but she was not afraid or even apprehensive, because she was wearing a maternity belt made of the skin of a mountain lion. It was a belt worn not for the sake of her figure, which did not matter very much, but worn because the mountain lion gives birth to young easily and with no trouble. To wear a belt made from a lioness' skin assures an easy birth to any Apache woman. Moreover, this particular belt had first belonged to her grandmother, then to her mother, and now to her. So it was a very fine belt indeed, and Kai-a knew that with its help she would have nothing to fear when her child was born.

They rode on another mile or two, and then Agocho found a slight trickle of water running down the slope of the beach from the chaparral and into the sea. He bent over and tasted it and was glad to find it fresh, but with a peculiar taste of mineral.

Kai-a waited while he followed this rivulet up into rising ground and into a greasewood maze. Some hundred yards in from the beach he came to a natural clear-

ing in the heart of the greasewood, and in the middle
of it were the perpetual desert signposts of fresh water—
cottonwood trees.

And beside them was the water hole, with the water
seeping up from beneath the ground, forcing its way to
the surface and forming a muddy pool four or five feet
across.

Technically it was a spring, but a very small one
with little claim on the word. A white man would have
found the water brackish and hardly fit to drink and
would have called the water hole a mud puddle.

Before the Salton Sea had been formed, this seepage
had run into the salt sink and dried up, but now it
emptied into the great body of salt water as a river
runs into the ocean.

To Agocho the entire place, lost in the greasewood
with fresh water on hand and cottonwood trees for
shade, was a perfect natural site for a camp. He went
back to the beach, found Kai-a, and together they forced
their horses through the brush and into the clearing.

They stayed there all day, and at night slept in their
blankets as usual. And the following morning they talked
about the possibility of staying for some time, and agreed
that it was the thing to do. There were so many elements
contributing to that plan that they adopted it at once.
It wasn't wise for Kai-a to travel any more until the
baby was born. This particular place was especially nice.
The River Spirit must know that they were there and he
would keep a protective eye on them. There were no
white men for miles around; it was a full day's ride or
more back to the ranch land they had passed through
and apparently nothing but desert for miles ahead.

There was a mesquite forest to the south and that meant plenty of mesquite beans. The soil around the water hole was rich and could grow things rapidly. And last of all there were no fish in the Salton Sea and that was a very good omen indeed, for an Apache will never eat fish or bear, both foods being a taboo that is never violated.

The next step after the decision to stay was to build a kowa. With so much mesquite wood and greasewood branches nearby it was easy. Together they constructed the little shelter in a day, building it in a circle converging toward the top but with an opening at the peak for smoke to go through if they ever wished to have a fire inside. Everything was so easy in this ideal spot that the Great Spirits must have been pleased with them indeed.

As soon as the hut was finished Kai-a examined the sprays of fig trees that had been given to her in Yuma. They could not live much longer. In fact one was dead already. If they were not planted at once they would be useless.

So she turned up the earth near the water hole and planted the six sprays of figs, expecting them to die, but with her economic sense of food, unable to throw them away.

With the six little green trees newly stuck in the earth before her, Kai-a went back to the wickiup. She was very tired and she lay down on the blankets with her hands on her swelling body. It was a very peaceful day, and the Great Spirits were kind and she was happy. She lay perfectly still in the absolute quiet with the pleasant acrid odor of greasewood floating into the hut from outside, and in a few minutes she was asleep.

Agocho stood before the small fig trees and looked at the new kowa, and the water hole and the surrounding wall of greasewood. It was an extremely satisfactory spot and he appreciated all its values. Toward sunset he threaded his way through the greasewood again to the shore of the Salton Sea.

The scene fascinated him. As the sun sank behind the mountains far to the west and the rapidly changing light spilled fantastic reds and yellows over the sky he stood perfectly still and watched and listened. And he knew that Na-yen-ez-gan-i, the War God, was in the sky, and that Tu-ba-dzis-chi-ni, the Water God, was at his feet, and that Ste-na-tlih-a, the chief Goddess of all the Apaches, and the mother of all fire and water, was everywhere. Never had he experienced this emotional response to all the powers at any one time or in any one place. And he wasn't surprised when he heard the voice of the Goddess telling him that his wife would bear him a son in this place, and that the fig trees would grow, and that the Gods of fire and water would watch over him and protect him as long as he remained. He stood very still, with his head thrown back and his hands at his sides, listening to the voices of the Gods in the song of the wind and the lap of the water.

Chapter III

THE days went by into weeks and the weeks made the moon of Sos-nahl-tus, December. The longer Agocho and Kai-a stayed in their camp the better they liked it, and Agocho knew that the Gods intended this place to be his. He began exploring the adjacent country, particularly the Santa Rosa mountain range to the west. And he found that its upper regions were thick with piñon which was a valuable find indeed for it had innumerable uses. It made several kinds of food, the bark was good for tea and the gum was a thick sticky substance from which was made the water-proof lining of the sumac water bottles. Not only was there piñon in the Santa Rosas but yucca and prickly pear cactus. The fruit of the prickly pear made a pleasant delicacy called "hush," and the yucca stalks were full of a sweet substance not unlike honey, and the stalks themselves were ideal tinder for fire. As long as there were plenty of yucca stalks and some sharp stones, there could always be a fire in no time at all. Then there were rattlesnakes in the Santa Rosas, and if well prepared they made a very fine food, too, not to mention jackrabbits, swifts, and chuckwallas.

So the Santa Rosa range, immediately to the west, so near at hand that it was only a few hours' travel, was a very rich source of supply. And that was only one little piece of the vast circle of country that Agocho had yet

to explore. On the opposite shore of the Salton Sea were
several ranges of mountains, and there was no doubt
that they were full of all kinds of useful things. He began
to think about a trip around the sea itself, estimating
that he would need six days in order to make it, allowing, of course, plenty of time to see everything.

With this endless opportunity for exploration, Agocho
took it very slowly, becoming thoroughly familiar with
all the surrounding country. On the north slope of the
Salton Sea watershed he found two more springs. One
was hidden away in an almost impassable canyon and
he had nearly overlooked it. After he had scrambled over
and under sharp rocks and bowlders and was about to
look no further, Agocho saw the tops of half a dozen
palm trees. He went on and found a spring of good
water at the base of the trees. It was an interesting spot
and a perfect retreat. The only thing that puzzled
Agocho was the presence of the palms. They were the
first trees of that kind he had ever seen, and he wondered why they were there and what they meant. Some
message of the Gods, naturally, but just what its significance was Agocho could not discover.

The place, nevertheless, was important, and Agocho
built a mound of stones about as high as his knees. On
the top of it he put a few twigs in the sign of his clan.
Perhaps he didn't understand exactly why the Gods had
picked that place for palm trees and fresh water, but
he certainly wasn't going to appear ignorant before
them. It was an incumbent gesture of homage made auto-
matically, as a white man removes his hat and talks in a
hushed voice when he walks into a church.

There were other springs on the north shore of the

Salton Sea, and close beside the sea itself, running parallel to it, was a railroad. Several times a day the long snake-like trains of the white men went over this railroad. Agocho often watched them from a distance. He didn't like the railroad, but it was a long way from his own settlement on the opposite shore, and he really couldn't resent it.

The only bad thing about it was that it brought white men into his desert country and it was impossible to tell what the white men might do. Wherever there were white men there was trouble. The history of the Apaches in Arizona proved that, and even such great men as Das Lan and Geronimo had been unable to do anything about it. Agocho remembered that he had seen the great Geronimo twenty years ago, just before he had been captured by the white soldiers. Nobody ever knew what happened to Geronimo after that. He and his warriors had been taken away and none of the other Apaches ever saw them again. But perhaps, some day, the great warrior might return. Who could tell?

The ways of the white men were always inimical. Even now they were building two or three houses beside the railroad and several white people were living in them. The place was called Mecca and while it was a few miles beyond the Salton Sea it was too close to Agocho's country to be comfortable. He hoped there wouldn't be any more of that kind of thing, and probably there wouldn't, for white men never like the desert country unless they can get water on it.

The fig trees were growing. In fact they were shooting up so fast that Agocho could hardly believe his eyes. But of course he had been wise enough to recognize a place blessed by the Gods, so after all it was no wonder that the soil was wonderfully rich and that green things grew faster than they had ever grown before.

Some three months after they had been in this marvelous place an event happened that made Agocho forget all about fig trees and springs and new explorations.

Kai-a had her baby.

Agocho was not really worried about her or the child, but it was an event important enough to rivet his attention and keep him by her side. There were certain things to be done that would facilitate the matter. He was not exactly sure of what ritual and what ceremony he could evoke to help her. He wished for the presence of Hashke Nilnte, the greatest of all the Apache medicine men. Hashke Nilnte would have known just what to do, what chants, what invocations, and what kind of medicine dance to perform.

Agocho was limited in this knowledge but he did the best he could with what seemed fitting to the occasion. He scattered pollen to the four winds and then at sunrise he went down to the beach of the Salton Sea. With the Water God at his feet and the Fire God in the sky he said a long prayer to Ste-na-tlih-a, the mother of both those Gods, so that she would understand and help and protect her earth daughter, Kai-a.

Then he went back to the clearing in the greasewood and a few hours later the child was born. It was very simple and very easy. Ste-na-tlih-a saw to that. Only once did Kai-a make any sound. From that time on she either clenched her teeth or gave forth a little desperate laugh. And finally she laughed more and more, and after that she forgot everything and went into a restless coma.

Agocho took the child from her—a boy as the Gods had foretold—and when she awoke it was lying on the belt of lioness' skin beside her. Agocho was sitting looking at them both. It was noon, and he went out to the spring to bring her some fresh water.

That day and all of the next he stayed in camp. On the third day Kai-a grew tired of having him continually watching her and their son. She chided him for being more apprehensive over the baby than three women might have been. So Agocho took a horse and rode off to the Santa Rosas. He was gone all day, and he returned at dusk with four rabbits and they had a feast.

The days went by rapidly after that. It was a very happy time and Agocho was pleased with life indeed. The Gods had been good to him in this place and he was content to stay on. He had no desire to return to the White River country, to live on a mere part of his own land called a reservation and to be hemmed in by white men and perhaps soldiers who were always interfering with everything that he wanted to do. There was freedom here in this place of the Gods, real freedom, and it was a possession worth keeping.

The months slipped by until it was spring and then the long hot desert summer.

The thermometer in the little railroad settlement of Mecca touched a hundred and ten, then a hundred and fifteen, and in the middle of August a hundred and twenty. It made the white men swear, but Agocho, who never went near Mecca, didn't know there was such a thing as a thermometer in the world and loved the heat. The fig trees flourished under it, and the baby, though he cried at times, laughed and chuckled just as much as he cried, and was growing larger and healthier every day. They called him, out of deference to the Gods, N'Chai Chidn, which means Great Spirits.

About the middle of September Agocho and Kai-a had their first visit from a white man; from what Agocho could understand he was a stranger more dead than alive. He had been traveling from the Imperial Valley to Mecca and he had been all that day in the desert without water. He had lost the trail and followed the Salton Sea, trying to make Mecca before his strength gave out. It was a great temptation for him to stop and lie down in the desert, but he knew that if he did so, he would probably never get up again. So he staggered on trying to abide by his good judgment, walking toward the sunset, moving at last only by instinct, finally falling to his knees in the sand and crawling desperately away from that torturing body of dead water that had mocked his thirst all that day. He reached the grease-wood and Agocho heard him as he clawed at the bushes and dragged himself on, no longer seeing or thinking, but remembering somehow to keep moving.

When Agocho got to him the sun was almost down. The man was hopelessly lost in the greasewood, and lay face downward in the sandy soil, inhaling long, deep, gasping breaths, no longer conscious of struggle.

Agocho stood in the fading light and looked down at the exhausted man at his feet. The stranger did not know Agocho was there. It would be a simple matter to let the white man stay where he was. In the morning he would be dead, and in a day or two the buzzards would come from nowhere and leave nothing but his bones. Even those would bleach and eventually turn to dust and all trace of him would be gone. That would be the easiest way to handle the whole business.

But Agocho, having been so happy himself, felt sorry for the gasping miserable flesh before him. He stooped over and dragged the man to his feet. The stranger was unconscious. His knees crumpled beneath him, his arms hung at his sides, and his head drooped on his chest. The man was too heavy to carry through the grease-wood, so Agocho walked backwards, holding the stranger under the armpits and dragging him along.

Kai-a was waiting at the edge of the clearing, curious to see what this strange thing could be that Agocho was laboring to bring into camp. And when she saw that it was a white man she was surprised and startled. She thought it might have been a coyote, but not a white man. She turned away rapidly and went back to the kowa.

Agocho dragged the man over to the water hole and poured water over his head and chest and arms.

Then he turned and called to Kai-a, who was watching from within the hut. She came out and slowly approached the prostrate figure beside the spring.

Presently the man groaned and sighed, and Agocho told her to rub his arms and to pour water into his mouth. The man lay prone upon the ground, but his breathing became easier. He opened his eyes and looked around, tried to sit up, and at once slumped over to one side, his arms slipping into the pool beside him. Kai-a moved away and watched.

"Water," he said with a hysterical grin. "Water."

He plunged his face into the water hole and swallowed

mouthfuls of the stuff, dipping his arms into the pool and making the water muddier than it normally was.

Agocho and Kai-a stood still and watched him, and presently Agocho seized him by the armpits again and dragged him away from the pool so that he couldn't drink any more.

The man was content. He raised himself on one arm and stared at Agocho and Kai-a, and at the fig trees and the cottonwoods and the Indian kowa. In the fading twilight it was a confusing scene to his eyes. He only remembered staggering on, trying to keep on his feet, and then nothing. These were Indians, peaceful Indians, and they must have found him and saved his life, and here he was in their camp. Nobody had told him there was an Indian camp between the Imperial Valley and Mecca. He must have wandered far out of his way, but it was a mighty lucky thing that he had done so.

"Hello," he said to Agocho and Kai-a.

Agocho sat quietly and looked at him, and Kai-a backed farther away, drew a blanket about her face and shoulders, and watched the stranger with one furtive eye. She laughed a little, almost giggled to herself behind the blanket.

The white man sat up and grinned at them.

"Guess I needed that," he said. "What is this place, anyway?"

Kai-a thought that the sounds he made were funny.

"His tongue makes silly noises," she told Agocho in Apache, and she laughed at the white man.

Agocho knew what the man had said, but he didn't like white men and he gave no answer.

"Don't savvy my lingo, eh? I want to get to Mecca.
Ever hear of Mecca? Pale face town—men, like me, live
in Mecca."

He found that sitting up and talking was a greater
effort than he had imagined. He was a little ashamed to
appear so done in before these Indians, but his head was
reeling and he stretched back and leaned on one elbow.
He wanted more water and he moved toward the pool.
Stretched beside it he cupped one hand and drew the
water up to his mouth, drinking part of it and splashing
the rest on his face and neck.

Presently Agocho got up and moved between him and
the pool and pushed him away from it with a foot.

"No," said Agocho.

"All right, chief," said the white man. "I'll take it
easy."

Kai-a tittered again when he spoke and he turned and
looked at her. Even in the dim light and with her face
partly concealed by a blanket he could see her bright
eyes peering at him and he decided that she was not a
bad looking girl as Indian women go.

"I'm sure much obliged to you for your trouble. I was
about all in, I guess."

Neither of them said anything to this, so the white
man leaned back and rested. He was suffering from complete physical exhaustion, but he was in good health and
he was feeling better every minute.

There was the cry of a baby from within the kowa.
The white man heard it and looked up, and Kai-a
went into the little hut and was gone for some time. The
baby stopped crying and presently Kai-a came out and
collected some brush and yucca stalks. Agocho then

made a fire by rubbing two stones together until their friction gave off a spark and ignited a thread of the yucca. The night was warm and the fire was small as it was not for comfort but for cooking purposes. Kai-a abandoned her reticence and let her blanket fall about her shoulders. She stuck some meat on a sharp stick and seared it in the flames. The meat and mesquite beans and fruit from prickly pear cactus was their supper. They offered the white man a portion and he ate it. The meat was not unpleasant, though extremely tough. But with the beans and the fruit and the water it made a good meal. The white man didn't know what his supper was made of, and he was curious.

"What is this meat?" he asked. And when Agocho and Kai-a went on eating and did not answer he leaned over and touched Agocho.

"What animal? What name?" he asked.

"Ba," said Agocho, which the white man took for an ejaculation of disgust at his ignorance, which was probably just as well for his digestion as "ba" means coyote.

After supper the white man tried to talk to Agocho again.

"So you no savvy Mecca, eh, chief?"

Agocho grunted.

"Mecca—town—white men—on railroad—big trains," explained the white man.

"Mecca nâ-ak-ku-se bi-yâ-yó," said Agocho.

"Well, we're gettin' somewhere if I could only understand it," said the white man. "Listen to this: Mecca—that way?"

He pointed toward the Santa Rosa range.

"No," said Agocho.

It was dark enough now for them to see the North Star and the white man began to get his bearings.

"Well, now let me see, I guess Mecca must be—*that way.*"

He pointed toward the north.

"Sure," said Agocho.

"What tribe you belong to?"

Agocho resented the question and did not answer.

"What name?" asked the white man. "Savvy name?"

"White men call me John," said Agocho.

"John what?"

"John."

"Well, you did a good job for me, John. You're all right and I won't forget it."

They sat and talked for half an hour. But the white man did most of the talking and he got very little information out of it. A few grunts, some native words, and an occasional "no" or a "sure" were all that Agocho had to contribute.

When it was time to go to sleep, Agocho gave the stranger a blanket and then walked into the little hut with Kai-a and left him beside the water hole. Rest was exactly what the white man wanted. He made the best bed he could out of a blanket and went to sleep.

Just before dawn a horse whinnied and woke him up. His body was stiff and cramped and his legs ached. He was unable to go to sleep again. He lay still and watched the sky get light and the stars disappear.

Presently Agocho appeared, and then Kai-a and the baby. The white man got up and stretched himself. Except for his stiffness he felt perfectly well.

Breakfast consisted almost entirely of figs and strong

acrid piñon tea. The white man was surprised to see fresh figs and he made several comments about them, but Agocho and Kai-a ignored them.

"Well, if your name is John, I suppose the little fellow's name is Johnny. Is that right?" asked the white man.

"Sure," said Agocho.

"John, I want to do something for you. You're my friend and I'm your friend. Savvy?"

Agocho listened.

"Now you saved my life and I want to make you understand that I'm grateful. And I bet you don't understand a word of all this, do you? No—well, all right. But I haven't got anything on me that I can give you except money, and I don't know what you'd ever do with that. Now listen to this because this'll do you some good."

Agocho understood a great deal more than the white man thought he did, but he stood still and continued to listen.

"Back there on the desert, maybe five mile, and then five mile more—" the white man held up his ten fingers— "is a pack with some food, some blankets, and some stuff you can use. I had to throw it way. You're welcome to it. Follow my trail back and it's yours. Savvy, John?"

"Sure."

"Now then: I see you've got two horses over there and I want you to get on one and I'll get on the other, and we'll ride up to Mecca. We'll go up to the store and I'll buy you anything you want—sugar, flour, coffee, pants, anything you like. Then I go on my way and you come back here with your horses. Savvy that?"

"No," said Agocho.

"Well, listen, we go to Mecca and I'll buy you a present—buy your wife a present."

"Not go to Mecca," said Agocho.

Then followed a complicated discussion as to the why and wherefore of going to Mecca. Agocho was very much against it as a matter of principle. Finally, however, he agreed to saddle the two horses and go with the white man more to get rid of him than to please him.

The sun was not very high in the sky when they left, and Agocho explained to Kai-a that he was tired of this loose-tongued white man and that he would return as soon as he had gotten him far enough away from camp.

So they mounted the horses and rode away, not toward the inland sea, but due north, parallel to the shore line. And when they had ridden about eight miles Agocho was surprised to see that much of the desert flora was being cleared away and that white men were busy cultivating the land. The town of Mecca was easily visible two miles ahead in the clear morning air, and the whole scene made Agocho furious.

He said nothing to his companion, but he looked at him in disgust that grew as they approached the town. Ranches were being developed. White men were beginning to run long pipes into the earth to tap the fresh water beneath the surface. The whole territory was liable to become a valley of ranches exactly like the other valley far to the south that had been made fertile by running the Colorado River into the desert. That was just like white men. They couldn't let a piece of ground alone, not even the desert. They always had to spoil everything that they touched. It was all exasperating,

aggravating, and wrong. Why the Gods ever allowed
white men on the face of the earth is something that
nobody can understand. And here he was, saving the life
of one, riding along beside him, going somewhere that
he had no desire to go, through a land that really was
his by right of personal conquest and was now being
ravaged by dozens of them. That wasn't right. Something
had to be done.

Agocho abruptly drew up his horse.

The white man rode up to the animal's head.

"Hey, come on—don't stop here. Come into town and
let me fix you up."

Agocho looked at him coldly. He said nothing, but his
expression was sullen.

"Come on," said the white man, reaching out and
slapping Agocho's horse on the flank. "There's nothing
to be afraid of."

Agocho glared at him, but he had no words to say.
"Afraid"—as if he were afraid of all the white men in
the world. Afraid of white men! This man was a fool.
They were all a race of blundering fools.

Raging within himself he allowed his horse to walk
into Mecca. Just before they reached the little cluster
of shacks they crossed the railroad. That was always
the beginning. Whenever a white man builds a railroad
he has the land by the scruff of the neck. He can pour
any number of his kind into that land on trains, and
anybody who thought he owned the place before had
better get out or they'll drive him out. A railroad is a
great evil.

Two or three people looked at the white man and
Agocho as they rode up to the general store. The white

man dismounted, but Agocho refused to get off his horse's back. He sat still in the sun and looked at the store building. He thought it was very ugly.

In a moment the white man came out and the storekeeper came with him. The storekeeper, a little round fat man with a bald head, was taking the cork out of a bottle, and he and the man Agocho had saved were talking rapidly.

"John, here, is a little ill at ease in a big city. Give him a taste to make him feel better," said the white man.

"Sure," said the storekeeper, handing over the bottle. "But don't let him drink too much. It drives 'em crazy."

Agocho took the bottle. He thought that it was full of dirty water, but when he sniffed it he knew that it was something else. He put the bottle to his lips and took a big mouthful. The liquid burned and choked him and he gasped after swallowing it and could not speak. He knew what it was or he would have been furious. The storekeeper thought it was a great joke. He laughed and pointed at Agocho.

"That's a new one on him! It's good for rattlesnakes, John. Heap big firewater!"

Agocho got his voice back but he did not use it. He knew the bottle contained whisky. He had drunk it before some years ago in the White River country, and he had seen white men drink it at Fort Apache. He liked it, and he wondered if they gave it to him for a joke or for a gift. At any rate, it was their mistake, for he intended to keep it.

"Now listen, John. I'm your friend," said the white man. "I want to treat you right. Come inside and pick out anything you want to eat or wear or anything you want to take back to your wife."

"Don't tell him that or he'll want the whole stock," said the storekeeper.

"Oh, no, John's all right," said the white man.

Agocho was willing to be a little more affable. He took another swallow of whisky and got off his horse.

"What's his name—John what?" asked the storekeeper. "I don't know. John something. John Fig Tree, I guess. He's got a squaw and a baby and they raise figs."

"Well come on inside Mr. Fig Tree, and don't let all the flies in the store."

The three men walked into the dingy little building. The general store sold everything that the pioneer rancher needed, all kinds of food and clothing and ranch supplies, and in one corner was a post office.

Agocho looked around. He was a bit bewildered by the heterogeneous mass of goods. He picked up a large broad-brimmed sun hat that struck his fancy.

"All right. He wants that," said the storekeeper, taking it out of his hand. "One hat."

"Well, suppose we get him some flour, some sugar, and some coffee," said the white man.

"Flour, one sack; sugar, ten pounds; and how much coffee?"

"Oh, two or three of those are enough."

Agocho paid no attention to this transaction.

"Now let's see," said the white man. "I think a pair of pants and a shirt wouldn't go so bad."

"About a sixteen neck would you say that was?"

"I think so. His wife can fix it."

"All right. Pants and shirt."

"Say, let me have that coffee pot over there and a couple of stew pans for his wife."

"How about a string of beads," suggested the store-keeper. "They love them. Or some nice red calico."

"That's right. Give me about six yards of that red cloth and throw in a string of beads and a side of bacon and that'll be all."

"All right, sir."

"Now let's see—how is he going to carry all this stuff. Better let me have a pair of saddle-bags, too."

"Right you are," said the storekeeper, bending under the counter and coming up with the article.

Agocho was still looking around. Such a wealth of goods interested him. Only once before in his life had he ever been in a white man's store. Many of the objects were strange to him and their uses he did not under-stand. The white men were apparently through with their trading. They put all the articles in the saddle-bags and carried the bags outside. The storekeeper put the large sun hat on Agocho's head and both men laughed.

"Come on, Fig Tree, that's all for to-day," said the storekeeper.

The white man was giving the storekeeper some of the round silver pieces called money, and Agocho, still carrying the bottle of whisky, walked out to the horses. He mounted his horse and tethered the other animal to the saddle of his mount. The two white men threw the saddle-bags over Agocho's horse and Agocho put the bottle of whisky in one of the bags.

"Now that's all, John," said the white man. "I'm going

on from here and you're going back, so we have to say good-by. Adiòs, savvy?"

"Adiòs," said Agocho.

"He understands, all right," said the storekeeper. "They play dumb but they're smarter'n you think they are. I bet he can talk English as good as you or me."

"Good-by, John, and good luck. You're a good fellow and I hope I see you again," said the white man.

"I wish he could see himself in that lady's straw hat," said the storekeeper, pointing and laughing at the same time.

Agocho knew he was being laughed at. He took the straw hat off and gave it a glance. Outside in the bright sunlight he could see that it was very poorly made. The weaving was very bad and not comparable to the skill of Kai-a's work. Both the men laughed as he looked at the hat.

Suddenly Agocho crumpled the thing in his hands, crushed it to a ball, and hurled it at the feet of the white men. Then he said "Ee-yah!" slapped his horse, and rode off at a gallop, sitting straight in the saddle and never looking back.

The white man watched him with a surprised grin and the storekeeper doubled up with mirth.

"He understood every damned word!" he roared. "Every damned word!"

Chapter IV

SULLEN and resentful, Agocho galloped away from the town. He was angry at the white men and annoyed at himself. He felt that he had handled the whole business quite badly.

He had done things that were not true to himself. He had no business going there in the first place. He knew better and he had permitted himself to be coerced. It was all a little disgusting. He should have ignored those white men, never spoken to them, never gone into that store. He should have denied their existence.

His good sense told him not to accompany that man to Mecca, and yet he had been a fool and played right into the white men's hands. He deserved what he got. He'd like to rip a hunting knife right through that storekeeper's round fat belly. One slash—so fast that the man wouldn't know what had happened—and when he grabbed his belly the blood would be running through his fingers. Then it would be Agocho's turn to laugh.

What right had that man to slap a hat on his head and then point at him and laugh at him? And to call him names—Fig Tree John. It didn't make any sense. They certainly never would learn his real name. He'd see to that.

And that man whose life he had saved, he was just as bad. He was a fool, too. He didn't understand anything. Agocho wasn't looking for presents. He didn't want gifts from white men. He never asked for their tizwin or their clothes or their food.

And just because they forced gifts upon him, that didn't mean anything. They were never trustworthy. They'd take them away from him just as readily as they gave them. Weren't they taking land away from him right now, right here, this instant?

He looked across the wide expanse of desert country. It wouldn't be desert country much longer. It would be a white man's land full of ranches and towns and white men and women. It was an outrage.

Instead of returning to his camp by the same route that he had come, Agocho rode several miles further west, making a circular detour, so that he could see just how much territory this white invasion was including. And it was appalling. Practically everything to the north had been touched by it. There were many white men at work clearing the desert of its natural growth. They worked in groups and they had teams of horses and mules. They watched as he rode by, but he stayed some distance away from them and ignored them.

One of the white men gave him a hail and waved an arm, but Agocho looked straight ahead and rode on without acknowledging the greeting. Perhaps they, too, would like to laugh at him. They'd better not do it too close.

To the south the desert was still untouched. That was a blessing. Perhaps the Gods would put a curse on the white men who continued to trespass against them. It would be a good joke, indeed, if none of their crops would grow and they had all their work for nothing. That might happen.

Gradually Agocho began to circle toward the south, leaving the traces of civilization to the rear. There were about eight miles of uncleared desert between him and his camp. But even as he reined his horse to the left he came upon another cleared area. Two men were at work burning the chaparral on the other side of the field and straight ahead of him was a house made of bright new boards. There was a well beside it and a white man moving about between the well and the house. This was simply too much. It was bad enough to have Mecca where it was, but here was this place too close to his camp to be endurable.

The white man, at work on the small two-room house, turned as he heard Agocho's horses approaching. He looked around and saw a stalwart well-built rider with a dark skin and long black hair coming toward him. He stood still, holding a hammer in his hand and watched the stranger as he rode up. He thought at first that the visitor was a Mexican and that he was bringing a horse to sell, but a closer glance told him that the man was an Indian. He didn't like his looks very much. The fellow had a grim mouth and a nasty stare. There was a pair of saddle-bags hanging over his mount, and the white man wondered if the Indian had come to trade. If he had he was an unsociable fellow, because he never opened his mouth or made any sign of greeting. He simply rode up within a few feet of the white man and stopped.

"Hello," said the white man.

Agocho stared at him, threw a glance at the house and the well and then looked at the white man again. It was not a friendly look. There was no mistaking that and the white man decided that this fellow must be a pretty rough customer.

"What do you want?" he asked.

Agocho stared at him with black eyes that made the white man uneasy.

"Savvy English? What do you want? Que quiere usted? Habla usted español?"

Agocho didn't answer.

"Can't you speak or are you deaf?" asked the white man. "Tell me what you want or get on along with you. Savvy? Que quiere usted aquí?"

He knew that this fellow was up to no good. He began to think what he would do if there were trouble. He gripped the hammer in his right hand a little tighter. There was a six shooter in the house, but the Indian was between him and the door. In order to get in there in a hurry and get that gun it would be best to throw the hammer at this fellow to disconcert him and then dash around to the back and enter the house from the rear door. Of course if the Indian were armed even that would be taking a chance. Suddenly Agocho spoke.

"Get out," he said.

"What's that?"

"White men get out. Go away."

Agocho pointed toward Mecca. The white man watched him closely, tightening and relaxing his grip on the hammer.

"My place," said Agocho. "All my place. You go back," and again he pointed toward Mecca.

"You mean this is your property? You want me to get out?"

"Yes," said Agocho.

"You're crazy," said the white man.

He felt that he dared not take his eyes off this fellow, but he was sure that out of the corner of his eye he could see his partner and the Mexican coming across the field. They had burned the chaparral and they were returning to the house and he was very glad of it. Another few minutes and they would be here.

"What makes you think this is your property? Have you got a title? Have you got any right to it?"

Agocho couldn't answer that.

"Now look here, you've got the wrong idea," said the white man. "All this land belonged to a company—savvy company? I bought it from the company. Paid for it. Now it belongs to me."

"White men go back. No come here. Get out," said Agocho.

There was no reasoning with that kind of thing. The white man decided to stall along until the other two men arrived. Then, if this nuisance still persisted, they'd get rid of him in a hurry.

"Listen here, what's your name?"

"Fig Tree John," said Agocho.

"Well, Fig Tree John, you've got to be a lot smarter than you are. Where do you live?"

Agocho wouldn't answer this directly.

"All mine," he said, with a gesture that took in half the horizon.

"That's all right by me. But this ranch isn't yours and you better get that in your head pronto."

Agocho looked at the two men approaching from the field.

"White men go away. Tluh-go nde hi e-na."

"There's a lot of desert over there," said the white man. "You can have all of it. But you can't have this and you better get that in your head right away."

The two men were in hailing distance of the house.

"Now here comes my partner. He knows this is our land. He'll help me keep it. You better ride on, savvy?"

"What you got, Frank?" called the approaching white man.

Agocho stared at him and the Mexican as they came up.

"This is Fig Tree John. He thinks this is his ranch and he wants us to get off," said Frank.

"He does, does he. Well he's crazy with the heat," said this other white man.

The Mexican smiled, and showed his white teeth, and said nothing.

"Tell him to go to hell," said the newly arrived man.

"He won't do it," said Frank.

"What's he got in them saddle-bags?" asked the other.

"Probably been stealing," said Frank, feeling much better now that he was not alone. "You better try to talk to him, Gil. You know more about 'em than I do."

The man called Gil took charge of the situation. He addressed Agocho in a loud voice and a belligerent manner.

"Try to get this in your head, Fish House Mike, or whatever your name is—"

The other two laughed at this.

"—this property belongs to us and you keep your

Goddam nose off of it. Savvy that? This ranch belongs to Wright and Hunt, and anybody who says it doesn't is lookin' for trouble. Now get the hell out of here and stay out or you'll get buckshot in your pants."

He spoke rapidly and Agocho couldn't understand everything he said.

"We don't want to see you around here. It ain't a healthy place for you. I know damned well you're off your reservation and you better hotfoot it back to where you came from or Uncle Sam'll have you in tow on a chain gang. Now get the hell out of here and stay out of here or I'll take a pop at you just for luck."

There was a pause. All three men stared at Agocho.

"Get out!" bellowed Gil.

He thought of taking the Indian's horse by the nose and leading him off and slapping him on the rump to keep him going. He made a motion to do so, but hesi--tated, and decided that this might be a bad hombre and he'd better not get that close to him.

Agocho stared at this vehement white man. He knew he was being challenged. He knew he was being ordered off his own land. He knew that the white men were enemies.

It wasn't Apache psychology to fight at that moment. The white men expected it and they were ready for him. And it is never Apache psychology to attack openly an enemy who outnumbers him. An Apache always strikes when least expected, without warning, and when he begins a battle he fights until he wins or dies. This was not the moment to attack. It would have been foolhardy. Agocho drew up his horse's head, dug his heels into its ribs and trotted off.

The white men watched him go. Gil was grinning with pride and the other men looked at him with admiration.

"You got to make 'em see you mean business," said Gil. "Tell it to 'em so they're afraid of you. Take their heads off. They'll only respect you for it. I've handled dozens of 'em. They're all alike. That fellow's a coward at heart, and if he ever comes back here again he'll be as meek as Moses."

To the south and east rode Agocho into the desert away from ranches. His sullen anger was blended with surprise. These white men were utterly unaccountable. It was beyond comprehension that any man could take something to which he has no right or privilege whatever, and immediately convince himself that it is his, has always been his, and will forever be his, and he will be ready to fight to prove it. That was why Apaches always fought white men. There was no alternative. It was impossible to settle anything with them, impossible to argue any dispute without fighting it out by force. That is what had happened in Arizona. That is why Mangus Colorado and the great Geronimo had fought and killed white men. The white men themselves made no other choice possible. They were the most warlike and stupid people Agocho had ever heard of. And, like most stupid people, they were surprisingly brave, even to the point of being fools. No Navajo or Zuni or Pimo could be as stupid as white men.

The conduct of those three at that ranch was utterly without reason. Surely they could not know that Agocho lived alone in the desert. For all of their knowledge he might summon twenty bucks and ambush that ranch in a day or two or three at some hour when the white men were separated and not expecting an attack. Then the Apaches would kill them all, hack their victims to show that they were the worst possible enemies, burn the house, take everything of value, and disappear. It would be easy. Ten Apaches could do it—eight—six. It was a battle for children, it was so easy. If only there were three or four good warriors in this country, Agocho would lead them on that ranch house and kill those white men and teach all the others a lesson.

But even that kind of thing was futile, for the other white men never heeded the lesson. They would always keep coming on in ever-increasing numbers, blundering, shooting, killing, stealing, taking whatever they wanted and driving the Apaches by sheer force of numbers into more and more remote country. Then they would have a pow-wow, make treaties and promises and tell the Apaches that they had to stay in whatever land they had been forced into which was to be called from that time forth a "reservation." That, of course, was impossible, and the result was more fighting than ever. That is what had happened in the Salt River valley, and Tonto Creek, and the White River country and all over the Apache lands. And now it was repeating itself in the great desert country west of the Colorado River. It was all very discouraging and hopeless.

Agocho threaded his way through the desert growth, crossed a dry wash full of smoke trees and finally reached the greasewood adjacent to his camp. When he rode into the clearing Kai-a was waiting. She was surprised to see the new saddle-bags and was curious to know what they contained.

Agocho wouldn't say anything about them. He lifted
the bags off the horse and threw them to the ground.
Then he continued to unsaddle and pretended not to
notice that Kai-a was fascinated by the things she found
in the bags.

The flour and the sugar were unusual foods, but she
knew what they were and they pleased her. The two
packages of coffee gave off a fragrant aroma. The pair
of trousers and the shirt she gave but a passing glance
because the shiny new coffee pot was an object of endless charms. She thought that it was a beautiful thing.
She held it up and looked at it, raised the top and
looked inside, and uttered exclamations of delight.

Agocho turned his back. He knew she would be
pleased with this white man's stuff and he was disgusted.

In the other bag she found a bottle of whisky, nearly
full, a side of bacon, two shiny tin pans that were
excellent for cooking food, a string of beautiful glass
beads, and a roll of red calico that was simply dazzling
to the eyes. These were treasures, indeed, and she
couldn't understand why her husband was so disagree-
able and uninterested in all these lovely things.

Of course that white man had given them to him.
He must have been a nice white man, and a very rich
one, too. He must have liked Agocho a great deal. Kai-a
called to Agocho to come look at all these new things,
but he answered that he had seen them all before and
that he had only brought them back for her to look
at and do with what she pleased.

He walked over to the water hole and drank and
then sprawled in the shade under a cottonwood tree.
Then he remembered the whisky and he wanted it. But

vanity made him spurn the idea of getting it in front
of Kai-a after he had pretended boredom with this white
man's goods. He lay still and watched Kai-a.

She put the beads around her neck and then carried
the calico and the cooking utensils into the kowa. The
baby laughed and she gave him a tin pan to play with.
Immediately he tried to put it into his mouth.

Agocho got up and walked over to the flour and
sugar and bacon and coffee. The whisky was there, almost a full pint. He picked it up and started off with
it. Kai-a came out of the little hut and saw the bottle
in his hand.

"What is that?" she asked in Apache.

"Tizwin," he said.

"What are you going to do with it?"

"Drink it."

And with that he walked off through the greasewood
and disappeared.

Chapter V

A GREAT number of moons went by until the group
of little stars that Agocho had learned were called Nus-
ka-u-ŭ-hú, but which white soldiers at Fort Apache had
called the Pleiades, were no longer directly overhead
in the middle of the night. They moved constantly westward until they were no longer visible at night, and
for many moons the Gods kept them out of the sky.
Then, slowly, they reappeared, at first only on the edge
of the eastern horizon, but every night climbing a little
higher in the sky, until the night came when they were
directly overhead again.

White men reckoned a great deal by the stars, and
Agocho knew that when a star or a group of stars had
completed its journey around the sky in approximately
twelve moons, white men called that a year.

Three times had the Pleiades made the circular journey since Agocho had decided to stay a while in the
desert beside the inland sea. There were a lot of ways
to count time. A very patient man could count the suns.
A more efficient man reckoned by moons. And Agocho
had even other methods of estimating time. The mare,
for example, had had a colt, and now the colt was
big enough to ride, and was more than twelve moons
old. Agocho's son, N'Chai Chidn, was big enough to
walk and could speak a few words and make himself
understood, not many words, of course, and not under-

stood very much, but nevertheless he had been on this earth for thirty-three moons, and just to look at him one would know it.

Agocho and Kai-a had stayed in one place for twenty-seven moons, and that was a long time, indeed. For it was now the moon of Buh-is-chi which the white man's calendar in Mecca called February, 1910.

For a long time Kai-a had been weaving baskets of all kinds and sizes. She was a bit bored and she wanted to see the White River country again. She wanted to talk and gossip with other Apache women. She was tired of the inland sea and the greasewood and the fig trees and the desert country. She had made a great many baskets because she had nothing else to do. There were the tus, or water bottles, the tutza, or burden baskets, and a great number of tsa-nas-kudi, a kind of flat bowl or tray-shaped basket. All of them had designs of the tribe or clan, or talismans of the Gods woven into them. She had a great many more baskets than she could ever use, but it was better than doing nothing. She wished to move on and she said as much to Agocho.

He was not as restless as she. And when she pointed out that this was all right for a while but it was not really Apache country and that the little boy should grow up in the White River country where he could have mountains and creeks and rivers as well as desert land, Agocho had to admit that there was truth in what she had to say. This desert might be very fine for a Zuni or a Hopi, but they were Apaches.

But then there were other elements, not as pleasant. Nobody could really own the White River country as the white men had made it a reservation and it didn't belong to anybody. Here the desert was his, at least most of it, and the white men weren't able to throw a boundary around it even if they had encroached on the north and taken land for ranches. And there were mountains here, too, for the Santa Rosas were near at hand even if they weren't like those in Arizona. Perhaps here it was not quite as desirable, but certainly there was more of it and more privacy and the country itself was smiled upon by the Gods.

So both places had their values and if Kai-a was tired of this and wanted to go back he was willing to consider the journey. It would be nice to see old friends again— Long Ears, and Alchise, and Datilye who said all white men would kill each other and die off in time because they all really hated each other and were afraid of each other and spent their whole lives planning ways to get the best of each other. Datilye said the white men were doomed and didn't know it because each one was too busy trying to get more than the other and couldn't see beyond his own covetous desire and thus learn that this very desire was making him do everything wrong. Datilye was very wise. It would be nice to hear him talk again. Perhaps the white men were already killing each other back there. It might be a pleasant surprise to go back and discover that.

The more Agocho thought about it the more it appealed to him, and he and Kai-a finally decided to return to the White River country. After all, they could always come back here. Then, too, Agocho had a couple of wives back there, and while they were older than Kai-a and not as nice, he might like to see them again.

The kowa they could let stand, and many of their

personal effects could be packed on the yearling colt.

Kai-a suggested that Agocho take most of the baskets she had made and trade them to the white men for food, but Agocho disliked the idea of returning to Mecca. He had not been there since his meeting with the white man and the storekeeper and he still remembered that storekeeper with misgivings. That laugh and that fat belly. They were irritating.

But there was no sense in taking all of Kai-a's baskets back to Arizona with them if they were good for barter here. Moreover, Agocho wanted cartridges for his rifle. He hadn't been able to use it for a long time and he enjoyed firing it. He might as well go to that store-keeper in Mecca and get what he could.

The morning after that decision he saddled the stallion preparatory to riding into the white man's town. He took the rifle with him because he wasn't sure just how to ask for cartridges without having it along. There was no point in taking Kai-a with him because they would have to come back the same way. She could stay and pack things into the burden basket and the saddle-bags, and the boy could play around and watch her. He was too little to ride and too heavy for her to carry, but they could find some way to fasten him on a horse or tie him to the saddle-bags. He'd see to that later. Taking all the baskets he could conveniently pack to-gether, Agocho rode off for Mecca.

In spite of the fact that he was riding toward the white man's country he was happy. It had been a long time since he had ridden up this way—many, many moons, in fact—but he had seen the country about Mecca from the steep sides of the Santa Rosa range whenever he had gone up into the mountains. These mountain outposts gave him a broad vista to the north, east, and south. To the south was endless desert; to the east the great inland sea with the desert on its opposite shore and mountains on the horizon; and to the north, the ranch country, looking unnatural in its regular lines formed by fences and ditches and roads. Mecca was visible if he climbed high enough, and beyond Mecca he was sure that he could distinguish other towns that the white men were building. But as he rode along the idea of that white man's world was not as aggravating as usual.

Several miles north of his camp he was aware of the presence of another person. He had not yet reached the cleared area where the ranches began, but he was close to it. He stopped his horse and waited.

No sound. Nothing.

He rode on again, perhaps twenty yards. Then the floor of the desert dipped down into a dry wash. As he approached it he stopped his horse again.

There were smoke trees growing in the sandy bottom of the wash. Most of them were small and scattered. But to his right across the dry river bed on the opposite side were a few smoke trees that were full size, six or eight feet tall. And as he looked at them, perhaps sixty feet away, a white man walked from behind the trees, followed immediately by another white man.

In a moment the first man saw Agocho outlined against the sky on the opposite embankment. He stopped with a start and raised a hand of warning to the man following him. Both men stood still, watching Agocho apprehensively.

Agocho sat on his horse and looked across at them.

There was something about them that was different from other white men, and at first Agocho did not realize just what it was.

The three of them stood looking. The two white men conferred together. Agocho was too far away to hear any words. He saw that they were talking and that they were perplexed and uncertain. That was unusual in white men. Then it occurred to Agocho what was wrong. They were afraid. Both those white men, whom he had never seen before, were frightened. He had surprised them and for some reason they feared him. They stood still in their tracks, not daring to advance, afraid to run away, completely at a loss to know what to do.

It struck Agocho as funny. He thought of brandishing his rifle, yelling a raucous war-whoop and charging across the wash at those men at full speed. That would be a great joke indeed. An Apache, armed with an empty rifle and his wife's woven baskets attacking two enemies on sight. He must remember to tell that to Long Ears back on the White River.

Now the men were backing away. They kept their eyes on Agocho and retreated to the smoke trees. Then they stopped again.

Agocho decided that they were newcomers, new ranchers that the white men called "tenderfeet," and that they had wandered away from their ranch without being armed. He would like to have scared the wits out of them—given them a shock that they would never forget.

But it wasn't worth the effort. He walked his horse down into the wash, crossed it, and rode up the other side. The two white men stood beside the smoke trees and watched him go. They made no sound, and except to follow him with their eyes they did not move until he was out of sight.

Agocho rode on through the desert flora, and soon after he had left the dry wash behind he came to the beginning of the ranch land. Mecca was still four miles away and he rode on at a leisurely pace thinking how to go about getting as much as possible for the baskets he had to trade.

As soon as he was beyond the sight of the white men, they began to talk excitedly. They were both men of medium height. One was about forty and the other perhaps twenty or twenty-one. The older man was a shade taller and quite a bit heavier than the other who was thin and hollow-chested. They were both dressed in makeshift clothes, and in spite of the fact that they needed shaving it was obvious that they both had pallid complexions that marked them as strangers to the desert sun.

The older of the two left the smoke trees and scrambled part way up the embankment of the wash, craning his neck in an effort to see if Agocho were riding on.

"Can you see him, Joe?" asked his friend.

"No," said Joe. "I think he's goin' right on. He was as surprised as us."

"What the hell was he?" asked the other.

"Looked like an Indian or a Mex," said Joe.

"Have they got Indians out here?"

"I don't know. But I know one thing. We got to get out of here. If he rides up to town and then starts tellin' people he seen two strangers down this way—well—we ain't got any horse and they'd pick us up in a hurry."

"Christ sake, what'll we do?"

"Are you game, kid?" asked Joe.

"Sure."

"We got to go on."

"I thought you said an east-bound freight train would—"

"I did. You got a good memory," said Joe. "That's just what I said, kid, an east-bound freight and we got a chance. But do you think we can go back to that little hole and get a freight without being seen by the whole Goddam little dump?"

"I guess not," said the kid.

"You *guess* not. They got a sheriff or a constable or something there, and that's just the fellow who is goin' to spot us. He ain't got a thing to do but sit in the sun and wait for us to show up. Well, we don't show, see?"

"Yeah."

"We move on. We get around this here dead sea, and down at the other end we hit the railroad again. Then we get on a freight at Niland or Calipatria and we get across the line into Arizona, see?"

"Yeah, I see."

"Then we tell California to go to hell and you go your way and I go mine, see?"

"All right," said the kid.

They started across the wash, looking back now and then. Joe changed his course so that he fell in line with the tracks of Agocho's horse, and they more or less back-tracked his route further and further into the desert.

It was difficult moving on foot. The sand made a footing unsteady, and sometimes their weight would break through the soft crust and they would plunge into a hole up to their ankles. This annoyed the younger man greatly.

"Say, I'm afraid of rattlesnakes," he said.

"You got more'n that to be scared of," said Joe.

The kid did not reply. They saved their breath and trudged on.

Once they stopped to rest. But they were both too ill at ease to sit still.

"I thought you said there wasn't anybody south of Mecca—just empty desert," said the kid.

"What do you call this?" asked Joe.

"But that Indian came from somewhere, didn't he? If there's one Indian there's more, ain't there?"

"Maybe," said Joe. "And maybe not. What do you think this is, the wild west?"

The kid said nothing. When they talked he was uneasy because their voices sounded loud and strident in the hollow silence. And when they didn't talk the hollow silence made him nervous. He contented himself with sitting still and picking up handfuls of coarse sand and letting the grains trickle through his fingers. This was a strange place and he was a little afraid of it. Because of that he hated it. And Joe was a strange man, and he was afraid of him and at the same time he hated him, too. So far he hadn't gotten a dime out of the whole business. It was his own fault for making friends with strangers. He suspected that Joe had at least a hundred dollars of the cash and certainly that fellow called Bub, whose idea it had been in the first place, must have gotten his hands on a load of the money or he wouldn't have ditched them both the way he had. It was his own fault for being merely the lookout while the older men had gone into the store and done the trick between them. Well, there was no choice now. Presently Joe stood up.

The kid jumped up at once. Joe started off, still following the tracks of Agocho's horse.

"This is a hell of a country," said the kid. But Joe trudged on without answering, and he followed, trying to walk in the older man's tracks. After some time the greasewood began to get thicker, and before long they were in a veritable maze of it.

"Sure we're goin' right?" asked the kid.

Joe had stopped and was looking ahead.

"Shut up," he said, quietly.

The kid looked over Joe's shoulder and saw a clearing in the greasewood. There were a number of green trees in the clearing, and that meant there must be water. And somebody lived there, too, because there was a crude hut made of branches and leaves, and beyond the hut two horses.

"Joe," said the kid in a whisper. "Look—horses."

"Shut up," said Joe, gripping the kid's arm. "Don't move."

For an endless time they stood still, watching the clearing. The kid tried to say things to Joe but he wouldn't listen. Then something moved in the clearing. The kid saw a woman, an Indian woman, come out of the hut. She moved around the camp and the water hole and once she looked in their direction. But she looked away again and went on moving about the camp. A small child appeared from the hut and began to play beside the water hole.

Still Joe refused to move. For almost an hour they stood still and watched the camp until the kid thought he must crash through the bushes and dash into the clearing and call out in nervous desperation. He finally backed away a few steps and sat down, unable to endure it any longer, leaving Joe to stare.

In a few minutes Joe motioned for him to get up. He walked up to Joe and listened to his whispered directions. The Indian woman had disappeared.

"Do what I do. Whatever I say, don't butt in, see? I think we're in luck. Get a hold of yourself and keep an eye out for anybody comin' into the camp. If we have to beat it, we come out this way and move fast, see?"

"But what are you—"

"Follow me. Keep your head."

Then Joe boldly and slowly made his way through the bushes into the clearing, making a lot of noise and calling, "Hello, there!"

The kid followed.

Then he saw the Indian woman again. She had been over beside the horses and she moved rapidly toward the hut, looking at them in open surprise.

Joe walked across the clearing toward her and the kid stayed at his heels. The Indian woman seemed uncertain. She stopped before the hut and watched the men come closer. The Indian baby, frightened by the appearance of strangers, ran from the water hole to the woman. The woman backed to the entrance of the hut and the child peered at the men from behind her.

"Where's the chief?" asked Joe as he came up to the hut.

It seemed to the kid that the Indian woman was both amused and alarmed by his voice. That she was fright-

ened was evident and that she was curious was obvious
by the way she looked at both the strangers. Then she
said something that they couldn't understand. And when
Joe looked at her closely and said to the kid, "Keep your
eyes open for anybody comin' in," she repeated the same
meaningless words.

"Where are the other Indians?" asked Joe. "Where's
your husband?"

Kai-a giggled at this.

"Chief—him go to town?" asked Joe, pointing toward
the north. "Ride horse—go see town?"

Kai-a nodded and laughed again. These white men
made the most ridiculous sounds when they opened their
mouths.

Then Joe turned to the kid.

"It's a cinch," he said. "All we got to do is work fast.
That fellow we saw lives here alone. This is his squaw
and there's his kid. Yonder's two horses and we take
them and ride to Niland before dark. Then we jump a
freight headin' east and we're safe."

Joe turned and walked about the camp. He wanted to
be sure there was no one else around.

"Hallo, everybody!" he bellowed.

There was no response except a giggle from Kai-a and
a whine from the Indian baby.

The kid was watching the Indian woman closely. She
was short, but not fat and her features were not bad at
all. Her figure was full but not quite plump. He hadn't
been that close to a woman for a long time. She looked
pretty nice. He wondered what she felt like. He wondered what she would do if he touched her. He wanted

to feel her. And while he stood and stared at her she looked at him and smiled.

"Tu," she said, and pointed to the pool of water.

"What's your name?" said the kid, grinning and stepping up beside her.

She said something that he couldn't understand. Then Joe came up.

"The coast is clear," he said. "Leave the woman alone. We won't hurt her unless she tries to stop us. Do you know how to saddle a horse?"

"No," said the kid.

"You better learn. Come on."

They went over to the horses and Kai-a watched them from the hut. She was surprised at this. The white men she had seen before were always looking for food or water. She didn't want them to touch the horses. She didn't know what to do about it.

They picked up the saddle blankets and seemed to be preparing to ride. Pretty soon, the younger one, the slim one whom she thought looked funny, left the horses and went to the pool for a drink. She watched him and he watched her. When he went back to the horses he touched her as he passed and she started in surprise. Then, in a moment, she was angry.

There was something different about these white men. They came bearing no gifts, they had nothing to trade, and they acted as if the place belonged to them. They weren't friends of Agocho. Perhaps they were thieves. Agocho often said all white men were thieves. They were going to steal the horses. That is what they intended to do. They were saddling the horses and they were going to ride away on them. They must not do it.

She picked up the baby and set him down in the back of the kowa. She picked up a knife and concealed it under the blankets she wore. Then she went out and walked over to the white men. She was not smiling now. Her face was serious and she addressed them in Apache words which they did not understand.

The older man had his horse ready, but the younger one was making a bad job of his.

"She wants something," said the kid to Joe, pointing at Kai-a.

"Get away from here," said Joe. "Beat it."

But Kai-a was angry. She began to pull the saddle blankets off the younger man's horse.

"Quit that!" said the kid.

Joe reached over and grabbed Kai-a by an arm. He pulled her away and gave her a shove that sent her sprawling.

"Leave us alone, see?" he shouted at her.

She lay on the ground and glared up at the white men. She didn't speak any more. She understood now, and there was no use in wasting words.

The kid kept an eye on her, but Joe went on with his work.

"I'll fix the horses," he said. "We don't want to waste time. You go take a couple of those water bottles over there by the spring and fill 'em up. See if you can find any corn or anything to eat and we'll take that along, too. Take anything we need."

"Sure," said the kid. He picked up the sumac water containers and hurried over to the water hole. He glanced at the Indian woman from time to time. Apparently Joe had taught her a lesson for she lay where he had thrown her and had not tried to get up.

The kid filled the two water bottles and then looked around to see if there was any food that could be stowed away. He looked over toward Joe and his heart skipped a beat.

"Joe!" he yelled. "Look out!"

Joe wheeled and bumped against Kai-a. She had crept up behind him, silently, was standing up, and was bringing her arm down toward his back with all her force, the glint of a knife blade flashing through the air. Joe ducked and leaped to one side.

"Goddam you!" he yelled. He slipped and rolled along the ground. Kai-a tried to strike again, but he scrambled to his feet and got out of her reach.

The kid came running over from the water hole. He picked up a stick of wood on his way. Joe stood facing Kai-a who had backed to the horses, holding the knife in her hand and glaring at Joe.

The kid stopped a few feet away. He held his stick in his hand, but he didn't know what to do.

"We've got to get that thing away from her," said Joe. "Don't come near me. Go at her from the other side."

He picked up a heavy club of wood of a variety known as desert mahogany or ironwood because of its great weight. Kai-a watched both the men like an animal, cornered but deadly. There was nothing they could do until they had gotten rid of her.

Joe moved slowly around Kai-a, holding his club of wood ready in case she rushed at him. The kid approached her from the opposite side.

"Careful," said Joe. "They can throw a knife."

"Wait. I know what to do," said the kid. "I'll get her. You keep her there. I'll show you what."

He grinned and ran back to the little hut. Joe saw him peer inside for an instant and then he went in. He was out in a moment holding a yelling frightened Indian baby in his arms.

Kai-a broke into guttural Apache as soon as she saw him.

The kid dumped the baby on the ground and held him with one hand and raised his stick of wood in the other. He appeared to be ready to beat out the child's brains.

"This'll make her give up," he called to Joe. "Tell her to surrender or I'll—"

He never finished the sentence because the shock of the scene was too much for Kai-a. She forgot all caution. She forgot Joe and his ironwood entirely. She let out a terrific shriek and rushed at the white man and the baby, waving the knife as she charged.

This turn about was a surprise. The kid had expected a meek surrender. Instead, Kai-a had apparently gone mad. Shrieking and yelling, with fury on her face, she raced across the ground toward her threatened child.

The kid was unprepared for this onslaught. He jumped up in a hurry and retreated half way across the clearing. Joe, meanwhile, had rushed to the horses. He mounted one, and reached for the other. But the other was the colt and it leaped away from him, frightened by all the noise.

The kid came around to Joe in a large semicircle. He wanted to keep plenty of space between himself and that crazy woman. He was pale and trembling. Kai-a put the screaming child back in the hut and stood before the doorway. She watched the white men and she still held the knife in her hand.

"Why didn't you get her with that club when I made her run?" asked the kid. "You could have caught her from behind."

"Why didn't you get her yourself? She was comin' right at you," said Joe. "Get that colt and we'll get out of here."

The kid tried to reach the colt, but it was too frisky to be caught. It stood still until he was close beside it and then it kicked up its heels and galloped across the clearing and turned and looked back at him.

The kid crossed the clearing and the colt repeated the performance, running back toward Joe. Joe tried to reach it as it came up, but it sensed his plan and dashed away toward the hut. It trotted up to within ten feet of Kai-a and stood still.

The two men swore.

"We'll never get the damned thing by running after it," said the kid.

Then Kai-a reached out a hand toward the colt and tried to coax it to come to her.

"Don't let her get it," said the kid. "She might kill it to stop us!"

Joe thought of that, too. And when Kai-a approached the animal and it did not bolt, he kicked his horse in the ribs, gave it a slap, and yelled. It started off at once straight toward Kai-a. The colt looked up and trotted around in a small circle so that by the time Joe tried to pull his horse to the left to avoid Kai-a the colt was in his way. The two animals passed shoulder to shoulder, and on Joe's right was Kai-a, knife in hand and slashing at him as he went by.

The kid's heart sank as he viewed the scene. For Joe, to save himself, was forced to let go of his horse and wield the heavy club of ironwood at Kai-a. She struck at him at the same time. The kid couldn't see exactly what happened. He saw Joe bring his club down with both arms, and the lurch threw him off the horse as he swung. He heard a heavy crack as if a branch were snapping and the thud of falling bodies.

And then suddenly there was the Indian woman crumpled in a heap on the ground, and there was Joe rolling around on the ground right beside her, and there were the two horses galloping across the clearing together.

Joe was yelling and groaning and trying to scramble to his feet. The ironwood club lay close beside the Indian woman and the knife was a little further away. The kid ran over and scooped up the knife, and Joe backed away, limping and rubbing his leg.

"Are you hurt? Did she get you?" asked the kid.

"She got me," said Joe. He showed a gash in his right leg that was bleeding. "But I got her for sure."

They stood still and looked at the woman. She hadn't moved. They were both afraid to touch her.

"I think she's done for," said Joe. "Now we got to get those damned horses and get out of here."

The kid gave Joe the knife and then he went after the horses again. The larger animal was standing still some distance away. It allowed the kid to walk up and take it by the horsehair bridle.

Joe picked up the ironwood club and cautiously approached the Indian woman. He could see that she was breathing, but he believed that he had fractured her skull.

This time the kid had little trouble in capturing the colt. It jumped away once but only ran a few feet. It was tired of playing, and stood perfectly still as he came up to it the second time. The kid threw a piece of Agocho's horsehair rope about its neck and it consented to be led. With both horses following him the kid called to Joe.

"I got 'em! I got 'em both!"

Joe was looking down at the Indian woman. He moved her body with his foot. In spite of the kid's announcement he didn't look up. He simply stood there looking down at the woman.

The kid led the horses up to the water hole and hung the water bottles over the neck of the larger horse. Then he threw a saddle blanket over the colt.

Joe hadn't said a word.

Then the kid took the burden basket and dumped everything loose into it; mesquite beans, figs, and strange stuff that looked as if it might be palatable. This, too, he slung over the larger horse. He was just about ready to go when Joe came over to him.

"Listen, you take the horses and lead them through the bushes off that way," he said, but he didn't look at the kid as he said it.

"Why?"

"Because the Salton Sea is over that way and we got to follow the beach line south. It's a sure trail and we won't get lost, see?"

"What are *you* goin' to do?"

"I'm goin' to wash this leg," said Joe, slowly, bending over and looking down at the wound. "I got to wash it out a little—and I'll take a last look around."

The kid hesitated for an instant. Was Joe trying any tricks? No, he couldn't be. Not if the kid had both the horses.

"All right," he said.

"Better lead the horses through the bushes. We won't try to ride 'em until we're out in the open. I'll meet you beside the sea."

The kid looked at Joe. He was a bit bewildered. Joe was up to something. Well, it couldn't be much.

"All right. How long are you goin' to be?"

"Just a little while," said Joe.

The kid started off toward the greasewood. The horses followed him. He stopped and fastened the colt to the larger horse's bridle with seven or eight feet of horsehair rope.

Joe stood and watched him. The kid noticed that he wasn't in any hurry to wash out that cut in his leg.

With the horses tethered together the kid walked on and they followed single file. Just as he turned into the greasewood, he looked back.

Joe was still watching him go, but it seemed to the kid that he had moved two or three steps nearer the Indian woman.

Chapter VI

AGOCHO crossed the railroad tracks and rode into Mecca. One or two people stared at him as they had done before as he drew up his horse in front of the general store. He pretended not to see them and went on about his business of unloading the baskets that he had to trade. Then he stacked them in his arms and carried them all into the store at once, making an entrance that went from dignity to bathos. For he yanked the screen door open with a sweeping gesture of superiority only to have it swing back at once on its spring and slap him in the back making him drop the two top baskets. And when he stooped over to pick up those baskets two more fell from the pile in his arms. So he put them all down on the floor and looked around.

Three men were watching him.

"What're you doin', John?" asked one.

Agocho looked at them.

None of the three was the round fat storekeeper he was looking for. The man behind the counter was a young fellow whom he had never seen. The other two were customers who had stopped to chat with this young clerk. They continued to look at him and Agocho didn't know exactly what to say to them.

"What can I do you for?" asked the young fellow behind the counter.

83

The other two laughed and one of them took a pipe from his mouth and blew a cloud of smoke.

"Got baskets," said Agocho. "Got nice baskets here."

"He wants to make a deal," said one of the customers.

"He's come in to trade," said the man with the pipe.

"Well, I don't know," said the clerk. "Petterman's gone up to Coachella."

"Let's see some of your stuff," asked the man with the pipe. He reached out a hand toward the baskets. Agocho picked up one and gave it to him.

Both men looked at the basket critically.

"The boss ain't here," said the clerk, leaning across the counter and speaking directly to Agocho.

"Man with round belly," said Agocho.

Then all three white men laughed.

"He's got Petterman's number, all right," said the man with the pipe.

"Wait'll I tell my wife that one," said the other.

"Have you traded with the boss before?" asked the clerk. "You know Petterman?"

Agocho said nothing.

"Well I ain't got anything to do with it," said the clerk. "You'll have to wait until Mr. Petterman gets back."

Then the two men who had been examining the basket put it down. Neither of them knew anything at all about it but they both wanted to act as if they knew what they were looking at.

"I'd say that's pretty nice work," said one.

"Yeah," said the man with the pipe. "Look at it, Tom," —and he handed it to the clerk. "It's a right nice basket."

"See round man. Trade baskets," said Agocho to the three of them.

"Mr. Petterman's out of town," said the clerk. "He'll be back this afternoon. I don't know if he wants to trade or not."

"Let me tell him," said the man with the pipe. Then he spoke very slowly as if he were addressing a child or a moron, taking great delight in showing off his ability to converse with a primitive Indian.

"Big boss with round belly, him go way," he said. "Him ride hoss up north then pretty soon by'm by him come back git-a-lap, git-a-lap"—here he pantomimed a gallop—"Him ride up before sun him go down and you wait and by'm by make heap big trade and pow-wow. Savvy?"

Agocho decided there must be something wrong with this white man. Certainly what he said was neither Apache nor English. He decided not to speak to him again, and turned to the clerk.

"Wait and see Round Belly," he said.

Then he picked up all the baskets and walked out with them, while the white men watched.

"It's all in knowin' how to make 'em understand," said the man with the pipe.

Agocho put the baskets down beside the general store and then sat down beside them himself. He gathered that the round fat man was away and was expected back, and as long as he had come this far he might as well wait until the fat man returned.

A very young white man was looking at Agocho's horse and at the muzzle of the rifle that was sticking out of a saddle-bag. He reached for it and touched it. Agocho got up at once and walked over to the young man. The young man let go of the rifle in a hurry and walked on. Agocho took the rifle out of the saddle-bag and carried it with him as he returned to his place beside the baskets. Then he sat down again with the rifle across his knees.

Time went by and the few people who came near Agocho walked around him at a discreet distance. Several people commented about him but none of them did anything. Then the men came out of the store and the clerk followed them as far as the door.

"Say, he means business," said one of the white men, pointing at Agocho.

"Christ a-mighty, Petterman better make him a good deal or he'll get his head blown off," said the other, laughing.

The clerk said nothing, but he looked serious and seemed to be a trifle upset by Agocho's determined stand and handy rifle.

The two white men walked away and more time passed. Several people who had intended to come into the store hesitated and seemed to be apprehensive of Agocho. But he continued to sit and ignored everybody. The clerk stayed inside and contented himself with occasional surreptitious peeks out the door. He wished Petterman would come back, but there was nothing he could do but wait.

Agocho was not annoyed. He was quite satisfied to sit still and mind his own business until the round fat man returned. He would wait all day, and if the man didn't

come by sunset he would go home and not bother about
trying to trade at this place.

Some time later a white woman came down the street
and approached the store. Agocho watched her with interest. He thought she looked nice. Her white dress was
very pretty and hung nicely about her figure. As she
came closer she looked at him and the baskets and the
rifle. She had none of the querulous looks that the
other people had given him, and she brushed by so close
to him that he could have reached out and touched her
skirt as she walked into the store.

Presently she came out with several packages in her
arms. Agocho looked up and watched her as she moved
away. He thought she was a very interesting woman and
he decided that some white man had an attractive wife.
He kept his eyes on the white dress until it disappeared
and he even leaned forward in order to see it as long
as possible. White women were beautiful. He couldn't
recall having seen an ugly one unless she were old. When
they got old they were just like Indian women; they lost
their charms. He hoped she might come back soon so
that he could look at her again.

More time went by and two or three customers went
in and out of the store. Three or four men sat and stood
in the shade across the street. They were waiting for
something, like himself, but Agocho was not interested
in them.

Once a train went by. It made a terrific and unpleasant noise, but it did not stop and the noise didn't
last long. He was glad of that.

About the middle of the afternoon a man rode into

town on horseback. He rode up to the store and tethered his horse to a hitching post beside Agocho's animal. It was the round fat man and Agocho was glad that he had waited. The four white men who had been waiting across the street came over and spoke to the fat man and the young clerk came out of the store.

There was a great deal said that didn't mean anything to Agocho, but he did notice that the fat man was armed. Agocho stood up but the white men were so busy talking, two or three of them at once, and asking the fat man questions, that they forgot about him.

The fat man moved toward the door and the others followed. Agocho was waiting beside the door and he caught some of the conversation.

"There were three of 'em, we know that much," said the fat man. "And one of 'em was young, only a kid."

"I saw a couple of tough-looking hombres over my way last week," said one of the men.

Agocho noticed that the fat man wore a shiny piece of metal on his shirt front. It was shaped like a star and looked very nice.

"How much did they get away with?"

"Did they shoot old Foster or did they beat him to death?"

"Who discovered it?"

"Which way did they go from Coachella?"

All the questions came rapidly and the fat man seemed to be overwhelmed.

"They got Foster with a blackjack. They got about a hundred dollars in cash. Nobody knows who they were, but everybody in Coachella seems to think they headed down this way instead of going north. But unless they steal some horses or hop a freight they're going to have a hard time getting away without somebody seeing 'em. Now it's our business to look over all strangers we see in Mecca. McCracken has deputized me and if any of you boys got any suspicions this is the place to bring 'em."

"Everything has been quiet to-day," said the clerk. "No strangers around except this Indian who's been sittin' here half the day with a rifle and I can't figure out whether he's on guard or if he's goin' to walk in any minute and shoot the place up."

The fat man and the others looked at Agocho and the fat man remembered him.

"Well, well," he said. "Where have you been all this time? I thought you must have moved away from these parts."

"Do you know him, Mr. Petterman?" asked the clerk.

"Sure, I know him. He's Fig Tree John."

"Say, maybe he was mixed up in that business up at Foster's!" said one of the men.

"No—no—" said Petterman. "Fig Tree, here, is a good fellow. He lives down the other way somewhere, and why he does God knows. Ain't that so, Fig Tree?"

The fat man grinned, and Agocho said, "Got nice baskets here."

"He wants to trade," said the clerk.

"No, Fig Tree wasn't mixed up in that mess," continued the fat man. "That was done by some professional criminals and I hope to hell they turn up in Mecca. We'll make it hot enough for 'em, Goddam their hides. Old Foster never did any harm and they must have overpowered him and never given him a chance."

"Did he die right away?"

"Did anybody see the thieves?"

"Who turned in the alarm?"

"I've told you all I know about it, boys. Just keep your eyes open and use your heads and one of you is sure to see 'em if they're still in this neck of the woods."

Agocho was watching the fat man.

"Like make trade for baskets?" he asked.

"Sure—you bet your life," said the fat man, feeling very happy and important and quite willing to make a gesture now that he was an authority on crime and a deputy sheriff. "Come on inside, Fig Tree, and let's trade."

Agocho picked up the baskets and walked in while the clerk held the door open for him. All the other white men followed.

"You know the only trouble with Fig Tree," said the fat man, "is that he don't like hats. He just hasn't got any time for a hat, have you, Fig Tree?"

Then the fat man proceeded to tell how Fig Tree had come into the store a long time ago and picked out a lady's straw hat, and how he had no sooner worn it outside than he took it off and hurled it to the ground. But of course the fat man enlarged upon the story and said that Fig Tree had torn the hat to pieces and stamped on it and then made his horse dance on it and then had ridden out of town "makin' the air blue with Indian cuss words, yes sir!"

"So there's no mollycoddle in Fig Tree," said the fat man, slapping Fig Tree on the back while the audience laughed at the story.

That was the kind of thing that white men invariably

did that was annoying, but Agocho was in Mecca on his own business and he was tolerant and indifferent, hoping to complete his trading and get away as soon as possible.

"Well, now let's see what you got here," said the fat man. "Baskets, eh? Well, I don't have much demand for baskets so I don't see how I can give you very much for them."

Agocho had twenty-six closely woven baskets of many sizes and shapes. All of them were decorated with symbols of Apache art in a manner extremely artistic according to Kai-a's taste. He said nothing by way of argument, but simply spread the baskets around as much as the counter space would allow.

"They're right nice for decoration," said the fat man, "but they ain't really useful like a kettle or pots and pans or a bucket."

In spite of this depreciating attitude, however, the fat man wanted to trade. He was the center of the local news in Mecca and he liked acting the shrewd bargainer before the half dozen men who stood by and watched. All in all he was about the most important man in town and it behooved him to prove that he could drive a smart hard bargain.

"Tell you what I'll do," he said briskly. "I'll give you three dollars in trade for the whole load of 'em and that's a deal I wouldn't offer anybody else, not even my own brother. You can have some canned stuff or whatever you want up to three dollars. How do you like that, Fig Tree?"

"Need bullets," said Fig Tree. "Rifle got no bullets."

"Well, for God's sake," exclaimed one of the men.

"He's been sittin' out there all day armed to the teeth and lookin' dangerous with an empty rifle."

The men reacted to that and laughed, and the fat man picked up the rifle and examined it for its caliber.

"Well, guess that's fair enough," he said. "Rifle's no good without cartridges no matter who fires it. Two boxes ought to be enough to last you a while. If I give you too many you might run hog wild and take a pop at somebody just for the fun of it. Now, let's see: how would you like some flour?"

"Sure," said Agocho.

"Well, I'll give you some flour. Do you know what to do with canned food? If you don't you better get wise to yourself."

"Got any whisky?" asked Agocho.

"Well—" the fat man hesitated "— no, I guess I haven't. If you got a rifle and two boxes of cartridges you better not have any whisky this time. I'll give you some coffee. Savvy coffee?"

"Sure," said Agocho.

"Tom, get this red gentleman a pound of coffee."

"Yes, sir," said the clerk.

"Try him on candy," suggested one of the white men.

There was a barrel of mixed hard candy beside the counter. The white man with the pipe picked out one and handed it to Agocho.

"Eat 'em up," he said. "Damn good. Taste nice. Chew 'em up."

He pantomimed eating something with great relish. Agocho disliked the man, but out of curiosity he put the candy in his mouth. All the white men watched his re-actions. It was a hard piece of red and white peppermint.

He rolled it around in his mouth and then cracked it between his molars with a snap that made the white men laugh and made the fat man wince in sympathy. When he got the full flavor of the peppermint Agocho found it very distasteful. He immediately spat it out on the floor and went on spitting to get the taste out of his mouth.

"Hey, cut that out," said the fat man. "Quit that!"

Agocho wiped his mouth with the back of his hand. He glared at the white man who had given him the candy and the man stopped laughing and moved back a step.

The fat man made light of the incident and at once addressed Agocho.

"Now, then, Mr. Fig Tree, here you have some coffee and some flour and two boxes of cartridges. I'll give you some matches and you'll be glad to get them. Look. See? Just a little stick with a bright round point, then—one scratch and you've got a fire."

Agocho was pleased with the matches. He had seen them before but he had never owned any. He thought they must be very expensive and he planned to use them sparingly. There must be a hundred of them in that box and he wished that he knew how the white men made them. If he could find out that secret he could make his own. But it was doubtless a secret that they would never divulge.

"Now I guess that doesn't amount up to three dollars so I'll throw in some tobacco for you and we'll call it a trade. Savvy that? All these things are yours now and all the baskets belong to me."

"Sure," said Agocho.

He felt that he had made a very good trade. This fat man whom he hated before wasn't so bad this time. He wasn't trying to make fun of him, and Agocho walked out of the store bearing no animosity. He felt that he had caught the white man in a good humor and that he had been generous. The things he had were worth a great deal more than the baskets, certainly, and he left all twenty-six of them in the store without a qualm. In time, as those baskets were sold and traded and distributed about the country they proved a source of great perplexity to a young ethnologist from a California university who insisted that the Arizona Apaches once lived in California, probably about 1800, because of certain baskets bearing tribal designs that he found in and about Coachella, Mecca, and Indio. He wrote a paper to prove it and probably got a degree for it.

Two men came up to the general store as Agocho was putting his new possessions into the saddle-bags. They were a little excited, not wildly so, but excited enough to talk fast and wave their arms. At first Agocho didn't listen to them. He was through in Mecca and he was ready to leave. Anything further that the white men wanted to talk about was no concern of his.

But the two newcomers talked enough to bring the fat man and the clerk and the rest of the white men out of the store. They all stood in a group and looked off toward the south.

Agocho looked, too, and saw that what attracted their attention and caused them to talk rapidly was smoke. Agocho watched it for a moment. That smoke was rising from some eight or ten miles away, rising from a point on the desert that must be close, very, very close, to his camp.

"Nobody lives down that way, Petterman," said one of the men. "What do you think it is?"

Petterman was inclined to discount it.

"Brush," he said.

After all, there was a lot of excitement among the people. A fire was just a fire and there was no sense in getting everybody excited about it and rushing down there and having the ride for nothing. Probably somebody was clearing land and that's all there was to it.

"It might be the murderers," said the clerk.

"They wouldn't be dumb enough to build a fire that big," said Petterman. "That's a regular brush fire. You watch and it'll die out in a little while. Probably two or three men clearing ground."

"Nobody down that way that I know of," said another man.

"Well, there's somebody down there now," said Petterman. "We could go ridin' down there huntin' murderers and be the laughin' stock of the valley. If any of you boys want to waste your time and horse flesh, why go ahead."

The black smoke was floating up into the sky, gradually thinning and disappearing into space. It was unusual, coming from that location, but as Petterman pointed out, it wasn't astounding. There was an answer for it, and the answer was probably right.

"That's a good sized fire," said somebody, "but looks to me like she ain't gettin' any larger."

"It must be a load of brush," said the clerk. "It's too

big for a bonfire. You couldn't see a small fire from that distance."

"I reckon it's ten miles away," said Petterman, "and I reckon it'll be out before you could ride one quarter of the way down there. Might have a hard time locatin' it by the time you rode there. Mark my words, the fellow who started that ain't got any reason to lay low. He'll be in here in a day or two wantin' to buy a plow for his land."

This was good common sense, and everybody knew it. Just because there had been a robbery and a killing at Coachella was no reason why people should get excited over the first strange brush fire they saw.

None of the men had looked at Agocho. For a moment he had watched the smoke without alarm and without the curiosity of the white men. But that smoke bothered him—no, not the smoke, but the place where it was coming from. That there could be anything wrong at his camp seemed impossible, and yet . . .

Suddenly Agocho moved to his horse's head. Quickly he unfastened the animal from the hitching post. That smoke meant something. That didn't happen by chance. Something was up. Something was going on that he didn't understand. Something must be the matter and that smoke was telling him so, and it was close to his camp; might be at his camp. He wouldn't waste time.

He swung himself onto his horse's back, adjusted the saddle-bags, and rode off. The white men were still watching the smoke and the fat man was talking. Agocho forgot them at once. He rode out of town, crossed the railroad and followed the trail through the ranch land. To save time he cut straight across a field instead of going around the ranch. He nudged his horse into a full gallop. Most of the time he could see the smoke and he kept his horse at a run while he was in the cleared area, knowing that once in the raw desert he would not be able to move as fast.

The smoke was still visible, but now much thinner. By the time he was two miles from Mecca it had become a faint wisp. But that was no relief at all, for the nearer he got to it the more certain he was that it came from his camp. He urged the horse on into the uncleared desert, worried, frightened by uncertainty, unable to guess what that smoke meant, falling an easy victim to the worst kind of fear, that which doesn't know what to be afraid of.

He came to the dry wash where he had seen the white men that morning. They were gone. He walked the horse down into the sandy bottom, galloped across the dry river bed, and scrambled up the other embankment.

Where were the two white men he had seen earlier in the day? A glance at the trail told him. They were on foot and they had walked south over the very trail he had left as he rode toward town. They had followed his trail back. They had acted like strange white men. They hadn't looked friendly. They must have reached his camp hours ago. Were they there now? Were they enemies? What had they wanted? What had they done? What did that fire mean? Had they started it? Had Kai-a started it? What *could* that fire mean?

The desert growth made speed difficult, almost impossible. It was maddening. The smoke had disappeared. The fire must be out. There was no trace of it in the sky.

Onward he rode, twisting, turning, avoiding salt grass, prickly pear, and sagebrush, occasionally whipping the horse's flanks by cutting too close to greasewood or mesquite, but always plunging onward, trying for speed in a country where speed is impossible, asking everything that the animal could give.

Chapter VII

THE kid stood waiting beside the two horses. He looked out over the Salton Sea and then at the desert horizon. At his feet was an alkali patch. There wasn't a sound or a puff of wind. Even the water was quiet and dead and the whole place was depressing and ominous. He was absolutely alone and yet he felt nervous and scared as if he were being watched. One of the horses flicked its tail and the sudden movement made him start. He wanted to get away from this place. A sudden attack from an unseen enemy would have thrown him into a panic. He kept looking around on all sides, afraid to keep his back turned to anything.

There was no sound from the greasewood. Why didn't Joe come? Why did he delay? How would it be if he were to take the larger horse and ride off and let Joe take his chances and go his own way on the colt?

No, that wouldn't be good sense. For if Joe had any of the money on him the kid would never see a cent of it if he left him. The thing to do was to stick to this fellow Joe until such a time as they were safe from pursuit and could divide up and separate. Then he'd never see Joe again. He wished that time had come now. That damned Joe. He was a tricky bugger and you had to be careful how you handled him. He never gave anything away. You never knew what was going on in his head.

He never said much and he always kept you guessing. The bugger.

It was well into the afternoon. The kid estimated that it must be after three o'clock—maybe almost four o'clock. If Joe didn't come pretty soon they wouldn't have many hours of daylight left to ride in. What was he thinking about, anyway? Was he really coming or was he up to some tricks? You can never tell about a fellow like Joe.

The kid thought of fastening the two horses and then sneaking back through the greasewood to the clearing. But if he did that Joe might appear on the beach from some other route, find the horses, and go off and leave him. You couldn't trust him. It was best to stick by the horses no matter what happened. Besides there was no way to really tie them securely and they might get away for good and then what a hell of a mess they'd be in.

The kid gave up planning and waited. He decided to wait one solid minute before doing anything. He began counting the seconds off to himself, and then he realized that he was counting too fast. And as soon as he thought about counting too fast he forgot what his count was and got himself all mixed up. So he began over and counted very slowly to sixty, making himself concentrate on the numbers.

At the end of that time everything was just as oppressive and desolate as before. Even the horses were restless and nervous. They moved around and threw their heads up and down. The colt, in particular, was hard to control. Just as the kid felt that he couldn't endure it any longer he heard a noise in the greasewood.

Who was it? Joe? Sure. It must be Joe, coming along

the trail and making a noise about it. Well it was time
he came.

But what if it weren't Joe? Suppose it was somebody
else? What would he do? There was nothing he could
do. He stood still and waited and stared at the greasewood where he knew he must see the figure of whoever
approached as he came out into the alkali patch.

Then the noise stopped.

The kid caught his breath. Somebody had stopped and
was standing still somewhere right there in the greasewood. Somebody was watching him from some unseen
point of vantage. Who was it?

The kid wanted to call out but he didn't dare. His
mind formed the word "Joe" but his vocal cords
wouldn't say it. He stood still, too frightened to move,
and stared into the brush. He could feel his skin draw
tight over his flesh and he could feel his heart beating.
His mouth went dry.

Then the noise began again and in a few seconds
Joe walked out of the greasewood, crossed the alkali
soil, and walked up to the horses. He gave the kid a
look.

"What's the matter?" he asked.

The kid didn't answer right away. He took a deep
breath and exhaled in a great sigh.

"Scared?" asked Joe.

"Let's get out of here," said the kid. "This place
stinks."

He began to untie the colt from the larger horse, but
his hands were unsteady. Joe reached over and gave the
knot a yank and it unfastened. Then he examined the

saddle blankets on the larger animal and swung himself onto its back.

"You take the colt," he said. "You're lighter."

"All right," said the kid.

Joe nudged his horse and slapped it on the rump. It walked down the beach line and Joe guided it fairly close to the water's edge.

The colt was a little frisky when the kid tried to mount. It shied away from him and tossed its head up and down.

"Quiet, damn you," said the kid. "Take it easy, now, I'm not goin' to hurt you."

Joe was riding on ahead. He didn't look back and the kid was afraid to call to him to wait for fear of scaring the colt. He came up beside the animal and tried to stroke its head. He found that he couldn't leap onto the animal's back and that he had nothing to stand on to help him mount. He became rattled and finally called out to Joe to wait.

Joe stopped his horse and turned and looked back. He stared at the kid and the colt. He offered no advice and the kid felt that Joe was disgusted with him. Once again he tried to scramble onto the horse's back and again the animal sidled away. The kid looked helplessly toward Joe.

Joe nudged his horse and walked it back to the colt. He turned his animal alongside of the colt so that the two animals were shoulder to shoulder. Then he held the colt's bridle with one hand and reached across the animal's back with the other. The kid grabbed Joe's hand and swung himself off the ground and Joe pulled him up onto the colt's back. Then Joe nudged his horse and said "gittup" and the animal started off again.

The kid didn't have to urge the colt, for as soon as Joe's horse moved the colt began to follow. The kid, unused to this kind of thing, held on tightly and dared not look around. But before they had moved twenty yards the kid's attention was attracted by something moving to the rear over his right shoulder.

He turned and threw a glance in that direction, and again he was startled, surprised, and afraid.

"Joe!" he called. "Look back! What's that?"

Joe looked, too, but he failed to react. There was black smoke rising from the center of the greasewood, rising straight up into the air, and disappearing into the sky.

"It's a fire!" said the kid. "Something's on fire back there."

"I know it," said Joe, calmly.

"What is it? What's burning?"

Joe didn't answer. He rode on and didn't look back again, but he made his horse move a little faster. The kid followed, keeping the colt as nearly as possible in the other horse's tracks. Every few seconds he turned and looked at the black smoke. It was quite a fire to make all that smoke. What was it? What had Joe done that for? Was it an accident? The kid couldn't make it out. Joe must have started the fire because he seemed to know it was there and to take it for granted. It didn't make sense to the kid and he couldn't help but speak of it again.

"What is it that's burning?"

But either Joe didn't hear him or else he didn't want

to answer. They rode on for a quarter of a mile and still that black smoke was curling up into the sky, but not quite as thick as it had been when the kid first saw it.

The kid wanted to talk to Joe, but he was self-conscious about asking questions. Finally he mustered the courage.

"Joe, how's your leg? Is it all right?"

"It's all right, what of it?"

"I just wondered how it was."

There was no answer to this. They rode on for another mile, and by that time the smoke had died away to a mere gray wisp. The kid stopped turning his head to look back at it for there was nothing more to see.

He looked at the back of Joe's head as they rode along. It was a funny looking head. It came down flat and straight to the back of his neck. The kid thought it was as ugly as Joe's disposition. He was a surly son of a gun and the kid would like to have told him so. He hated Joe, now, and he knew that once they were separated he would never see that nasty cuss again.

"He better not try to cheat me," thought the kid. "He better not try to do that."

But Joe didn't seem to care if the kid were there or not, for he rode silently on and never looked around. The kid gave up all efforts to make conversation and occupied himself with despising the man ahead of him. And finally he gave that up and occupied himself with trying to be comfortable. He had no saddle, only blankets and a surcingle and the blankets were little protection from the hard bony spine of the colt. The small of his back hurt, his legs ached, and his buttocks were sore from the constant vibration of a trotting horse. Occasionally the animals walked, but that was no help for the slower rhythm was even more agonizing and racked more of his body than the rapid one.

Late in the afternoon, when the sun was near the mountains far to the west, Joe drew up his horse and looked back. He had gradually edged inland away from the beach until now they were riding in desert country. They were on a slight rise of ground and the beach of the Salton Sea was several hundred yards to the east. Joe looked back to assure himself that nobody was in sight. The kid drew up the colt beside him.

"Jeez, what a rotten country," he said.

Joe drank from one of the water bottles and then handed it to the kid.

"Let's eat a little while it's light," said Joe, "and then we'll go on."

"All right," said the kid. "Think we ought to ride in this country at night?"

"We better," said Joe.

"Think somebody's followin' us?"

"Maybe."

"What makes you think so, Joe?"

"You're pretty damned dumb," said Joe.

He dismounted and stretched and examined the contents of the saddle-bags.

"Can't say much for this grub," he said.

"I took everything that looked like grub," said the kid.

He managed to climb off the colt and he tied it to the pommel of the saddle on Joe's horse. His muscles ached and the opportunity to stand and stretch was a relief.

"Shall I get some wood and make a fire?" asked the kid.

"There ain't any wood layin' around, is there?" asked Joe.

"No," said the kid.

"Then how are you goin' to get any?"

"Well—"

"No fire for me," said Joe. "I've built all the fire I'm buildin' for to-day, see?"

"What did you start that fire for, Joe?"

They sat on the ground and tried to eat some of the food that the kid had stowed in the saddle-bags. Joe wasn't in any hurry to answer but he was thinking, that was plain to see.

"I don't know," he said, slowly. "I don't know why I thought of doin' that."

"What was it you set fire to?" asked the kid.

"I guess I wanted to cover up," said Joe. "I just naturally took that way of coverin' up. Funny the way a man'll do somethin' like that to protect himself when it's the worst thing he can do if he stops to think of it."

"What do you mean, Joe?"

"Of course I didn't know that it was goin' to make that much smoke. I'd have thought twice if I'd known it was goin' to make all that Goddam smoke, see?"

"Sure," said the kid, not understanding at all.

There was silence for a moment and then the kid spoke again.

"You know she wasn't a bad looker, was she?"

Joe gave the kid a glance.

"Do you think that crack on the head got her?" asked

the kid. "Was she breathin' when you looked at her last?"

Joe watched the kid.

"She wasn't doin' much breathin'. Not much," he said. "And she ain't doin' much now, I can tell you that."

"I touched her once there in the camp when I walked past her," said the kid with a grin. He stretched out flat on his back in an effort to relax and stared up at the sky. "She felt kinda nice. I never thought of goin' for an Indian woman before. Seems kinda funny, but I bet I could. How 'bout you?"

Joe went on eating and didn't answer. The food was unpleasant and the water in the water bottles was flat and warm. He was irritated by the kid. He had no desire to hurt him but he would like to have kicked him and roughed him up. The kid was a damned fool and Joe hated damned fools who blundered in everything and talked too much nonsense. All kids weren't like that. Joe hadn't been that way when he was a kid. This youngster was a fathead and Joe had no time for fatheads.

Anyway, that sun was getting pretty far down in the west and they might as well keep moving while it was light. If they followed the same course toward the southeast and rode all night, keeping the Salton Sea on their left, they couldn't miss Calipatria or Niland by dawn and there they would strike the railroad again. And that would put them a good fifty miles from Coachella, fifty miles of solid desert between themselves and suspicion. There was no reason why a couple of strangers couldn't turn up in Calipatria or Niland, was there? Then Joe would abandon the horses and hop the first eastbound freight and the kid could go to hell his

own way as far as he cared. It would be a lot wiser to
ditch the kid anyway. He was too easy to spot and too
damned dumb. So that's the way it would be. Joe got
up and left the food and the saddle-bags on the ground.
No use carrying that stuff any further. He gave his horse
some water and was ready to move on.

The kid jumped up and grabbed the colt.

"Joe, don't you want that stuff and the bags and all?"

"No."

"Well, we're takin' this other water bottle, aren't we?"

"Sure."

"All right, I'm ready, I guess," said the kid.

The kid held the colt for a moment and then managed to scramble onto its back. Joe took another look
at the sun, estimating at least two hours of light, perhaps three before it was dark. He turned his horse
toward the southeast and rode off. Again the colt followed.

The kid was glad to be moving again in spite of the
soreness of his body. He wanted to get it over with. The
rising ground gave him a view to the rear and he turned
his head and looked back over the long expanse of
desert. Not a thing moved in all that vast emptiness,
nothing but desert all the way back to the clump of
greasewood, now no longer visible twelve or fifteen
miles to the rear. And nothing was moving back there
either, the kid thought—nothing but a clearing in the
desert with some water and some trees and an Indian
woman who, by this time, might be dead. He wondered
about her. He recalled the scene in all its detail. The
spring, the trees, the Indian hut, the horses, the woman,
the child, the fight. What had become of that child? He

had forgotten it. He thought of asking Joe, but Joe was such a surly cuss there was no use trying to talk to him. Probably it was yelling its head off, scared to death, not knowing what it was all about, squalling, yelling, and screaming. . . .

The cry of a child, a persistent whining and sobbing of a child in distress came through the greasewood. In spite of the noise that the horse made as it brushed past the bushes and snapped twigs Agocho could hear the crying of his son before the horse carried him into the clearing. For the last mile he knew that fire had been at his camp. He broke into the clearing almost prepared for the scene that awaited him.

The kowa had been burned. It had been completely destroyed and was now a heap of smoldering ashes.

The little boy was standing over by the fig trees. He was sobbing dismally. Agocho rode over to him. Kai-a was gone. The whole clearing smelled of the odor of burned flesh. Agocho got off his horse and picked up the little boy. The child was unable to tell him anything. He was incoherent. Agocho carried him in his arms over to the burned ashes of the hut. The child screamed louder. Agocho didn't need to be told. The charred corpse of Kai-a told everything. And then the footprints, the tracks of the missing horses, the positive marks of fight and scuffle, the missing water bottles—the whole story was there.

Agocho looked at this evidence quickly. He read it all in a few glances. His face froze in hate. Confronted with an outrage that challenged his soul his face remained set in deadly acknowledgment of the significance of that challenge. There was only one answer for

that. There was only one thing to do. And by the power
of the Great Gods how he would answer that!

He moved quickly from that moment on, quickly but
with deliberation. He knew what he had to do. And he
had to do it now. There was no time to consider. He
didn't need to consider.

His first glance was at his horse. How long could it
go on? It was a hardy animal used to long rides, used
to the mountains and valleys and scorching deserts of
Arizona. It had done twenty miles to Mecca and back
and the last ten had been hard, but it had more to give
if he asked for it. It would be good for hours. He placed
the boy beside the spring. The child stopped crying and
watched him. Then he lifted the saddle-bags off the
horse. It wanted water and he let it drink from the
pool while he opened one of the new boxes of shells
and loaded the rifle. Then he filled the one remaining
water bottle, and hung it over the pommel. That was
all and he was ready.

But first he picked up the child again. He tried to talk
to him very slowly in Apache and he was sure that the
boy understood some of the words. He tried to tell him
that he must be a brave warrior. He must stay in the
camp and wait. He mustn't cry; he mustn't talk; he
mustn't make a sound. He must wait—just stay and wait
very patiently. Maybe all night. Maybe all the next day.
But he must understand and stay and wait right here
beside the spring. Then he put the child down and it
sat beside the water hole and watched him. He went to
the fig trees and gathered several handfuls of fruit. From
a burden basket he took some mescal pulp and ground
beans. He placed the food beside the child.

Then he swung himself onto the horse with the rifle across the saddle. The trail was plain to see. Through the greasewood toward the beach he rode, not looking back as the bushes enclosed the clearing from his view. He rode out of the greasewood and across the alkali to a point beside the sea where the horses had waited. There the trail turned southeast along the shore line. It was a simple trail to follow. There had been no attempt at concealment and it was only a few hours old.

The temptation was great to let the horse go at full speed, but that would be foolish and tire the animal too soon. He kept the horse at a gallop, a fast gallop that maintained a rhythm that he held for several miles.

Then he hauled up and made the horse stand still while he examined the trail again. It was fresher. He was gaining. And the two horses ahead were not running. They were alternating between a walk and a jog trot. He could tell that by the imprints of their hoofs. They couldn't be much more than an hour ahead now. He had cut the distance in half. He could cut it again.

He mounted and rode on, loping now at the animal's natural speed, not taxing it to its utmost but keeping at a steady consistent pace. The sun disappeared. An hour or two to follow the trail, and then night to stop him altogether. He planned to let the horse go at full speed for the last half hour of daylight. Until then he maintained his rhythmical pace.

Presently the trail curved in from the shore of the sea. What did that mean? He slowed down to a walk. The ground rose slightly up to the right. The trail led up toward the hummock. Were they up there now? He moved on slowly, screening himself from the top of the hill by bushes and turning at right angles and riding around the side of the hill until he was on the opposite side from that of the trail. Then he started up. Half way up he dismounted. He left the horse and went on foot carrying the rifle. Slowly he gained the top of the rise and found all his precaution for nothing.

The white men were gone. They had stopped there and eaten and abandoned a pair of saddle-bags. He emptied them in a hurry. Food. And a knife. He picked up the knife, glanced at the trail as it led on down the hill to the east. That knife was a good omen. It was a very good omen indeed. The Gods meant that he should use that knife, and he would know what to do with it. How long had it been since the white men left? An hour? Possibly. Not more. He went back to his horse, unfastened the water bottle and drank. Then he mounted, stuck the knife in his belt, and again the rifle across the saddle, and rode around the shoulder of the hill to where the trail came down toward the east.

There wasn't much more daylight. The trail was getting harder to see. He dug his feet into the horse's sides and urged it on. He leaned forward with his head close beside the animal's ears and spoke to it as it ran. He asked it for all it had to give. He wanted every last atom of energy now and the horse sensed it. Down the hill they raced, dodging the bushes, following those tracks on into the desert, the dull thud, thud, of the hoofs the only sound save for the whisper of sand as it was thrown up in the rear. Down the hill, hard on the trail, thud, thud, thud, they rode, man and horse riding, driving, straining.

Chapter VIII

BY midnight the kid was sure that it wasn't worth it. His tired body, continually tortured by the slow plodding and jogging of the horse, was ready to quit. He gave up altogether trying to speak to Joe. He hoped that he would never see Joe again, and the next minute he was terrified at the thought of getting lost from Joe in the dark and finding himself alone in the desert.

He had no idea where they were. A few feet ahead of him was a form riding a horse, and that's all he knew. He followed, or rather the colt followed the mare and the kid endured it. All sense of direction was gone; the inland sea was somewhere around and the kid vaguely thought it must be to the rear. The night was dark. There was no moon, but there were thousands of stars, more stars than the kid imagined ever existed. He wondered if he were going a little daffy. There were too many stars up there. Something was wrong. Sometimes the desert made men crazy.

No use thinking about that. No use thinking about anything. Just keep following that form ahead. That Joe. At least he couldn't see the back of his head. He could only see where the back of his head was, and he couldn't see that flat shape coming straight down to the neck the way it had looked in the afternoon. He wondered what it felt like. The idea was unpleasant. Joe's head. Why should he think about touching Joe's head?

113

He didn't give a damn about his ugly head. It comes straight down to the neck and the back of the neck is yellowish and has three wrinkles. He hadn't thought about those wrinkles during the day. He didn't know that he had seen them. But now when he couldn't see them he remembered them.

Many times Joe stopped his horse and the colt would walk up beside it. Either Joe was taking his bearings or picking his way down into a dry wash or avoiding scrub growth. The trail veered crazily back and forth, never moving in a straight line for more than fifty yards. By midnight Joe was trying to go due east, but when he did a short distance brought them to that everpresent damnable body of dead water, and they would be forced to veer to the southeast again. It seemed they would never get around the Salton Sea so that they could move northeast toward the railroad that was somewhere on the other side. The kid gave up all efforts to figure the plan of the thing. He simply followed.

As the hours passed he caught himself nodding. He was tired out; he needed sleep. It was plain hell. The night was never going to end. He and Joe were riding on forever, going around and around very likely, going on this way forever. There was no use in keeping on moving, only Joe didn't know it, and it was impossible to tell him.

After an endless period of this the kid's sleepy eyes recognized things a little more clearly. He could distinguish more of Joe. He could see the shape of the animal ahead of him and he could see the difference between the horse and Joe whereas before they had been a vague shape. It was getting light. That was it. It was getting light. The sky was getting lighter, but strangely enough this dawn was breaking over his right shoulder. Dawn was breaking in the south instead of the east. What a hell of a country. It's crazy. The sun is going to come up in the wrong place. The damned fool sun—no better sense than to come up in the south. The kid grinned and then slipped to one side and almost fell off the colt. He shook his head. Here, this won't do. What's the matter, anyway? Was he asleep or something? He'd have to get a hold of himself. Well it was getting light, that was some relief. There wasn't any sun yet but he could see where it was going to be. So that was east. They must be riding northward then. If that's the case they must have rounded the inland sea. Did Joe really know where he was going? There was no railroad in sight. No nothing. This part of the desert had even less in it than yesterday's. There was hardly anything here, nothing but some of those funny little bushes and alkali flats.

Joe turned around and looked at the kid. He grinned a little. The kid looked desperate. His eyes stared, his mouth was open, his lips were cracked. He couldn't stand much more of it before he dropped off.

"Hang on, kid," said Joe. "This is the home stretch."

"Where's the railroad, Joe? Can you find it?"

Joe turned back. He tried to urge his horse on but the animal refused to change its pace. It plodded along in an aggravatingly slow walk. It refused to move any faster. Far ahead Joe could make out a black spot on the horizon. That looked good. Another mile, but the spot was just the same. But finally, at last, that spot grew. By the time the eastern sky was bright red and yellow, just before the sun came over the rim, Joe knew that he was riding toward some trace of civilization, probably a few cottonwood trees, and, unless his eyes were lying, a black square object that was going to turn out to be a water tank. And if that was a water tank what would that long black thing be? Wouldn't that be a freight train? Wasn't that beginning to look like a whole row of box cars standing on a railroad? Wasn't it?

Then the dawn burst and the sun shattered the bright reds and yellows as it rolled up over the horizon. And the rays of the sun fell upon that objective and some of the pieces of the long black thing turned yellow. Yellow cars—box cars; fruit cars from the Imperial Valley. A freight train, standing at a junction of the Imperial Valley spur. That would be Niland, and that freight train would be eastbound. How far away was it now? Two miles, three miles—four? Would it stay there? Could they make it? Goddam these horses. Goddam that bright sun. Goddam that train—they *had* to make it.

The bright round orange disk rolled on upward, and as it did it lost its orange color and turned a brilliant golden yellow. The sky turned a light blue and the blue absorbed all the colors spilled by the sunrise and dried them up. The bright sunlight fell over everything and fell full upon a horse and rider galloping out of the night with a soft thud, thud of lightly touching hoofs.

Agocho raced on. He had been wise. He was fresh. His horse was fresh. That trail couldn't hold out much longer at this rate. Night had stopped him. Three times he lost the trail in the dark and the third time he couldn't find it again. Although it had run generally

southeast it wavered so much that there was no telling
which way it might change. There was no use in guessing and riding on blindly in the dark. Wiser, much
wiser, to wait for dawn. That would rest him and the
horse, and even if the white men had ridden all night,
Agocho and a rested animal could soon make that up.

Onward he galloped into the new day. The trail was
clear. It weaved in and out, back and forth; obviously
the men had been blundering on at night. Now, though
they may have gained as much as fifteen miles, their animals must be exhausted, and Agocho would soon make
up the distance he had lost.

Yes, this day would end it. He would overtake them
now, there was no doubt. It was only a matter of
hours, and not many of them. Agocho rejoiced as he
saw it and rode straight on to the southeast, allowing
the white men's tracks to veer first to one side and then
to the other while he kept to a straight course.

In a little over an hour he had covered the ground
that it had taken them five hours to pass over at night.
Suddenly the trail shifted to the east and then gradually
to the northeast. It was plain. The men were trying to
round the lower end of the inland sea. Once they had
done that they wanted to go north. That was a foolish
thing for them to do and if they had been clever they
would have avoided following the outline of the inland
sea. For it made a constant barrier to their left and
would make their escape practically impossible. That
inland sea that hated white men—it knew.

Suddenly the trail became straight. The veering had
stopped. Why? Because this is where the white men

were when it became light. From here on they could see well enough to ride in a straight line. And it wasn't very long ago. One more hour—then . . .

Agocho urged the horse on. He had them. His pursuit had been well done. It was a matter of minutes. The country was wide open, nothing but salt grass and alkali, no greasewood, no mesquite, no hills, not even any more washes, just flat desert land. They would see him coming; they would struggle to go on; they would urge their exhausted horses; and they would see Agocho rapidly gaining. Then, if they were smart, they would separate, each a different way in order to make Agocho split his trail. That would save one for a moment or give that one a chance to shoot him while he shot the other. But it wouldn't work. For Agocho planned to attack the man who rode the mare first. Then he could easily outmaneuver the man on the colt. He would shoot both the men with the rifle as he came on because they might have revolvers for closer range. He was sure neither man had a rifle. Then, he had the knife, and he would use that later.

It must be soon now. It must be soon. Yes: there they were, far ahead, at first only one figure but later two because the men were in single file and at first looked like one person.

They didn't see him yet. They would soon. They seemed to be making for something. Trees, and perhaps a ranch over there, still a long way off. No, not a ranch, but the railroad. The white man's railroad came down here and they were going toward that. He swung the rifle from its position across the saddle and gripped the stock in his right hand. He lifted it to his shoulder and set the cocking piece. The magazine was loaded. He let his trigger finger rest on the guard rather than the trigger. It was too soon for the trigger.

They must have seen him. Something was happening. They were dismounting. He could see them beside the horses. So that was it. They would wait for him using the horses for ambush, and let him come within revolver shot. He was too smart for that. He would ride around them in a circle while they wasted bullets and tried to keep their horses broadside to him. Then Agocho would gradually close in that circle, until they couldn't move the horses fast enough, and then one of them would get in range and he would fire. And if that didn't work he would shoot both the horses and then take the men at will.

He was almost happy now. He was nearing the kill and never before had he wanted so much to kill. There was a battle in the air and he was going to win it and he knew it. He rode steadily and deliberately on.

Joe saw him first. He had dismounted and looked back. Somebody was following them. He was too far away to tell anything about him, but in the clear desert air there was no mistaking the sign of pursuit.

Joe thought quickly. Should he remount? His horse had been barely moving. Now it was standing still and wouldn't budge. To hell with it. The kid was sliding —really falling—off the colt. He saw Joe's look, and he turned and saw the pursuer.

Joe didn't waste any breath. He turned and ran straight toward the freight train three hundred yards away. The alkali soil was harder than sand and Joe didn't stumble or fall. The kid went into a panic. He tried to run after Joe but his throbbing legs made him call out in pain.

"Joe!" he screamed. "Wait for me, Joe! I'm comin', Joe!"

He stumbled, scrambled, and half fell across the desert. His voice choked and tears ran down his face. He threw a glance back at that rider. He was much bigger now. The kid ran on, gasping, choking, begging Joe to help him, while Joe widened the gap between them.

Agocho began to swing his horse to the right as he came on. His plan was to encircle the two standing horses. But suddenly he swerved and charged straight at the two horses, for the white men had surprised him. They were not using the animals for ambush. Instead they were running on foot, running toward the railroad. They might have been a half a mile away and Agocho dug his heels into his horse and raced on at full speed.

Panting for breath, Joe dashed up the embankment to the side of the freight cars and swung himself on to the first car—a flat car, empty. He then turned and looked back. The pursuer had cut the distance in half. In another minute he would be up to the place where they had abandoned the horses. The kid had cracked under the strain altogether. The damned fool was yelling and wasting his breath as he ran. If he would use his head he could make it.

The train gave a lurch, and Joe almost lost his balance. The engine away up ahead had finished taking on water and had backed, breaking the tension between the cars preparatory to starting ahead. Then, slowly, with a painful, taunting deliberateness the train began to move ahead. At first it was just a crawl, but slowly the rhythm increased. The kid, seeing the train move, made a last effort and clawed his way up the embankment. He reached the end of the car that Joe was on as the speed of the train accelerated to a fast walk. Joe, from the middle of the car, watched the gasping, crying kid pull himself onto the car and fall prostrate and exhausted face down on the rough floor. He lay there choking and sobbing, not looking up, as the train gained momentum. Joe looked from the kid across the desert. The horseman had just passed the two abandoned animals and was bearing down on the train. He threw a rifle to his shoulder and fired as he came on.

Joe threw himself to the floor. Over the rumble of the wheels he could barely hear the report of the rifle. Faster and faster went the train, and if there were any more rifle shots Joe could not hear them. After a few minutes he looked up. The train was moving along now and the horseman, well to the rear, was making a terrific effort to stay within rifle shot. It was a hopeless job. Slowly but surely the train was pulling away from him.

When he was far to the rear, only an indistinguishable figure, Joe waved his hand. The train was still gaining momentum. Let the sucker ride until he dropped. He couldn't catch the train. Pretty damned lucky.

Joe grinned. If they hadn't ridden all night it would have been another story. He was pretty smart. Guess he had a hunch and knew a thing or two. Maybe he had been a damned fool to start that fire, but he wasn't such a damned fool not to know what to do next. Guess he could take care of himself. Look at that fathead kid. Bawling. The damned fool. The Goddam little jackass.

Chapter IX

ALL day long is a long time. A lot of things can happen to make life exciting or amusing or thrilling or at least worth living. But when nothing happens it is annoying and disturbing if you stop to think of it. The little boy wasn't old enough to think of it very often. But once or twice he became apprenhensive because there wasn't enough going on to occupy his thoughts.

He might play for an hour and not worry about anything, but at the end of that time he would remember that his mother was missing and that his father was missing and that the horses were gone. He wasn't used to that. It was out of the ordinary and he didn't know whether to cry about it or not. He wasn't used to being left alone all day.

And when he thought of the day before he was frightened again. That had been a terrible day. Perhaps the white men had only been playing a game, but it was a game he didn't understand and it seemed full of danger. His mother hadn't liked those white men and his father had ridden off with the thunder stick the same way the white men had gone. They had scared him terribly and they had made dreadful sounds and they had built a great big fire that was bigger than any fire he had ever seen before. If he had understood what it all meant he might not have been so frightened, but to have strange and terrifying things going on is enough to frighten any-body.

To-day was just the reverse. Nothing happened. And because of that he was frightened, too. But there were sticks to throw in the pool, and ants to chase and watch, and trails to build from the pool to the first cottonwood tree, and soft mud to make into all kinds of funny shapes, and all that was interesting to do.

Following ants, or putting sticks in front of them and watching them crawl over and explore stones was all right for a while, but why didn't something happen?

Then there was a bad smell that seemed to get a little worse as the day went on. It came from the place where the big fire had been, and he was afraid of that place and stayed away from it.

When he got hungry there was food to eat and water to drink and he remembered that his father had put those things there for him. So gradually the day went by and nobody came to say a word and there was nothing around to make him afraid except his own apprehensive-ness at being left alone.

Then, well into the afternoon, there was something new—not exactly new for he had seen them before high up over the desert and he remembered that his mother had told him they were chi-sho-gi and that they ate dead animals. He wasn't afraid of them and they seemed to be afraid to come very close. He watched them as they circled and banked high up there in the sky—a couple of black specks, moving gracefully against the light blue.

"Chi-sho-gi!" he said aloud, and then the sound of his own voice in the silence frightened him and he didn't speak again. They seemed content to stay up

there and if they came down he was going to throw a
stick at them. He would like to throw a stick at them.
He wished they would come down so he could give them
a good scare and chase them away. They were cowards
all right.

He got back under the cottonwood tree with a
stick and some stones and he stood very still to see
if the chi-sho-gi had courage enough to come down and
look around. His black eyes were shining and he made
no sound. He wouldn't throw a stone right away. He
would wait until the birds had perched and weren't
expecting an attack. Then he'd let them have it. That
would be great fun and he might be able to kill one.
Then he could show that to his father and mother and
wouldn't he be proud.

But though the instincts of the hunter were there, a
little boy of three doesn't have the perseverance to wait.
He found a loose piece of bark on the cottonwood tree
and in picking it off and making it float in the pool
he forgot all about the buzzards. There was a water bug
swimming around in the pool, and the boy tried to make
the water bug climb up on the piece of bark. The bug
didn't want to do it and he darted around on the surface
with a piece of bark propelled by a brown hand pursu-
ing him. Both the bug and the boy got a lot wetter than
they intended to, and finally the boy sank both the bark
and the bug just to see if they would rise again. Then,
for the sake of variety, it was possible to put pieces of
mud that were men on the bark and let them chase the
bug around the pool, and by the time all these interesting things had been done it was almost sunset.

Nobody had come back yet. And those chi-sho-gi, they

had gone home to sleep. And what was he going to do now? He was afraid again and he wanted his mother. It wasn't the way things ought to be. He wanted to cry again, but he didn't know why except that he didn't know what else to do.

So he sat quietly beside the pool while the sun went down and the heat of the day melted away. And the longer he sat in the spreading dark the more frightened he became. There was just no way to stop it; he was going to cry again because this wasn't right and he wanted his mother and father and he had no business to be left all by himself and he couldn't help it if it made him cry.

Sitting by the spring, crying softly to himself, he peered into the night. He didn't howl; he just cried softly to himself, and when the earth began to get cool he curled up and put his arms around his head and went on weeping. Then he must have slept for he had no recollection of stopping crying, but suddenly he was awake.

There was a noise in the clearing. He sat up quickly. Horses. He could see horses in the clearing—two horses that he couldn't make out, but beside them was a smaller horse that he knew was the colt, and thus he recognized all three animals as his father's. And there was his father coming from the horses toward him, calling him, looking for him, and how glad he was to see him.

He laughed and spoke to his father and his father picked him up and rubbed him and patted him and they both knew they loved each other.

Agocho was very tired and the horses were tired, too. He built a small fire and prepared his supper and he and the boy sat together and ate it. The boy told him all about the buzzards and how he would have killed them if they hadn't been such big cowards that they were afraid to come down.

The talk about the buzzards made Agocho look toward the ruined kowa, but the fire gave off such little light that he couldn't distinguish anything, and he didn't want to see anything in that direction anyway. Like the child, he hated to go near the burned kowa.

After the supper he wrapped the boy and himself up in a blanket and they lay down together and the boy went to sleep. Exhausted as he was Agocho could not sleep. There was so much to think about and so much that he didn't understand and couldn't reconcile to what should be right, that he lay in the dark beside the dying fire and thought and wondered.

He saw the pattern but not the meaning. He knew there was a meaning. There was an idea in back of it all. But what was it? Why? Why should this be? What could he do about it; and what was he expected to do about it?

He had followed the obvious course. He had tried to do what he knew was the right thing. He thought he was going to succeed. But he had not, and in that failure there must be some ignorance. There was part of the pattern that he did not comprehend even though he could see it. The Gods meant something else. Something more.

He had not been allowed to kill those white men. Even after finding the knife, the best possible omen, the Gods let them get away from him on the white man's railroad. It was a crushing blow, and at the time he couldn't

believe it. He was sure that the train would stop and
he had ridden after it for several miles until it entirely
disappeared. Now why was that? Just what could that
mean? How could he have done anything else? The
hollowness of that ending was exasperating and he
tossed and fretted for several hours before he could go
to sleep.

In the morning the boy woke up first.

Agocho, still tired from his journey of nearly a hundred miles in two days, slept until the sun climbing up
in the sky, fell upon his face and woke him.

The boy had something to show him. He pointed up
to the sky.

"Chi-sho-gi," he said.

Agocho saw the buzzards circling above. He rose and
ate a few figs. He picked up his rifle and examined it.
The day before in a frenzy of rage as he watched the
train pull away from him he had swung that rifle over
his head and hurled it to the desert. He had forgotten
that foolish act, prompted by violent temper, and he
looked at the rifle carefully to see if it were in working
order. He threw it to his shoulder, sighted a fig on a
tree twenty feet away, and fired. The shot tore the fig to
pieces and convinced him that he had not injured the
weapon.

And then there was nothing more to see about. There
was no other duty he could attend to first—no other ex-
cuse for waiting—no reason, now, for not attending to
the ruined kowa, and to her. It had to be done at once
if the chi-sho-gi were already in the sky.

He left the clearing and went out into the greasewood
and selected a place he thought would do. There he

dug the grave, and when that was finished he returned to the clearing and placed the body of Kai-a in a blanket. He didn't say anything to the boy, and the boy didn't seem to attach much significance to what was going on. Then Agocho carried the body to the grave and placed it within. If there were any things that Kai-a owned and wanted in the next world he could place them in the grave and she would take them with her. He couldn't think of anything unless it might be the string of beads that the white man had given him his first time in Mecca. He went back to the clearing, found the beads, and returned with them to the grave.

But as he stood looking down he remembered that they were white men's beads and he hated them and Kai-a hated them now. He broke the cord and the beads fell loose in his hand. With hatred and disgust he threw them out over the greasewood as far as he could and they scattered in the air and disappeared from sight.

He thought of the boy and he went back to the clearing and picked him up and carried him out into the greasewood beside the grave. The child was too young to understand the ritualistic significance of what had to take place, but Agocho wanted him to be there. He believed that the meaning of the scene would eventually make itself understood to the child if he were exposed to it. He placed the child down in the sand and told him that this was an important moment in his life, that his mother was going away, and he would never see her again, and that he must remember this and sit perfectly still for a long time. Then, slowly, Agocho filled in the grave until the sand made a mound slightly higher than the floor of the desert. He hunted around

and found two stones each about the size of his fist.
He placed these on the top of the mound and then
said a prayer to Ste-na-tlih-a for the safety of Kai-a's
journey. The boy, not comprehending any of this but
fascinated by the unusual procedure, sat still and
watched Agocho with interest.

Later on Agocho would place more stones on the
grave, but for the first few days he couldn't do that as
the spirit has to rise through the grave and if it is heavy
with stones the spirit might be weighted down and
wouldn't be strong enough to leave the ground—especially in this case as the spirit was not that of a strong
warrior, but only a young woman.

He would wait four days before placing any more
stones on the mound. At the end of four days Kai-a's
spirit would have left and gone by way of I-kutl-ba-ha,
the Milky Way, to heaven, where Kai-a would be re-
created in a land of neither death nor disease and
would live there forever in happiness.

They were strange days to the boy. And as they went
by he began to realize a little what it all meant. His
father rarely left the mound of sand out there in the
greasewood. Day and night he stayed there. He seemed
to be thinking, concentrating, praying. There were great
and serious things going on in a realm that the boy did
not understand. It was a very critical and important
time. There was a distinct feeling of awe and fear hov-
ering about. Something terrible had happened and was
still happening. His father didn't want him to play. He
was expected to sit for hours and do nothing, sit for
hours beside that mound of sand.

Sometimes he would pick up the sand and toss it in

the air, and sometimes he would build things and make designs and trails. Then his father would stop him, not angrily, but firmly, and he would have to sit still again for a long time and do nothing. This had never happened before.

Gradually it dawned upon him that his mother had not only gone away in the usual sense, but gone away into this mound of sand. He began to understand that she was dead. Dead. It was a word he knew nothing about. He hadn't thought of people dying at all. Animals died. Rabbits, coyotes, snakes—they all died. And now people died, and some day his father would die and he would die and they would become mounds of sand. It was a curious awakening. He had learned something that was true all the time, but he had never thought of it before.

That first night that they sat beside the mound was a trying one. It was hard to stay in one place so long. It was hard to stay awake, too. But his father wanted him to be there and to stay awake as long as he could.

In the clear desert air there were thousands of stars, and Agocho pointed out the Milky Way and explained to the boy how the spirit was rising from the grave and would travel on the Milky Way to heaven. He was very serious and he tried to make the boy understand. The boy was serious, too, All this was something immense and profound. It was a first lesson in philosophy and religion, and while he didn't know that, he did know that it was of great significance and that he must try to understand it because his father wanted him to.

He looked at the avenue of stars and he tried to imagine his mother crossing it, to heaven, but his eyes got sleepy and wouldn't stay open. He tried to think what all this meant, but his head nodded and all the ideas blurred together.

The second day and the second night were repetitions of the first, but on the third day a thrilling and fascinating thing happened. It had nothing directly to do with death but it might have had. At the time the suddenness and the action appealed to him, and in contrast to the two solemn days that had just passed it was a welcome interlude. It drove everything else out of his mind.

It began very simply. He was sitting by the mound, when his father, whose ears were wonderfully sharp, heard a noise out in the bushes that he didn't like. He picked up the rifle that he had kept within reach ever since these strange events had begun, and moved toward the clearing. He motioned for the boy to follow him and they concealed themselves from the clearing by keeping back of the bushes. When they were well hidden, but had a good view, they stopped. The boy was excited by this strange adventure and he stood beside his father and watched and waited.

Presently, across the clearing on the opposite side, something moved, and a horse and rider nosed out of the bushes and stopped. The rider looked all around. He didn't get off his horse. He was a white man, and he sat perfectly still and looked at everything—at the trees, the pool, the horses, the burned remains of the kowa.

"Hello!" he called. "Anybody home?"

There was the crack of a rifle and the whirr of a bullet close to his head. He wheeled the horse and dashed back into the bushes as two more shots were fired. He urged the horse through the greasewood as fast as it could go and drew a revolver from a holster as he rode. He had no desire to fight but if he were being chased he intended to fire back. He kept the horse racing through the bushes until they were in the open desert, and he rode on, straight north, as fast as he could, taking no chances of letting a possible pursuer overtake him. It was a pretty narrow squeak.

The child beside Agocho was thrilled by this ambush attack and he watched his father as he skirted the edge of the clearing, keeping out of sight, until he was near one of the horses. Then Agocho mounted it bareback, and rode off in pursuit of the white man. At the opposite edge of the clearing he thought of the child. He turned his horse, rode back to the boy, lifted him up and sat him on the horse, holding him and the rifle in place with one hand. They followed the trail through the greasewood until they came to the open desert. Then Agocho drew up. The white man wasn't far ahead, but he was out of sight and Agocho was not disposed to chase him further. Probably there was only one of them, but Agocho had the boy with him and he didn't want to ride on. But even that was better than leaving the boy alone in camp, a possible victim of another attack which might be imminent if this had been just a blind to lure him on. If that had been their idea it hadn't worked. Agocho rode back to the clearing by a roundabout route, looking for signs of other enemies and finding none. They finally arrived back at camp and the child had had an adventure that he never forgot.

Straight to the nearest ranch rode the white man

where he told a breathless tale of the attack and his escape.

It seems that there had been some smoke down that way four or five days ago. And Petterman—you know Petterman, the deputy in Mecca—thought it was brush, but nobody ever found out for sure and somebody said an Indian called Fig Tree John lived down there and maybe the fellows who killed and robbed old Foster in Coachella might be hiding down there at the Indian camp. Nobody really thought so because those fellows flew the coop long before this, but anyway he thought he'd ride down there and have a look around. Well, he found the place all right, found the clearing and the camp and the horses, but the Indian wasn't in sight. And just as he gave a hail to see if there was anybody around a half a dozen shots landed all around him. He thought quick or he'd have been a goner. He turned the horse and rode off into the brush and he knew damned well that Fig Tree was after him. But he set him a pace and gave him a few shots himself just to discourage him. Fig Tree meant business and he must be a pretty tough hombre to shoot first and ask questions later. He must have gone crazy. That's the only way he could figure it out. Petterman had been a damned fool to trade the redskin some cartridges and this was the result. Believe me, you better stay away from that neck of the woods unless you're looking for trouble. Funny about Indians: that Fig Tree John was in Mecca just the other day, as meek as Moses, sat around Petterman's store the whole day, and now here he is acting like he was on the war-path or something. You got to watch 'em all the time, yes, sir. The only good Indian is a dead Indian, and the fellow who thought that up knew what he was talking about. But say, it might be a good idea to get a bunch of armed men together and go down there and teach that Fig Tree John a lesson. What's he doing here, anyway? It's not safe to have him around if he's goin' to act like that. It would be a good idea to get together sometime and go down there and clean that place out once and for all.

The little boy had the same idea. All day he played at being attacked by white men, and fighting back and driving them off and trailing them over the desert and catching them by short cuts and sheer power of pursuit.

Hadn't that game been played in reality with his father? Hadn't he been told what white men were? They were all bad. His father told him that it was because of the white men that his mother had gone away. The white men had done it. Because of them he would never see her again. So there was only one thing to do with white men. Chase them over the desert, catch them, and kill them.

All day long he pretended he was fighting them. They met, and fought, and chased each other. The battles were quick and bloody. Sometimes the white men wounded him, but always in the end he killed them all. Then they were dead—that curious state of being and not being at the same time. And they became mounds. As soon as they were dead they went into mounds and their families sat around the mounds for four days and put stones on them. And nobody said anything and it was very solemn. Then all of a sudden some more white men came sneaking up and the battle started all over again. It was great fun.

Chapter X

GOING back as far as the association of ideas could retrace itself into the fog of memory, the boy could always recall three or four early events that stood out like islands in the hazy recollection of life in the clearing. He thought of them as he sat on the ground and looked at the figure before him. She was a white woman and she looked strange. She stood before Agocho and talked to him very slowly. The sounds she made were harsh and unmusical, and the words had little or no meaning. Occasionally she spoke Apache, and when she did it was strange to hear, and sounded distorted, but most of the time it made sense. The only trouble was she didn't speak enough Apache to make herself clear, and the rest of the time her white woman jargon had no meaning.

Standing there, talking to Agocho and calling him Fig Tree, and pointing now and then to N'Chai Chidn and calling him little Fig Tree or little Johnny, she made a surprising figure, and the boy sat quietly and looked up at her, ignoring most of her words and allowing the ideas she stimulated in his mind to take form and recall many things that belonged to the time that was past.

She was a woman—yes, a white woman, but nevertheless a woman. She stood for something that he didn't know much about. Of course, at the age of nine he wasn't interested in any kind of women, but he had seen so little of them that this figure standing there and jabbering away kept his attention.

Back in his memory there was a vague figure, difficult now to visualize in concrete image, of a woman to whom he had clung and to whom he was indebted for the simplest kind of knowledge. What she was like he couldn't say, but she had been there and he had been aware of her and he even remembered the inflections of her voice. He could hear her say "chu-ga-na-ai," and "kle-ga-na-ai," and "tit-so-se," words which he remembered entirely by hearsay and not because they meant sun, and moon, and stars. This woman, standing before him, brought back the other one who had been his mother and who had been dead almost as long as he could remember.

There wasn't much before that. Memory curved away out of sight back beyond that figure. There was a day when white men came and a big fire had been built, and a day when he had played all by himself beside the pool. There was a time when Agocho, now so positive a figure, was equally as indistinct and intangible and hard to remember; for instance, the time they sat for days and nights beside the mound of sand. What was Agocho then? Was he this same man? Yes, he was this same man, but the boy was just beginning to know him and understand him then, and now he had known him so long and understood him so well that it seemed as if he were another man back there in those days and nights beside the mound in the greasewood.

He sat still and watched and thought. It was strange to hear a white person speak his language. Of course she couldn't speak very well, and she kept trying to

speak in the white language and that didn't make any
sense at all. She was the only woman who had ever been
there, and that was strange, too. She was the only woman
to be seen in the clearing since that vague figure who
had been his mother and who had been a woman, too.
She had been something like this. It was curious to see
a woman and to think his mother had been one of these.
It was a very curious experience.

Before this he had never seen a white woman except
from a distance, for he and his father seldom went north
into the ranch country and only twice in his memory
had they gone to the town. The last time was a year
ago and the time before that had been almost three years
ago. And both times they had stayed but a little while—
just long enough for Agocho to trade with a fat man
who called him Fig Tree and slapped him on the back
and who had tried to shake hands with the boy and say
funny sounds to him. His father didn't like the town
and when he found that the fat man wouldn't give him
what he wanted he told the boy he was never going there
again. And they never had, which was disappointing
because it was an interesting place and the kind of a
place he would like to know something about. But
Agocho didn't like to talk about it and the boy had to
try to remember it from the two times he had seen it.
That town had a lot of white people and some white
women just like this one standing here in the clearing.
His father hated all of them.

It was a wonder he let her stay. That was a surprise.
He remembered the time a white man rode into the
clearing long ago when he and his father had been
sitting beside the mound. Agocho had fired at the white

man and chased him away and he would have killed him if he hadn't run for his life. Not many white men bothered them after that, and those who did got the same welcome. Every one of them got shot at, and once there had been one who had been in such a hurry to get away that he had lost his hat. Agocho had kept that hat ever since and it was in the kowa now and the boy knew exactly where it was.

If he and his father had little to do with the people and land to the north, they made up for it by their knowledge of the rest of the world. They had been everywhere to the south, all over the desert country. And many times they had explored the mountains to the west, and several times had ridden to the east around the big water to the other side and explored that part of the world, too. But very seldom did they go north into the white man's country. Agocho said it was a bad place, and any country that white men took became a bad place and was best left alone unless there were enough Apaches to drive the white men out. And that was impossible here because there were hundreds of white men and only two Apaches, his father and himself. So they were content to stay away from the white men and the white men had to stay away from them. If they didn't they would get shot. And every one of them who had come snooping down from the ranches had found that out in a hurry.

But this was different. Here was the first white person who had ever been allowed to come peacefully into the clearing.

The boy looked at his father. Agocho was watching the white woman. Probably what she said was interesting because he could understand the white talk even though he never used it any more himself and never explained any of it to the boy.

N'Chai Chidn wondered how long this was going to last. Possibly Agocho would pick up the rifle and kill this white woman. It would be easy. She wasn't armed. She didn't appear to have even a knife. And there was the rifle a short distance away from Agocho. All he had to do was reach for it. But he didn't. He just sat and looked at her and listened. It was strange.

She had come walking into the camp a little while ago as if it were the most commonplace thing in the world. They had been sitting before the kowa and she had walked right up to them, speaking as she came. It was so astonishing to see a strange woman walk into the clearing and say in Apache, "I come as a friend and Ste-na-tlih-a has sent me and you must listen with both your ears," that Agocho and N'Chai Chidn had been unable to do anything but sit still and listen. The boy wondered if she could be a Goddess, but later he dismissed it because the Gods aren't white. No, she was just a white woman who seemed to have a great deal to say and who wasn't afraid to say it. But the details of what she had to say and what Agocho was going to do about it, he couldn't imagine.

The boy was wrong about one thing. Though Agocho sat quietly and looked at the woman and seemed to be listening to her, he really gave little thought to what she had to say. She brought a number of thoughts and recollections to his mind. Here was the first woman to come to the clearing since Kai-a. It was a surprise that he hadn't expected. White men, yes, but why a white

woman? There were two white men in the world whom
he wanted to kill and whom he would surely kill some
day. But this woman—what relation could she have to
that? He hesitated and looked at her and wondered what
her existence really meant. She had begun talking a
mixture of Apache and English and he ignored her
words and tried to see just how she fitted into the peculiar
puzzle that the Gods had placed before him.

Six years now, and a little more than that, he had
been trying to solve it. It was very difficult, but the Gods
had a solution and a meaning, and if he thought carefully this might be a clew. There was a balance, a justice,
that was eventual and inevitable. There was absolutely
no doubt of that. The death of Kai-a and the outrage
committed against him by two white men had never
been settled. The way to do it had never been made
clear. After his futile pursuit of those two men six years
ago the Gods had turned their backs on his problem
and everything had come to a standstill. He had thought
about it a thousand times. He had tried to find the
way that they wanted him to go, and the only way he
could find was to wait. If he were very quiet and very
alert he might see the way. He had fasted time and again
to purify his body, and he had sat perfectly still and
tried to keep his mind blank for days in order to have
it completely clear so that he could pick up some message from the Gods. None came. He had made no rash
effort as time went by. He hadn't lost his head in wild
anger; he hadn't made any attack on other white men
unless they came after him; he had done nothing but
wait and search within himself for some clew as to what
the Gods really wanted him to do.

All he could think of was that there must be some
reason for delay. The Gods wanted to wait. They wanted
him to wait. And yet delay had nothing to do with
the certainty of eventual justice. It might be that those
two men would return. It might be ordained that he
was to kill them both at the very spot in which they
had killed Kai-a. That was a possible solution. If the
Gods meant that, they would bring the two white men
back and all he could do was to wait until they came.
That seemed possible. And if that is what the Gods
meant he must surely not return to the White River
country until justice had been done here. There was
no way to find those two white men. A vague pursuit
would be hopeless. Time means nothing, and the Gods
never consider time for their world is timeless. It might
be that they intended to bring those white men back,
and if that were the case, the only thing to do was to
wait until they did it.

He looked up at this white woman and wondered why
she had been sent. She said that Ste-na-tlih-a had sent
her, but that was probably a lie. Still, she meant something. It was so unusual that it must be part of the
scheme. It was up to him to find out what part. He
listened for a moment.

"—and this school is for his own good. It will help
make little Johnny a useful citizen. It will teach him to
use his brains. It doesn't cost any money. All he has to
do is to go to it. It makes skhin n'chai kots-its-in. Savvy,
Fig Tree? Kots-its-in and ko-za very smart. Savvy?"

Agocho stared at her but he didn't know what to say.
Her words sounded like a lot of nonsense. She touched

her head and pointed to her tongue and then to the boy.

Then she went on talking and Agocho looked at her closely, but his mind was full of ideas apart from her speech.

For six years he had thought of white people in relation to only one idea—justice. Until that score was settled he would never abandon it. He would never cease to think about it.

And there had been one or two distinct signs from the Gods, one in particular that was easy to read. It had occurred about two years after the death of Kai-a. It was the first intimation he had received that the Gods were watching him and he rejoiced in the knowledge.

It had come about quite naturally. Two years had gone by. The white men had not returned. He had been discouraged and he had decided to give up and return to the White River. He had old friends. He had two other wives there. Probably they had all given him up for dead. N'Chai Chidn was then almost five years old and was big enough to be able to travel. So he made all arrangements for departure. Everything was packed and ready and he was about to leave the spring and the greasewood probably forever. Then the Gods spoke and he saw that it was the wrong thing to do and that they didn't want him to go. They showed their disapproval by storm. The wind blew and the clouds gathered and it rained for a whole day. For over five years Agocho had been living beside the inland sea. It had been more than five years since he and Kai-a had found that place. And never in that time had it rained. It was a land of no rain. But that day it rained and rained hard and the Gods brought it about to show him that he was about to do the wrong thing. It was so very obvious that he unpacked the horses at once and never since then had he made the slightest effort to move back to his own White River country. And that must be right for never since that day had it rained again and now that was four years ago.

So there was a reason for staying on and the Gods wanted it that way. And that way it was going to be until justice had been done in this spot or until the Gods gave a sign which meant for him to leave.

Then to-day this strange event took place, and a white woman who spoke some Apache had appeared from nowhere and talked a lot of gibberish about smart heads and smart tongues and how the boy should go to a place where he would get a smart head and a nimble tongue and a lot more foolish talk that made little or no sense. Agocho had just about decided that this woman was an impostor and had no reason for talking to him when there was a noise on the far side of the clearing and a white man stepped into view followed by a second white man. Both men were armed.

Agocho reached for the rifle and stood up. N'Chai Chidn watched the white men and looked from them to his father. The woman was between Agocho and the strangers. They stopped as soon as they came into view and Agocho hesitated. Had it not been for the woman he would have fired at them.

"Is everything all right, Mrs. Reeves?" called one of the men.

"Yes, we're getting along all right," said the woman.

"You were a long time," said the second man, "and we were a little anxious."

"He's friendly enough," said the woman.

"He's got his rifle," called the first man.

"That's because he doesn't know you," said the woman. "He's all right. He's been listening to me for fifteen minutes. If you'll both go back to the buckboard and wait I'll come along pretty soon."

"We'll be right out here in the brush if you want us, Mrs. Reeves," said the second man.

And still looking back at the scene they walked out of the clearing and disappeared from view.

"They're members of the school board," said the woman, apologetically. "And they told me, Mr. Fig Tree John, that you would shoot anybody who came on your land. That's why we let you alone. But when Mr. Petterman at Mecca said he knew you and said he thought you were an Apache, I said, 'Land's sakes, my husband and I lived with the Jicarilla Apaches for five years and with the San Carlos for two, and I guess I can talk to any Apache who has ears to hear with.' So I came right down here in spite of what they said about you because I know your people and I've always been able to get along right well with them."

Agocho listened to this and looked across the clearing and held on to the rifle. He couldn't see any reason in all this.

"Why do you come here?" he asked in Apache.

The woman asked him to repeat his question.

"Why you here?" he asked in English. "What those white men want?"

"Now, Fig Tree," she said, "I've just told you why. Now don't you pretend no savvy, because I know you savvy all right. I'm not going over all that again. But we've got a school and it's paid for by county tax and it's right that all children should have an equal chance. If you put your boy in that school he'll bless you for it some day and you know that as well as I do. I know your people and I always do the right thing by you. Now you think it over and I'm going to come see you again. What is your boy's name, Fig Tree?"

Agocho looked at her and thought it was none of her business. He didn't answer.

"What's your name, little boy?" asked the woman.

The boy looked at her in open-mouthed surprise. His shiny black eyes appraised her critically but he said nothing.

"M'mm," she said. "A plain case. He's backward and he needs schooling the worst way. It's the only hope for your people, Fig Tree. It's their one salvation—education. Now I'm coming down here and see you again. And if you want any advice you come up to Coachella and ask for Mrs. Reeves. Everybody knows me. Martha Goddard Reeves. Good-by to you, Fig Tree."

Then she turned and walked across the clearing. Agocho watched her disappear and he heard her voice and the voices of the men when she met them. Then the voices faded away as they moved westward through the brush to a wagon road that ran from the ranch land southeast across the desert to the Imperial Valley, many miles away. The road had been there a year or two and Agocho objected to it, but so few people used it that he rarely saw any one on it.

He stood looking after her, bewildered by her many words, still hearing her and seeing her figure after she had disappeared. He put the rifle down, and wondered why he had done nothing. It would have been so easy to kill her as she walked away. He could have shot her in the back and then slipped into the bushes and shot both those men when they came running back at the report of the rifle. And that is exactly what they would have done. Those weren't the two men he wanted to kill but he would not have been wrong in shooting them. But he had not done it and now it was too late. It wasn't quite the moment.

He understood how Qulba Bachu had felt many years ago when Agocho's uncle had stolen Qulba Bachu's wife. Any Apache can kill a man for stealing his wife. Yet Qulba Bachu had done nothing when Agocho's uncle had stolen his wife. He had done nothing for a long time. All the relatives of Qulba Bachu thought he was a coward and was afraid to reclaim his wife and kill the man who had stolen her and taken her away to live in his kowa. It was only an hour's ride on horseback from Qulba Bachu's kowa across the mountain to the home of Agocho's uncle. Yet Qulba Bachu shunned violence and sought another wife. The whole clan laughed at him and Agocho's uncle met Qulba Bachu several times in the course of a year and nothing happened.

Agocho remembered it, even though he had been a little boy at the time, and he had grown up with a great respect for his uncle and scorn for Qulba Bachu.

Then one night, four years after the theft of his wife,

Qulba Bachu rode over the mountain. At dawn he waited outside the kowa of Agocho's uncle. And when his uncle came out he shot him nine times through the body and then walked over the prostrate form, placed the rifle against the head, and blew out the brains. Then he rode back over the mountain to his own kowa without taking his former wife. He hadn't shot Agocho's uncle on her account. He had shot him because he had the right to shoot him and he felt like doing it. He had acquired a new wife in the meantime and he didn't want the first one. And everybody knew that Qulba Bachu was a proper man after all and that he had only waited to be sure that he really wanted to kill Agocho's uncle. When he was sure of it he had done it and done it well and everybody was sorry for the things they had said about Qulba Bachu. That ended the trouble and Agocho's relatives and Qulba Bachu's relatives became friendly again.

And now Agocho knew exactly how Qulba Bachu had felt about it. He hadn't been sure and he had been careful not to make any mistakes. Agocho hadn't been sure that he ought to shoot the white woman and the two strange white men. He had hesitated and delayed, but it wasn't cowardice; it was uncertainty. He sat down and wondered again how justice could eventually be brought to bear and by what means he would some day find a way of actually consummating it.

The three members of the school board walked to the desert road, climbed into the wagon and rode north toward Coachella.

"Well, I take off my hat to you, Mrs. Reeves," said

the driver of the wagon. "There's not a man in Coachella or Mecca who would walk in on that fellow. He's a bad one."

"Yes," said the other. "He's got a bad name around these parts, but I guess you know how to handle his kind."

"Never be afraid of them. That's the secret of Apaches. Never let them think you're afraid and never take your eyes off of them," said the woman. "I've lived among them for years when Mr. Reeves was in Arizona and New Mexico. That fellow sat perfectly still and behaved himself. He listened to what I said and hadn't the least animosity toward me at all. And he's an Apache, all right. What he's doing over here, I don't know. But he's from Arizona, all right. I can tell that by the kind of kowa he's built."

"What did he say about sending his kid to school?" asked one of the men.

"He didn't say much. He just listened and took it all in. I know he was interested because he asked me to repeat it all over again."

"Think of that," said the driver. "Why if a *man* walks in there he starts shootin' first and talkin' later."

"Well, they're like animals," said Mrs. Reeves. "They know who likes them and who doesn't, and if you handle them right you can do anything with them."

They rode on for another mile, discussing the civilization of the savage and the various means of bringing him around.

"I wonder what happened to his wife," said Mrs. Reeves. "I forgot to ask him. Did she die in childbirth, does anybody know?"

"Well, there's a story about her," said the man who was driving. "It's not a very nice story and it's hard to say how much truth there is in it but it seems he's got one terrible temper. Some of the boys around here have had a brush or two with him and they all agree he's a bad hombre. Not trustworthy, you know. He'll walk up to a ranch and order a man off. Claims all this country is his. Well, he had a wife and—oh, I guess it must have been six or seven years ago that he went into Mecca with a lot of baskets she had made. He wanted to get rid of them and Petterman gave him some tobacco for them. Well, while he was there, there was a big fire down this way and everybody saw the smoke but nobody could figure out what it was. But Tommy Middleton rode down a day or two later to have a look around. And what do you suppose he found?"

Mrs. Reeves didn't know, so the man went on with the story without waiting to be questioned.

"Tommy rode up to the clearing, and he said he found it by the smell. He said there was the worst smell he'd ever run across and he figured that Fig Tree was roasting a coyote or something. He took a peek at the clearing and the—the—uh, what do you call that hut they build?"

"The kowa," said Mrs. Reeves.

"Yeah. Well, he had set fire to his own kowa and burnt it up. And he didn't want anybody to know it and he took a pot shot at Tommy as soon as Tommy stuck his nose in the clearing. Tommy ducked and beat it right away. Well, I'm not saying yes or no to this, but nobody ever saw Mrs. Fig Tree John after that. You can draw any conclusion you want, but there he goes and sells all her baskets to Petterman, and then she disappears, and Tommy Middleton goes down there and there's a funny smell, and Fig Tree has set fire to the kowa for some good reason and doesn't want anybody around the place. Of course, nothing was ever done about it, but the boys who were here at the time generally feel that he got tired of her and maybe got drunk and beat her up and got rid of her in a way that seemed mighty plain to see. Mighty effective, too, I guess."

"Land's sakes!" said Mrs. Reeves with a shudder. "Land's sakes alive!"

Chapter XI

THE road was paved in 1921. Traffic between the Imperial Valley towns and the Coachella Valley towns and the markets in, around and about Los Angeles warranted it. From Banning, up in the mountains, the road ran straight down into the desert country, jogged through Indio, skirted Coachella, ignored Mecca, and then ran parallel to the southern shore line of the Salton Sea for a long straight sweep across the desert and finally reached the Imperial Valley towns of Brawley and El Centro.

Traffic and trucking had made this highway necessary. Cotton, alfalfa, lettuce, and melons were brought up from the Imperial country that had once been a sterile sandy desert below sea level. And alfalfa, grapefruit, and the famous Deglet-Noor dates, the first sprays of which had been imported from Morocco, were the chief products of the Coachella country. First the railroad and then the highway opened these valleys to prosperity.

The road passed within a mile of Agocho's home in the clearing, but there was no way to tell that from the highway. Motorists sped by without stopping and only the local people knew that Fig Tree John had a water hole over there somewhere. Fig Tree was seldom seen on the highway. He was not a man to seek publicity. But if you looked carefully, even before the road had been paved, you might see an Indian boy sitting back from

151

the road in the sagebrush, or perhaps get a glimpse of him jogging along on horseback anywhere between Coachella and the lower end of the Salton Sea. In the old days your own dust flew up so much that a fleeting glimpse of him was all you could get. And then the road was often corduroy or sandy or both and there was no time to take your eyes off the tracks ahead of you. But with the pavement, driving was easier and those who passed over the road many times had been sure to see, at some time or other, a young Indian boy who stared at them as long as they were in sight. He was Fig Tree John's son and whenever any one mentioned him they called him Johnny. He was fourteen years old when the paving began and he was fifteen before it was finished. Most people would have said he was older. But fifteen years of brilliant sun, and an active life on foot and horseback across the floor of the desert from the Chocolate Mountains to the Santa Rosas, and simple food and good hours and no dissipation, had given him a physique beyond his years.

But the white civilization so close at hand and so accessible piqued more and more his interest. One day, a year or two before the road was paved, he sat beside an ironwood tree and watched the automobiles. There might be two or three of them in a few minutes. And then an hour might go by with only one car passing in that time. They were interesting things, and thrilling, and he had a great desire to ride in one. Sometimes they were painted in bright colors, but most of them were dark. He liked the bright ones best. But no matter what the color, they all threw a lot of dust and sand into the air and he was sure that riding one of these things must be more fun than riding the most spirited horse.

That he might ever ride in one of these white man's speed wagons seemed impossible. After the road was paved there were many more of them and he thought about it a great deal and even considered going to one of the nearby date ranches and getting in one of these cars when nobody was looking. But then he wouldn't know what to do to make it run and probably the white men would be angry and might take a shot at him.

The opportunity, however, of riding in a white man's car came about more quickly and simply than he had expected. Agocho thought they were one of the white man's many inventions, all of which made the world more unpleasant to live in, and N'Chai Chidn gave up trying to talk to him about it. It was hard to talk to Agocho about such things anyway because there were no words in Apache to describe the things he wanted to say. And he knew so little English that it was impossible to talk very much in that language. Still, he was learning more. He was old enough to ride anywhere he pleased by himself, and once he had gone into Mecca and stayed there all day in front of the fat man's store listening to the white men and watching everything they did. Nobody molested him, in fact most of the white people paid no heed to him at all, and the round fat man called him "Fig Tree Junior," and "the young sprout," and "the chip off the old block" and other funny names. It must have been all right because the fat man smiled when he did it and nobody seemed to mind his being there. N'Chai Chidn didn't speak to anybody at all, but he listened and watched and learned a lot. He never said anything to Agocho about it because Agocho hated and mistrusted all white men and would have been angry if he thought his son had been in the white man's town all day.

For several days after that Agocho and N'Chai Chidn went hunting together. They went up into the Santa Rosas, across the ridge to what the white men called Clark's dry lake and around through the Borego country and the Vallecito Mountains and back to the Salton Sea by way of Kane Spring. About white men they said nothing and thought nothing, and it wasn't until they were almost home and were crossing the highway that the boy thought of automobiles again. It had been a good trip. They had the carcasses of a mountain lion and two mountain sheep and a burden basket stuffed with piñon. Agocho wanted the boy to be a good hunter. After all, he himself was nearing sixty and not as active as the boy. Together, with Agocho's skill and experience and N'Chai Chidn's youth and vigor they had all the requisites of the hunt.

Two days in camp, and the boy was ready for more activity. Agocho was not. He had plenty to eat and his only concern was to get some corn so that he could make tizwin. The boy knew where there was some corn and he said that he might be able to get it. He wasn't sure. Agocho didn't ask any questions, so the boy saddled up and rode north.

The date ranches now came down to a short distance from the clearing. It was only two miles north to Mack's ranch and one mile straight up the beach to Paul's property that had been set out in dates the year before.

These were the nearest ranches, and between them and the clearing the country was still raw desert. Water below the surface of the ground and irrigation was the answer to successful date farming. Agocho's own property had a quantity of alkali soil around it or the white men would have found a means of getting him out before this.

N'Chai Chidn rode west to the highway and then north until he came to the Mack ranch. After his experience in Mecca he had no fear about boldly riding up to a ranch house. He felt that white people were not as dangerous as Agocho had led him to believe.

At the Mack ranch there was a Mexican youth named Jose who was perhaps twenty-one, and who was Mack's hired man and jack of all trades. Jose had seen N'Chai Chidn before, and while they had never spoken, they knew each other by sight. Jose had a wife and baby, and they lived in a little shack near the main house. As the Indian boy rode up he could see Jose moving about near a carpenter shop and tool shed. The water pump was making a chugging noise and Jose was busy beside the carpenter shop. He did not see the boy until he turned around. He started over toward the water pump, a wrench in his hand, and looked up quickly. The Indian sat on his horse and said nothing.

"Hola!" said Jose. "What you want, huh?"

"Hola," said N'Chai Chidn, believing that it was an English word.

Jose went to the water pump, placed the wrench on a nut, and slowly tightened it.

"Sì, you devil," he said. "Old son of a bitch. He go bust when I very busy."

He looked at N'Chai Chidn and grinned. "I know you," he said. "Usted es Juanito Fig Tree. Verdad?"

Juanito Fig Tree grinned back.

"Say, you listen to me," said Jose. "Maybe you like to work some. Maybe you like for to get little job."

Juanito Fig Tree didn't say yes or no.

"You get off caballo and I show you some work, muy pronto," said Jose. "I very busy. Mr. Mack he go Los Angeles and water pump go bust and I try all day to fix him and now very busy. Mucho trabajo y alguno trabajo para usted."

He picked up an ax and pointed to a pile of wood.

"I have too busy time to chop kindling for Mrs. Mack's stove. You chop him up. Sabe usted?"

Not far from the woodpile was Jose's Ford roadster. It was an old model and had seen a lot of service. But in an idle afternoon Jose had painted it a brilliant green. Johnny Fig Tree looked at the woodpile and the ax and the Ford. He understood that Jose wanted him to cut the wood, and he swung himself off his horse, tethered it to the tool shed, and said the single word "work."

"Bueno muchacho," said Jose, taking the ax and chopping a few pieces of the wood. Then, grinning broadly, he handed the ax to the Indian.

"Little pieces. Not too big," said Jose. "Chop it all and I give you something nice. What you want? Que quiere usted, Juanito?"

Johnny was looking at the Ford.

"Nice car," he said.

"Ho, no, no," said Jose. "I no give you the Ford car. Ford car cost plenty dinero. You like him?"

Johnny admired the Ford. He walked over toward it and looked it over carefully without getting too close to it. The Mexican was flattered by this admiration of his property.

"Say, I tell you what," said Jose. "I got to go to the store and buy new washers for that damn water pump. I let you ride to town and buy you a smoke if you cut up all that wood like a good Juanito. Sabe? You, me, we go ride in Ford after you chop woodpile."

He pantomimed steering the Ford and made a buzzing noise with his mouth as if he were spinning the engine.

"You and me in the Ford," he said.

Johnny got the idea. It was exciting. Certainly he was willing to chop a little wood. He took another look at the green roadster and then went to work on the woodpile with a great display of energy. Sticks flew up in the air and chips and splinters went flying in all directions. Jose was a friend and he wanted to make a trade. He wanted that wood chopped into pieces and into pieces it was going. He threw the ax over his shoulder and brought it down with terrific force. Blow after blow he struck, and Jose, satisfied with this exhibition, went back to work in the tool shed.

For something more than half an hour Jose worked in the tool shed. At the end of that time his assistant was still cutting wood, but his pace had slowed down considerably, and the willing grin with which he had started had changed to a look of persistent determination. Sweat was standing out on his forehead and running down his neck. He gritted his teeth and swung the ax again. Jose was pleased to see so much wood cut. Probably he wouldn't have to cut any to-morrow.

"Bueno muchacho," he said. "Bastante."

Johnny looked up. He had done enough and he had decided that for himself. He swung the ax over his head and hurled it twenty feet away.

"Ee-yah," he said, breathing deeply.

"Careful that ax," said Jose. "I got to use him again. Now we go to town. Say, you work good."

Jose stepped into the Ford and beckoned to Johnny to get in beside him. Johnny did so, looking at everything with great interest, while Jose stepped on the starter, pulled the choke, and the engine opened up in a series of loud explosions.

"Gettin' warmed up," said Jose, cheerfully. "Damn good Ford car."

He backed it around in a half circle, threw in the clutch, and they were off with a jerk that snapped Johnny's head back. Jose's idea of driving was to grip the steering wheel tightly and step on the gas. He maintained the same speed whether the road was rough or smooth. They bounced along the ranch road, hit the highway with a thud and rattle and then clattered along on the hard surface at thirty miles an hour.

"Paid fifty dollars for this Ford car," Jose said, raising his voice above the rattle of the engine, "and paid thirty more dollars gettin' it all nice. Damn nice now."

Johnny didn't say anything. He was thrilled beyond his limited vocabulary. Never had the world raced past him like this. Never had a horse been as smooth under him as Jose's Ford car. He sat straight in the seat and let the wind blow on him. It was an exciting and delightful experience.

About a mile from Mecca an element of danger appeared, and for a moment Johnny was frightened. Another car was coming toward them from the opposite direction. That strip of highway wasn't very wide and Jose didn't seem to see the oncoming car. At least he paid no attention to it whatever. And just as Johnny had almost decided to leap out of the Ford the approaching car whisked by in the flash of an instant so close that the two drivers could have leaned out and touched hands as they passed. Johnny looked back at the other car rapidly disappearing in the rear and then he looked at Jose. But Jose seemed to take it all as a matter of course and nothing at all unusual or worth mentioning.

Presently they banged across the railroad tracks and came to a stop before Petterman's store. Jose climbed out of the car and went into the store. Johnny didn't move. He was proud to sit in a white man's Ford and calmly wait to be driven back to the Mack ranch. He felt very important and he admired Jose who was able to come and go at will in so handsome a vehicle. He hoped that the white people in the town might see him and think that the car was his. He wished that he were as smart as Jose and able to own a fine car.

In a few minutes Jose came out of the store. Mr. Petterman wasn't in sight and Johnny was sorry because he wanted Mr. Petterman to see him in the car. Jose had a paper bag with some washers in it and two packs of cigarettes. He gave one pack to Johnny and tore off the top of his own pack. Then he struck a match and lit a cigarette for himself, and gave the packet of matches to Johnny.

Again Jose spun the car around in reverse and again they started off with a jolt. Johnny knew what to do with the cigarettes for he had seen white men use them before. He had a difficult time lighting a cigarette in the moving car, and several times the matches burnt his fingers. Finally he succeeded, but as he did so the Ford was banging over the railroad tracks and Johnny bit off the end of the cigarette. The tobacco flakes got in his mouth and the wind made the cigarette burn up one side. It was not as pleasant a sensation as he expected and he looked at Jose who kept his cigarette going nicely and hanging loosely between his lips. Johnny took a couple of long puffs and swallowed some pieces of loose tobacco and found bits of paper on his tongue. He became disgusted and threw the thing away. Then he looked back to see where it landed, but the Ford was spinning along so rapidly that his eyes could not follow it. He enjoyed every bit of the ride back to the ranch house, and this time, when an oncoming car sped past them, he was not afraid of a collision.

Jose swung the car off the highway, bumped and rattled across the sandy road, and came to a stop right beside the tool shed where Johnny's horse watched them arrive with signs of alarm.

For the rest of the afternoon Jose was busy about the ranch. He turned the water into the date palms, and slowly it made its way along the shallow ditches and furrows until it had flooded most of the grove. He returned to the tool shed and did several mysterious things with tools that Johnny had never seen before. He went to the corral and fed and watered the stock. He was a very active Mexican boy and Johnny was greatly impressed with his many duties and the ease and importance with which he carried them off. He had come to admire Jose very much.

Toward sunset he untied his horse and rode back to the clearing. It had been one of the most interesting days of his life.

Agocho was mending a horsehair bridle as he rode in. He looked for the corn that Johnny had started off to get, but Johnny had forgotten all about it. Agocho wanted to know why he hadn't brought it and Johnny tried to tell Agocho all about the exciting events of the day. It was hard to tell in Apache and he had to use a mixture of Apache, Spanish, and English words that made the story complicated indeed.

Agocho went on mending the bridle and didn't say much, but the story annoyed him more than he let the boy know. Such free mingling with white people was bad. It was undignified and wrong. The boy was young or he would have known better. Agocho saw the cigarettes and the matches and he wanted to know where they came from. And when he discovered that the boy had actually worked for them, earned them by cutting wood at a white man's ranch, he was furious. He tried to explain to the boy that working for a white man was beneath contempt. If he had wanted some wood and had cut some wood, he should have brought the wood back. That would have been all right. But to work for a white man's profit and advantage was something that no right thinking man would ever do under any circumstances.

Johnny was confused.

Among the white men everybody seemed to work. That seemed to be the thing to do. But Agocho, who knew everything and was wise beyond belief, said that it was all wrong. The boy couldn't reconcile these two opposite ideas and he wondered if the white people were living the wrong way. He tried to think it out carefully, but he couldn't reach any conclusion. Yet he was sure that his father must be right. He always was.

Agocho was greatly annoyed by the boy's experiences in this white intruder's world. That was no way for him to grow up. Here he was at the age of puberty with none of the advantages and education that he would have had back with his clan in the White River country. He was growing up in ignorance. It was time for him to take part in a tribal ceremony. He should mingle with other Apache boys of his own age, and they should fast for three days under the direction of the medicine man and then they should all take part in the puberty dance. Then they would be men. The clans for miles around would gather for this event. It would be a long tribal holiday and the dancing and ceremonies would last for three or four days.

And there would be a dance of young girls, virgins also at puberty, and at the end of the festival at dawn on the fourth day, the girls would run a foot race and the boys would pursue them. It would be their last dash for virginity and the boys would overtake them and catch them and claim them and then they would all be men and women. That was the way things ought to be, but here, so far from the clan, all that was impossible. It wasn't right for N'Chai Chidn to be handicapped by being kept away from his own people. Agocho thought again of packing up his possessions and beginning the long journey back to the Apache country. It would be the fair thing to do for the boy.

But then, there was this other situation. There was something yet to be done here. There was something not yet completed that had to be done, and by the dictates of the Gods, it had to be done at this place. He had waited a long time. He could wait a little longer. There was justice to be executed here and the day was coming when that justice was sure to take place. It might be tomorrow; it might be any time. Foolish, indeed, would he be to leave now with the old score incomplete when, any day, the Gods might show him the way. And when he saw it and he knew it he would act at once; swift and terrible, he would balance that score, an eye for an eye, with all the pent-up venom of twelve years' waiting. It was the one outstanding desire of his life, and when that moment came he would wipe out that old outrage with every atom of his strength, energy, blood and bone. May the Great Spirits bring that justice soon!

Then, back to the White River, and back to the clan where N'Chai Chidn could live a proper life. Perhaps he would be retarded a year or two or three. But he was a strong, smart boy and he would soon catch up to the activities of the others of his own age who had lived normal lives.

That night Agocho was in no hurry to sleep and when the boy was ready to wrap up in his blankets Agocho told him that they had things to do and that he must come along and help. N'Chai Chidn did not understand

and Agocho wouldn't explain any further. About the middle of the night Agocho saddled one of the horses and told the boy to saddle another. Agocho threw a pair of saddle-bags over each horse, and then, leading the way with the boy following, he rode north through the desert toward the ranch country.

It was only a short ride to the Mack ranch. They left the horses out under the date palms and went on foot toward the main house and the outlying buildings, carrying the saddle-bags with them. Agocho asked the boy where the woodpile was and the boy showed him. Quietly moving around Agocho examined the property and told the boy to put the wood he had cut into the saddle-bags. The boy did as he was told. Agocho found the ax a short distance away and he picked that up. The tool shed had not been locked, but it was dark inside and he was afraid to go in and run the risk of knocking something over and making a noise. There was a small screwdriver beside the water pump and he handed that to the boy, too. Then they each swung a pair of loaded saddle-bags over their shoulders and started back to their horses. Agocho stopped on the way and added to the booty a number of grapefruit from a grapefruit tree. Then they threw the saddle-bags over the backs of the horses and quietly rode away.

For several days N'Chai Chidn did not ride north. He and Agocho went down the shore line of the inland sea and rode back across the desert to the clearing. They found nothing on the trip and it was not particularly interesting. Life went on in its casual way, and the boy was soon thinking about the country to the north and wondering what interesting things he might find if he were to ride up that way again. But his father did not want him to do it and he put it out of his mind.

One day, however, when he was starting out alone for the Santa Rosas, he changed his course and rode north along the highway. Several cars passed him and one of the drivers waved to him.

At the entrance of the Mack ranch he turned in. It would be nice to see that Jose again and have another look at that Ford car. Jose was sitting in the shade doing nothing. His wife was washing some clothes near their little shack and the baby was crawling around on the ground.

"Hallo, Juanito," said Jose.

Juanito smiled and dismounted.

"No work to-day," said Jose. "Plenty time."

Johnny said nothing.

"Say, you didn't think I give you that ax last week for workin' here, did you?"

"No," said Johnny.

"I can't find that damn ax no place. Beat hell where he go to."

"Sure," said Johnny. He stood beside his horse and looked at Jose.

Jose lay almost flat on his back with his knees raised and his hat well down over his eyes. He felt lazy and comfortable and happy. He had nothing to do for half an hour until Mr. Mack called him and then they would go to work at pollenizing the dates. He carried on a desultory conversation with Johnny and he thought that Johnny wasn't very bright.

"Cuantos años?" he finally asked, and when Johnny said nothing he asked in English, "How old are you?"

Johnny didn't know what to answer. He was sixteen but he didn't know it.

"You're kinda dumb," Jose said. "Didn't you go to school?"

"No," said Johnny.

"Don't you know nothing?" Jose asked.

"No," said Johnny.

"If I was you I'd go to school and learn something. Reading and writing. Everybody has to read and write. Why don't you go to school and learn something, huh?"

"No sabe," said Johnny.

Jose laughed. He rolled over on one side and rested his head on his arm and elbow. He chuckled at Johnny, and presently he spat, and then spoke some more.

"You're never gonna get no place," he said. "You're never gonna get any money, or any wife, or any Ford car. I went to school and now I got a job and wife and a Ford car. I speak English just like American and I'm the best dancer in the valley. You don't know nothing."

Johnny didn't understand all of this but he understood the reproach and the criticism. He felt that Jose was a superior person and he envied him.

"You don't know the first lesson they say in school," said Jose. "Who was the father of your country? Can you tell me who was the father of your country?"

"No," said Johnny.

"Everybody knows that," Jose said. "I know it. My wife knows it. Mr. Mack knows it. Everybody in the valley knows who was the father of your country. Everybody except you."

"Who," said Johnny.

Jose laughed again.

"George Washington," he said, and sat up. "George Washington. You don't know it. George Washington."

"George Washington," said Johnny.

Then Jose rolled on the ground in glee, but Johnny failed to see anything funny in the strange words "George Washington." He didn't like to be laughed at. This place wasn't amusing him at all. He swung himself onto his horse and rode away. Jose called something after him but he couldn't hear what it was. He went back to the highway and rode on north.

Instead of crossing the railroad tracks and going into Mecca he rode further north than he had ever been before, and a few miles brought him to Coachella. He was surprised to find this town larger than Mecca. It was almost in the center of the valley and the main highway intersected its one main street which ran for a quarter of a mile from the highway to the railroad. Where Mecca had ten or a dozen buildings, Coachella had four or five blocks of houses and stores. Johnny thought it very impressive, and if he hadn't seen Mecca and white men before this he would not have ridden into Coachella.

There were a number of people in the main street and a dozen automobiles standing around the store buildings. There were white men and there were darker men who were Mexicans like Jose, but nevertheless white men, and there were one or two men who were darker still and different from the white men in many ways; and while he recognized the superficial differences of the darker men he didn't know that they were Indians like himself and that they were Cahuillas from the San Jacinto Mountains. Indians or not, they were strangers to him, and he classified all of the people he saw under the grouping of white men.

He saw a store that was something like the fat man's in Mecca and he rode up to it and dismounted. It had a window full of clothing and canned goods and saddles and rifles and revolvers. It was very interesting to look at, and when he tired of that he sat down on the curb beside his horse and watched everything that went on in the main street and listened to everything that was said by the people who passed within earshot. Sometimes people stopped in front of the store and talked and when they did he found he could understand a lot of the words if they didn't talk too fast.

He tried to think of the significance of Jose's words to him, and he understood that all of these people were saying and doing a lot of things that he knew nothing about. Jose had been right. He didn't know very much. He had never been to a place called school. Without a doubt every one of these people knew that the father of the country was George Washington. But now he knew that, too, and if he kept his ears open he would probably learn everything that they knew. Yet his own father thought that these people were all wrong and shouldn't be listened to, and his father knew everything. Perhaps he ought to ride home and forget this. But no, he was here, and he might just as well sit here for a while. If this weren't right he could forget it later.

For the rest of the day he sat on the curb in Coachella and let the white civilization explain itself to him in whatever way it could. Late in the afternoon he got up and mounted the horse and rode out of town. It was a day of wonder—a curious world indeed. He decided to try to talk to his father about it again and to see if his father couldn't give him a better idea of just what it all meant.

There was no use. Agocho was sullen and angry because he had gone to Coachella. He couldn't understand why the boy had any curiosity about it at all. He hoped he would outgrow it. He told him that white men would ruin his life and make a slave out of him. He didn't want that, did he? No. Then leave the white men alone.

The boy wanted to know what was meant by school. Agocho had an idea of the meaning even though he had never been in a school. There had been a government school in the White River Reservation and he knew that the young Apaches went there and learned a lot of useless things.

To the boy there was something unconvincing about Agocho's adamant remarks. That white world was there and it didn't care whether you came to it or not. But Agocho's world was here and it insisted that you belonged to it. He wondered how wise Agocho would be in the white world. He wondered for the first time in his life if his father were really the greatest man on earth, which he had always supposed him to be. For the first time he questioned it. And in questioning it a test occurred to him. Even while Agocho was talking the boy interrupted him in English.

"Who is the father of your country?" he asked.

Agocho stopped speaking. N'Chai Chidn was learning a lot of white talk. He must find a way to stop it.

The boy was waiting intensely. That question meant a great deal. Everybody in the white world knew the answer. It was the first thing they learned. If Agocho knew it too, then he was wise, completely wise, not only in the white world but in his own world. If he could give the answer to that he must be right about everything.

Agocho looked at him.

"Who is the father of your country?" the boy asked again.

Agocho didn't know what he meant. The question had no meaning. Mangus Colorado and Geronimo had been the greatest warriors. And the Goddess, Ste-na-tlih-a, had conceived two Gods, one by the sun and one by the sea. There was no father unless it be those two powers.

He looked at the boy and said in Apache, "The fire and the water."

The intensity left the boy's face. The answer was a disappointment. An idol had crashed and he felt sorry.

"Nope," he said, in newly acquired English, "George Washington."

Chapter XII

NEVER before had Agocho been corrected. It was a critical moment. George Washington: what did that mean? It was white man's heresy, and it had no real meaning, and the boy's thinking was being corrupted. But even worse, he had raised his voice against his own father; he had dared to challenge his wisdom; he had repudiated a truth in favor of two white words. George Washington.

Agocho was angry and offended, and he wanted the boy to know it. He got up and walked out of the clearing without another word and disappeared through the bushes in the direction of the inland sea.

Johnny was sorry. He wanted to tell his father that he loved him just as much, after all, even if he didn't know the answer to one simple question that all white people knew. He wanted to grin at Agocho and have Agocho grin back at him and he wanted a mutual understanding to exist between them that made them impervious to difficulty and chagrin over mere factual information. But he didn't know how to go about saying all this, even to himself, let alone to an indignant parent. He had exploded a bomb and he didn't know what to do about it except to sit still and let the pieces fall all over him. It was an awkward moment and he wanted to forget it. He knew he would never say the words "George Washington" to his father again. That

incident was closed forever. The trouble was that it left
a mark.

George Washington had done something that Johnny
hadn't intended to do at all. He didn't understand inevi-
tability. He hated George Washington for being the
agent that he was. He had brought about unpleasant
feeling between his father and himself and that was too
bad.

What was it white men said when they didn't like
something? Damn. That was it. Then damn that father
of the country. That was the way they did it. They
seemed to like doing it and it made them feel better.

"Damn it," Johnny said aloud.

It sounded nice and made him smile and he said it
over and over. It was a nice thing to know how to say.

Later Agocho came back. He didn't say anything
about the incident and the boy ignored it and acted as
if Agocho had not been away. But they both knew that
a seed of disagreement and dissension had been planted
and neither one of them could completely forget it.

Johnny stayed away from the ranch country and the
towns for several weeks, but all that time he thought of
the country to the north and he wondered what was going on up there. He fully realized the fact that he was
ignorant and while he was in no way unhappy about it,
he was curious to know a little more. Perhaps some day
he would.

Agocho also realized that the boy was ignorant, but
his realization of the fact was entirely different. He
knew that the boy was ignorant of life, ignorant of
ideals, experiences, and ceremonies of tribal living. To
some degree he could correct that and he proposed to

do so. If he were a medicine man he might do a pretty good job of it, even though he and the boy were alone. But Agocho did not have the supreme powers of a medicine man and he knew that at best his efforts would be crude and superficial. At any rate they would be better than no efforts at all.

He went to work at making a drum. He used the tough mesquite for the frame and he stretched the hide of a mountain lion tight over the outside. It was not a bad drum at all and he put the sign of his clan on one side and a figure representing Hadintin Skhin, Pollen Boy, on the other. Pollen Boy represented youth scattering his seed over the land and was an important figure in a puberty dance.

One night he rode north alone, and when he returned a few hours later he had a saddle-bag full of freshly plucked ears of corn. Paul's ranch had plenty of corn and Paul's ranch was on land that was rightfully his by priority and so naturally the corn was his, too.

Agocho cut most of the corn off the ears. Later on he would plant some of it near the fig trees so that he might have corn of his own and wouldn't have to ride north every time he wanted some. But the bulk of it went into the brewing of tizwin. When the sun had properly fermented the crushed pulp he would add water to it and within a day it would be ready to drink.

The boy watched these preparations with interest. Agocho gave him a vague idea of the ceremony that was about to take place, and he explained that it was incomplete and unsatisfactory, but better than none, and absolutely essential to his future well-being. It would take three whole days and nights, and during that time they would not eat a thing. For the first two days they wouldn't do anything but wait for the time to pass. These were the days when the older warriors would be dancing and the period would be taken up by medicine dances by various members of the tribe under the direction of the medicine man for whatever purposes were necessary—good hunting, the driving away of bad spirits, the healing of the sick, the curing of senility, and whatever functions the medicine man deemed worthy. On the third day the boy must spend hours in solitude. He must be alone in order to commune with the Gods and prepare his body and mind for the change that was about to take place in his life. By sunset of the third day he would begin dancing, and that would go on all through the night. At dawn of the fourth day there should be the race between the young men and the virgins. That was impossible, but later, when the Gods had allowed them to return to the White River, the boy could take part in another puberty dance and then that part of the ceremony could be consummated. In the absence of the Apache virgins they would end the ceremony by getting gloriously drunk on the tizwin. They would drink huge quantities of it and stay drunk as long as possible. That was decidedly an incomplete ceremony, but it had the time element and the dance element and if they went into the spirit of it, body and soul, it would make a decent substitute for the real thing.

He made a trip to the lower end of the Salton Sea where there were geysers which constantly bubbled up hot mud from the interior of the earth. Some of this mud was a blue-gray and some of it was red and some of it yellow. It made a perfect natural paint, and was ideal for the ceremony.

Meanwhile several days went by and the tizwin was almost ready and Agocho decided that it was time for the event to take place. So for two days they sat around the clearing and did nothing. Agocho was arbitrarily pretending that the older members of the tribe, members of his own generation, were going through the preparatory dances, and on the first night and the second night he performed two dances himself. First he had to take off his clothes and wear only a loin cloth. He painted his chest and arms with red and yellow lines and blue-gray circles and he put two long bars of red across his forehead. Before they could begin he had to teach the boy how to use the drum. He had to show him how to strike it so that the rhythm actually had a meaning. The boy soon learned that and he beat the drum for a long time while Agocho performed a series of gyrations and stampings that would have astounded and perhaps terrified a casual white man had there been such a white man to see it. Agocho at fifty-nine, circling a small camp-fire in the middle of the night, his body decorated with red and yellow pigment, stooping, bending and stamping, and emitting chants and yells for his own accompaniment to the rhythm of a primitive drum beaten by a sixteen-year-old boy who also chanted and yelled in an effort to assist him, was a strange scene in the civilized state of California in 1924.

To the boy there was nothing ridiculous in this. The spirit of it and the rhythm touched him and he found himself enjoying it. It was unpleasant not to eat, but if

that were a requisite he was willing to abide by it. Only
Agocho himself knew that it was ridiculous and meaningless for one grown man and a sixteen-year-old boy to
attempt to carry out a ceremony that needed at least a
clan, and perhaps a tribe, and at least one medicine
man and preferably two or three, to execute it with any
degree of dignity, meaning, and success. But the boy
had never seen a dance before and was unable to criticize
this one. This was part of his education and it was
better this way than not at all. Some semblance of the
significance of it was bound to break into his consciousness and that is what he needed to counteract his exposure to the white men.

Then came the third day, the day that the boy was
supposed to spend most of his time alone preparatory
to his own climax in the affair. Agocho sent him away.
He told him to sit in silence for a long time preferably
near some outstanding work of the Gods, and he told
him to go up to the rocky slopes of the Santa Rosas or
down to the shore of the inland sea.

This part of the ritual didn't mean much to the boy.
He chose the mountains and started off toward the west.
Agocho remained in the clearing and finished the prepa-
ration of the tizwin.

The dancing and the chanting had been fun because
they had been something new, but this sitting all day
in silence was an anti-climax. The boy crossed the highway and started for the mountains, and then changed
his course, and doubled back to the hard surface and
walked north. He didn't intend to go anywhere in particular, but it was easier to walk on the highway than

in the desert. He plodded on, and without thinking of it he came to the entrance of the Mack ranch.

He hadn't been there for a long time. No harm in seeing what Jose was doing to-day. He walked along the ranch road and passed Jose's little shack. It gave forth a delicious aroma of enchiladas and frijoles. The boy didn't distinguish the food by the smell, but whatever it was it smelled good to him after two and a half days' fast. Jose's wife was busy inside, and he caught a glimpse of her and he could hear things sizzling on the fire as he went past the door. Jose was a mighty lucky man.

He wondered how it would be to have a wife to cook for you and to sleep with and to do anything you told her to do while you were busy all day long doing things that white men wanted and making the stuff they called money which was useful in trade for anything you wished—a Ford car, for example. That life seemed attractive to him and it didn't seem possible there could be anything wrong with it.

He found Jose in the carpenter shop. A white man was with him and the boy knew that he must be Mr. Mack. They were talking and Mr. Mack was giving Jose directions for doing certain things with the tools and some boards. Jose was very respectful and polite to Mr. Mack. They looked at the boy as he stood in the doorway but they went on with their conversation.

"What's he want?" said Mr. Mack, finally, nodding toward Johnny.

"He never want nothing," Jose said. "He come around to-day and mañana."

"Isn't he Fig Tree's son?"

"Yes, sir, he's Juanito," said Jose.

"Well, Johnny," said Mr. Mack, "if you're anything like your father we haven't got much use for you around here. Savvy that?"

Johnny looked at him and grinned.

"Can't he speak English?" asked Mr. Mack.

"Juanito, habla usted a Señor Mack," said Jose, sharply, believing that Johnny understood Spanish better than English.

But still Johnny said nothing.

"No savvy English?" asked Mr. Mack of Johnny.

"Sure, damn it," said Johnny, cheerfully.

Mr. Mack threw back his head and laughed. Then Jose laughed too, but not as loud, and Johnny grinned broadly and looked at Mr. Mack.

"He's learned to cuss all right," said Mr. Mack. "Now Jose, you get these ladders finished by to-night. We'll need them first thing you know and won't have 'em. Get him to help you if you want to. If he can learn to cuss he ought to be able to learn to work."

"Yes, sir," said Jose.

Then Mr. Mack walked out of the carpenter shop and went toward the main house, and as soon as he was out of sight Jose started for his own shack where he knew his lunch was waiting for him. Johnny followed him, and when Jose went in he waited outside. The food still gave off an appetizing aroma and Johnny was very hungry. He wished Jose would offer him something to eat. Presently Jose came out with a plate of beans and an enchilada. He sat down on the steps and began to push large forkfuls of beans and enchilada into his mouth and he talked to Johnny at the same time.

"Say, you want more work?"

"Sure," said Johnny. He looked at the food and he watched the obvious relish with which Jose ate it.

"What you want to work for me—cigarettes?"

"Wanta eat," said Johnny.

"You work all day in shop buildin' ladders with me and do what I say do?"

"Sure," said Johnny.

"All right," said Jose. "I let you eat." He turned his head and called into the shack: "Nasaria, alguna cosa para comer para Juanito."

In a minute Nasaria handed him another plate of beans and an enchilada and Jose gave the plate to Johnny.

It was strange food and very hot and the juice got all over his hands, but Johnny didn't mind that. He ate everything on the plate and he could have eaten more but it didn't occur to him to ask for it. When he finished Jose was puffing a cigarette, and he took the plate from Johnny and put it inside the door on the floor. Then he got up.

"Now we go make ladders for Mr. Mack or he raise plenty hell if he come around and find us loafin'."

They went to the carpenter shop, and for the next two hours Johnny was busy picking up nails, getting boards from the woodpile, holding boards while Jose sawed them into pieces and doing whatever he was told. Once Jose hit his own thumb with the hammer, and then Johnny listened to a string of profanity in Spanish and English that increased his vocabulary ten-fold. Late in the afternoon they had completed two ladders about

eight feet tall and Jose seemed to think they were very
well built.

Then Jose went to the corral to feed the stock and
Johnny walked to the highway and then south toward
the clearing. It seemed strange to be going back to the
clearing. It was only two miles, and yet that clearing
was so far away from the world of the Mack ranch that
Johnny was a little bewildered in changing from one to
the other. He had almost forgotten the dance and the
drum and the rhythm. He felt like a different Johnny in
each place, and he didn't know what to make of it.

Agocho had been in the clearing all day. He knew
that the boy should be left to himself and he made no
attempt to follow him. But when his son returned late
in the afternoon he sensed that something was wrong.
He had been among the white men. He knew it. He
didn't know how, but he knew it. He looked at the boy
and the boy avoided him. He had been up to the ranch
country, there was no doubt of it. He had wasted the
whole day and violated one of the fundamental princi-
ples of the ritual.

Agocho was first angry and then discouraged. His son
was a weakling. He hadn't been able to follow the routine
of the ceremony. He was full of sin and poison. He would
make him dance this white craving out of his soul. He
would make him dance until his body and brain were
numb.

Agocho wore only the loin cloth, and his body was
still adorned with painted decorations. The boy had to
strip and wear a loin cloth, too, and Agocho painted
his chest with the sign of Pollen Boy, the lightning, and
the sun. Then he painted tribal designs on his arms

and cheeks and forehead. The boy endured the decoration but he displayed little interest. He was wondering what Jose would think if he could see it.

At sunset they started. Agocho sat near the fire and beat the drum and the boy began the steps he had seen his father do the two nights before. It didn't mean very much to him. He couldn't get into the spirit of it as he had before. He stamped and pranced around and danced very badly. On and on it went for several hours until he was tired. He wanted to stop, but Agocho would not let him. Agocho seemed to be in a frenzy. He yelled and shouted and the boy had never seen him so wild, so furious, so crazy with emotion. He began the prayer to the Gods, and he chanted it to all of them, over and over, in time with the drum.

> "Ste-na-tlih-a, you are good.
> I pray for a long life.
> I pray for your good looks.
> I pray for good breath.
>
> Na-yen-ez-gan-i, you are strong.
> I pray for a strong life.
> I pray for your great power.
> I pray to kill my enemies.
>
> Chu-ga-na-ai, you are life.
> I pray for your good warmth.
> I pray for your good crops.
> I pray for your good health."

Then he prayed to Tu-ba-dzis-chi-ni, and to Pollen Boy and to many others. And when he finished he began it

again and repeated the prayer over and over. He
thumped the drum until his fingers ached, and on and
on the boy danced until he stumbled in exhaustion
and half fell to the ground.

Agocho rushed at him. His eyes were flashing. He
yelled in the boy's ear and forced him to his feet.
Then that constant *thump*-thump-thump-thump, *thump*-
thump-thump-thump began again, and the boy danced
again, and Agocho yelled the accompaniment. On and
on again it went until the boy could not see. His body
ached and throbbed. He moved by instinct. He hardly
knew what he was doing and once he nearly fell headlong into the fire. But on and on went that eternal
rhythm, that endless reverberation, that fundamental
command that would not let him stop. He moved his
throbbing feet with that same *thump*-thump-thump-
thump until he reached a point where his brain ceased
to tell him of the pain.

Then it got him. Then all the laws and rules of
heredity came into their own. It had been almost six
hours that he had been obeying that rhythm. Now that
rhythm was obeying him. He was master, now. He was
God of the rhythm. He was Man. He raised his stooping body, arched his back, drew his knees up high as he
danced and yelled the chant at the top of his lungs:

> *"Ste-na-tlih-a, you are good.*
> *I pray for a long life.*
> *I pray for your good looks.*
> *I pray for good breath."*

He shrieked the prayer to all the Gods and Agocho
shrieked it with him. He danced now with a fury that

knew no command. He danced defiance at that endless rhythm, defiance at the sky above him and the earth beneath. He was one: he was all. The tempo had not increased itself. He had increased it. He challenged it. Faster and faster he went. *Thump*-thump-thump-thump, *thump*-thump-thump-thump. He shrieked and leaped in ecstasy—he couldn't see—he couldn't hear—he had gone completely mad—and then nothing.

When the boy collapsed flat on his face, gasping and choking and unconscious, Agocho rushed at him again. He was in a frenzy, too, but he was happy for he was sure that the boy was winning. He was pure. He was defeating all bad spirits. He was asserting himself. He was pure ego. Quickly Agocho rolled him over on his back. The panting, heaving body must not have time to react. There wasn't a moment to lose. He grabbed the boy by the shoulders and shook him, but there was no response. He tried to lift him to his feet, but he was dead weight. He mustn't stop here.

Agocho looked about. He wanted a knife. He found it, and grabbing the boy's hand he stuck the point of the knife blade under the thumbnail of the right hand. Then he gave the knife a sharp blow driving it down deep under the nail and the acute pain touched a consciousness that nothing else could arouse.

The boy yelled and squirmed. Agocho dropped the knife and with all his energy he yanked the boy to his feet. He staggered and reeled and Agocho dashed back to the drum. *Thump*-thump-thump-thump it went again, and Agocho yelled again, and the boy gritted his teeth and danced to that rhythm. He danced again, on and on and on. He danced with a super-consciousness that passed understanding. And as the tempo slowly increased so he increased the movements of his feet. He danced out of consciousness into hysteria and out of hysteria into insanity until everything—sky and earth, fire and water, the entire universe—ended with a terrific crash and there was nothing.

The drum stopped. Agocho did not rush at the boy this time. He leaned back and looked at the sky. It was almost dawn—another hour and the eastern sky would be getting gray.

Slowly he got up and walked over to the prostrate form. The boy had fallen on his face again and one arm was outstretched. Again Agocho rolled him over on his back. It was all over now. He had done well, too. Surely he must have won. Surely the boy must have conquered everything in that orgasm of the ego. Now, when he revived, if there were only a young virgin for him the whole ceremony would end with a reasonable degree of success. But that would come later. Now they would rest and drink and probably get very drunk together for several days.

He went over to the tizwin and tasted it. It was satisfactory. Then he brought two sumac bottles, both full of it, and set them down beside the boy. Then he sat down himself to wait for the dawn.

Chapter XIII

THERE was a great roaring. It wasn't any one kind of a noise, but a cacophony of many sounds all clashing at once. The earth vibrated like a drum. Sometimes it stood still, occasionally it swung around in a circle, and often it spun on its axis. The sky was bright and the sun was up and he lay still and watched the bushes go around in a circle. Then N'Chai Chidn drank another long draught of the tizwin, and when he had emptied the bowl Agocho refilled it and the bushes were all going around in the opposite direction.

His body ached and he lay still. Deep within the earth he could hear the throbbing. *Thump*-thump-thump-thump, *thump*-thump-thump-thump it went and everything on the surface moved in that rhythm. He watched Agocho drink. He took one big gulp followed by three smaller gulps. They went in fours like that, one after the other, *thump*-thump-thump-thump.

He raised himself from the ground and sat up. All his muscles hurt and he drank more tizwin. It was good. It burned his mouth but it was good and it made him forget that his body ached. Suddenly he wanted a lot more of it and he stood up and looked around. Agocho was pouring it out of the sumac bottle and he walked over to him and they both drank again.

Agocho was very happy and after a long time the boy understood that Agocho was drunk. Then he must be drunk, too. And that was good. That was the way to be. This tizwin was wonderful stuff. It took all the aches and pains out of his body. He drank more.

Agocho was talking but the words didn't mean anything. He told Agocho that the words didn't make any sense, but somehow Agocho didn't seem to understand him. They stood beside each other and drank more tizwin. They swayed together and bumped into each other and the boy said that the words didn't mean anything. He told Agocho several times that the words didn't mean anything. Agocho didn't seem to know it.

The boy walked across the clearing. A small pebble got in his way and when he tried to step over it the pebble was a big rock and he fell against it and slipped to the ground. Then he reached over to touch it and it was a little pebble again. That was a joke and he got up with the pebble in his hand. When he started back toward Agocho and the sumac bottle the earth dipped to one side and he almost slid across the clearing to the horses. Presently it righted itself and he walked back to Agocho. Then they both sat down and drank again. After a long time Agocho tried to walk over to the kowa and as he did the earth dipped again and threw him. But instead of falling down hill, he fell up hill, and it was so ridiculous that the boy laughed. His father must be the only man in the world who could fall up hill. But then that was his father, and he knew everything; even how to fall up hill.

Time went by and the boy wasn't aware of it. He sat still and sometimes moved around and he continued to drink tizwin. Presently all awareness of the world he knew disappeared and he was living and moving in a strange place that he had never been in before. Sometimes he sat still and sometimes he walked. Agocho wasn't in sight. He had stayed in the clearing and now the clearing was gone.

There were people here, but he couldn't see them. He could hear them because they were chanting and he recognized the chant because he had danced to it. It began "Ste-na-tlih-a, you are good." Then there was another sound that came over the chant and the chant disappeared. It was an automobile horn and it sounded very loud. And the automobile itself whisked past him in a flash just the way the automobile had whisked past Jose's Ford car that day when they had ridden into Mecca. This time the man in the other car yelled something at him, but he stayed in Jose's car and they drove on along the highway. Jose's car made a funny noise and it vibrated *thump*-thump-thump-thump and Jose said, "Damn good Ford car." Then he was moving along the highway but Jose and the Ford car had gone somewhere else. And the chant was on the highway in front of him and it was hard to move through it. He could see it now, and the chant had color as well as sound. It was red and black and yellow and white. It was green now, but it changed to brown while he looked at it.

Then it turned into a man and the man was Mr. Mack. Mr. Mack said, "He can cuss all right," but Johnny wanted to tell him they weren't words at all. They were beans and Jose's wife had cooked them and they tasted good. He would like to see Jose's wife sometime. He knew what Jose did with her and he would do that, too. He had seen the stallion go into the mare and he would like to do that to a woman. He would like to do that now and he would do it now if only there were a woman.

Then the highway slipped out from under him and he reeled over into the desert. It was hard to get back on the highway, and when he did there was Jose's green Ford car coming right at him. Jose stopped it right in front of him and he stood looking at the car and Jose and the two women beside him. They all looked at him and Jose got out of the car and came toward him. He didn't want to see Jose because he wasn't Johnny any more. He was N'Chai Chidn now and never had been Johnny. He walked around the car and he looked at the two women who sat in it. One was Jose's wife and he remembered her, but the other he had never seen before. For an instant he looked at her and she looked at him. That was the woman he wanted. He remembered now that he had known her all the time. She was just like Jose's wife and she had a light skin and dark hair and dark eyes. That was the one and that was the one he would have for himself just the way Jose had the other one. That was just the way it should be. And then Jose grabbed him by the shoulder and pulled him away from the Ford car. The highway slipped out from under him again and he had a glimpse of the women and the Ford car as they disappeared.

He was in the desert and he fell over the salt bushes and Jose had gone away. The Ford car had gone away and so had the highway and there was nothing around but desert.

He got up and he realized that he must have been lying in the desert, and his arm was bleeding where cactus had scratched it. He wanted to find the highway or the clearing. He wanted to see that girl again because she was the one he wanted but there was no highway and there was nobody around. He staggered through the bushes and they scratched his body but the scratches didn't hurt.

Then he felt very sick and discouraged. The girl had gone; and everything, the highway, the Ford car, Jose, and his wife—they had all gone. He wanted more tizwin, and then suddenly he was very sick and he fell down in the sand and vomited and drooled and he didn't want any more tizwin. He crawled on a little further and he wanted to sleep. He was going to sleep; he had to sleep, and for a long time he didn't know anything at all.

Agocho lay perfectly still and let the world come back to him. It came gradually. His numbed senses came to life and the clearing and the fig trees and the kowa and the horses began to take shape. He was thirsty, but instead of moving toward the pool he lay still and looked up at the sky. The sun was only an hour high and climbing higher. It was morning but he didn't know whether it was the second or third day since he had begun drinking tizwin. He remembered everything up to the drinking, but the liquor had affected him almost at once because of the three-day fast. He had gotten drunk rapidly and he had stayed drunk and so had N'Chai Chidn.

The boy was not in sight, but Agocho was not alarmed. He couldn't be far away. The effects of the liquor left him weak and shaky and his craving for water overpowered his desire to lie still. He rose and walked slowly to the pool. The two sumac containers had held almost six gallons of tizwin and they were both empty. Together they had consumed it all in twenty-four hours. He hadn't drunk that heavily in years. But it was worth it. Somehow it seemed to round out the ceremony. He decided it must be the morning of the second day after the drinking had begun. Whatever it was it didn't matter.

His mouth was dry and his tongue was thick. He squatted beside the pool and rinsed his mouth with water and spat the water out on the ground. Then he drank a large quantity of water, and finally he lay beside the pool and stuck his head in it. He felt much better and he was surprised to find that his body did not yet crave food. His system was recuperating but he wasn't hungry. He looked at his body and the daubs and the decorations upon it. He was surprised to find that he was naked. He had lost the loin cloth somewhere in his drunkenness but presently he saw it out in the middle of the clearing.

The day was hot and he was content to stay naked. The horses needed water and he led them over to the pool and let them drink from it. When they had finished he let them roam about the clearing at will. They nibbled the salt grass, and he went over to the shade of the cottonwoods and the fig trees and sat down.

He felt very well satisfied with the whole procedure. It had been even more successful than he had hoped. He reviewed the ceremony in his mind and he felt that it couldn't have been much better had it been back among his own people. The boy had responded as he knew he would and the only catch was that there was

no Apache girl for the final part of the puberty ceremony. As for himself, he would probably have gotten
drunk no matter where the ceremony had been. All in
all it had worked out well.

Before mid-day the boy came back to the clearing. He
had never been drunk before and the liquor had affected
him more than it had Agocho. He, too, was naked. He
still felt sick and his body was a wreck. His right arm
had a deep cut and his legs were cut and scratched.
The thumbnail of his right hand had been broken off.
Once he had fallen on his face and there was a bruise
over his left eye. The ceremonial decorations had been
smeared and were meaningless. He felt very badly but
he made his aching body walk to the pool where he
drank and spat and threw water over his head and
shoulders. Then he rested for the remainder of the day,
and the very thought of tizwin made him ill. Toward
sunset he rubbed the ceremonial paint off his body and
when the sun went down he put on his clothes and
drank a lot more water. He was feeling a little better,
and he began to think about everything that had happened.

Agocho didn't have much to say about it and the boy
couldn't remember everything clearly. There were a
hundred memories and visions gliding through his mind
and he couldn't define any of them or assure himself that
they had really happened. He shook his head and tried
to think what it had all been about. He didn't know.

Agocho was hungry. Suddenly he was ravenous and
he began to prepare food. He made a small fire in the
ashes of what had been the ceremonial fire and he
cooked mescal and mesquite beans and piñon tea. He

ate a great amount of it and the boy came over and ate
a little. It tasted better than he thought it would and
he ate more. He and Agocho talked, and Agocho seemed
pleased and happy and certain that life was proving
itself just and worth living. He thought the boy ought
to feel happy, too, and he was surprised when the boy
seemed pensive and uncertain. The exhilaration that
Agocho expected was missing and there was depression
in its place. But then that was attributable to tizwin and
would not last.

As soon as they had had enough rest—say three or
four days—Agocho wanted to take the horses and go on
another hunting trip. He wanted to cross the Santa
Rosas and explore the next range beyond. It would be
a five- or six-day trip and they would see new things
and get many supplies. The only difficulty was that he
needed shells for the rifle. And the rifle wasn't in good
working order and he didn't know what to do to repair
it. Nevertheless, he had a few shells left and if they
were good hunters they would make them do. The boy
agreed to this.

They did nothing for two days, and Agocho thought
of riding to Mecca and trying to trade with the fat man
for more shells. He gave it up, however, because he had
nothing he could spare that he might offer in exchange.
It was just as well not to go up into that country anyway.

The boy was confused by the incidents that floated
through his memory about the ceremony. Jose had been
in it. He remembered seeing Jose and Mr. Mack and
Jose's wife, and another girl he had never seen before.
And it was that figure above all others which interested

him most. Who had she been? What had she meant? Had he really seen her or had it been a kind of dream? Was the whole business a wild mixture of meaningless ideas? Had the tizwin done it all? He seemed to think he had been riding in Jose's Ford car and walking on the highway. And why were all these elements of the white world in the midst of an experience that was purely Apache and had nothing to do with the white world?

He asked Agocho about it and Agocho said he was wrong and that he hadn't seen any such people. That was a mistake. It might be that he had had a vision of an Apache maiden. That would have been quite natural. Agocho explained it that way.

It was not a satisfactory answer. The boy wanted to be sure. If he had really seen Jose, then he must have seen them all. She was a girl like Jose's wife. It was a curious and inexplicable jumble of facts and faces. Jose would know. If he were to see Jose again, just once more, and ask him about it, Jose could tell him if it were fact or fancy. If Jose knew nothing about it as soon as he started to ask him, he would know that it never happened and he would say no more about it.

He tried to put it out of his mind and evade it, but the vision kept recurring. Seeing that girl at that time meant something. If that girl really lived then she was the girl who was intended for him. Apache, Mexican, or whatever she was, if she had appeared before him at that moment the great magic and great powers evoked by the ceremony had brought her to him for a reason. He had to solve that. It was too significant to be ignored.

Three days of recuperation from the tizwin and he

felt as well as ever. There was only that one question, and he was going to settle that point to his own satisfaction.

Agocho was preparing for the trip to the mountains. There was nothing for the boy to do so he took one of the horses and rode out of the clearing. He didn't say where he was going and Agocho didn't ask. It never entered his head that the boy might ride north again.

Up the highway he rode at a gallop. He turned off to the Mack ranch and walked his horse along the sandy road. He passed Jose's shack but there was nobody in sight. He went on to the tool shed and dismounted. He left the horse and walked around. The Ford car was missing, and by the tracks of the tires he could see that it had been driven out toward the highway. Perhaps Jose had gone to town. If that were so he wouldn't be gone long. Mr. Mack was home because he could see Mr. Mack's car over near the main house. It was a bigger car than Jose's but it wasn't as pretty a green. He was too reticent to try to find Mr. Mack and talk to him, so he decided to wait around until Jose came back.

He walked back toward Jose's little house. The ranch was strangely empty without Jose. He seemed to be an important part of it. There were two or three Mexicans over in the date grove. He could see them as they worked but none of them was Jose.

He reached the corner of Jose's house. He stood still for a minute and then walked around the corner toward the front. Then he stopped in astonishment.

A young girl in a bright red dress had just come out of the house and she saw him at the same time. The boy stared at her, and she, equally surprised at seeing him, stared back.

As he looked at her, memory carried him back to that meeting on the highway. She was that one. That day, after the ceremony when he was full of tizwin, the road, and the Ford car, and Jose and his wife, and now this girl. She wasn't Jose's wife but she looked like her. She had a pale skin, and black hair, and very dark eyes. These features, contrasting with the bright red dress, made her a striking person indeed. She was young. The dress outlined, even accentuated, her figure.

He could do nothing but stare. So she was that one. He stood still and looked, unable to take his eyes from her.

For a moment she seemed to hesitate. She wasn't expecting to meet a stranger, especially one who stared at her that way, so close to her that he could reach out and touch her. She was bewildered for a moment and then she turned and went back into the house. There was only a screen door but she closed that emphatically and disappeared from view.

The boy was overcome by the understanding that the moment brought him. It had been real. There was such a girl. She was here. There was no refuting this. That ceremony and its delirious climax had meant something. It had meant something. He moved a few steps away and let the meaning of the whole thing register in his mind.

At first he could hardly believe it. He was pleased; he was delighted. He became almost ecstatic within himself, but externally he simply stood still and looked at the little shack and the screen door. It was a wonder-

ful experience. He felt immensely happy. He didn't
know what to do about it so he did nothing but stand
still and think. So she was the one. She was the one.
It was perfect. And everything about her was perfect.
She was exactly right. It was a grand moment—a glorious
moment. He felt like yelling, "Ee-yah!" but he was
afraid to yell, afraid to move, afraid to break the consciousness of the moment.

After a long time he stepped further back across the
road, perhaps twenty yards from the front door of the
house, and sat down. He would wait until she came
out. The next thing to do was to see her again. He sat
there for a long time. Once in a while he thought he
caught a glimpse of the red dress moving around inside the house. He watched the door every instant. Once
she came up to the door and looked out through the
screen. He could see her plainly then. He looked at her
and she looked out at him. Then she turned away
quickly and disappeared. It made his heart beat faster.
It was fascinating and thrilling. Never had he experienced anything like this. Never.

Suddenly there was a flash of a red dress moving
among the date trees. He jumped up. She had gone out
the back door. She was walking through the date trees
toward the tool shed. She hadn't used the road. She
had avoided it and seemed to be trying to keep out of
sight.

He followed her at once. She looked back and she
saw him. When she came to the tool shed she walked
over to the sandy road and then she started to run. He
followed, and he ran, too.

Straight toward the main house she ran, and he followed as far as the tool shed. He wasn't trying to catch her. He simply wanted to see her and keep her in view as long as possible. He stopped at the tool shed and watched her red figure as it went around the side of Mr. Mack's car, up onto the porch, and into the front door of the main house. Then he couldn't see her at all.

He waited a long time beside the tool shed but she never appeared again. He waited until late in the afternoon, but still she didn't come out. He didn't mind. He was happy just to be there. And when she had run toward the house—that was wonderful. He loved to see her walk and run.

Toward sunset he decided to leave. Jose had not come back. Jose's wife was not in sight so probably she was with him. But what did it matter about Jose? He didn't need to ask Jose anything now. He knew. He understood. It was a wonderful understanding. Life was wonderful. Everything was wonderful. It was wonderful to be alive.

He would leave now, but he would come back. Come back? Nothing could keep him away. It was truly wonderful to be alive.

He swung himself onto his horse. Then with a last look toward the door of the main house where she had disappeared several hours ago he galloped away. He raced the animal to the highway, turned south, and tore down the hard surface at full speed. He breathed deeply of the desert air and he slapped the horse on the flanks.

"Ee-yah!" he yelled. "Ee-yah!"

Chapter XIV

THE boy endured the hunting trip with growing impatience. Normally it would have interested him but now he had a greater interest and he was anxious to get back to that. Agocho had no intimation of the boy's state of mind. He was directing the trip and he was enjoying it and he delayed the return for several days. Instead of taking six days the traveling and camping took ten. They roamed about the mountain country and visited new canyons and valleys and had good luck. They got a couple of sheep and Agocho was lucky enough to bag a deer. They journeyed so far into the mountain country that they crossed the divide of the coast range and found creeks and rivers that flowed westerly toward the Pacific Ocean. They passed ranch country and once they saw the town of Julian in a valley below them. Back in the mountain recesses they discovered other Indians, and once they camped near them in a place called Los Coyotes Indian Reservation. They had little to say to these people. Agocho explained to the boy that they were obviously inferior to Apaches and that they had succumbed to the force of the white world and were not Indians worthy of respect. The Indians around Volcan Mountain lived like white men and all their children went to a government Indian school. They were very inferior people and it was a good thing for them they didn't live around the White

River or the Apaches would have wiped them out.

The boy wasn't interested in them in spite of the fact they were the only other tribe he had ever seen at close range, and in spite of the fact that Agocho thought they lived like white men. Compared to the people of the Coachella Valley they were stupid. They had no big date ranches or Ford cars. There wasn't one of them as smart as Jose. If that were tribal life he preferred to work and learn things and have a Ford car and a beautiful girl in a red dress for a wife. That was living. These people on a reservation didn't know anything. He was glad when they rode east again and down the mountain slopes to the desert and finally back to the clearing. It seemed good to be coming home.

The next day there was work to do. They had to cut the meat into long strips and preserve it, and dry the hides of the animals. They had to store away the piñon and the yucca stalks they had collected. Agocho was very happy. Life was smiling and his son had become a man. There was only that one old injustice that had yet to be satisfied. And that would come. Some day it would please the Gods to settle that and then life would be normal again.

Two days after their return from the hunt the boy rode out of the clearing. He was going for the day and Agocho watched him ride away without any resentment. He sat beside the kowa and made a belt from the hides and added the teeth of the deer for decoration.

The boy didn't want his father to know where he was going. He wouldn't understand and there was no use in telling him. Ten minutes after he left the clearing he was at the Mack Ranch.

Jose was repairing an inner tube for Mr. Mack's car. He looked at Johnny with a grin and coupled with the grin was amazement.

"Hallo," said the boy.

"Where you been all this time?" asked Jose. "It's a month since I seen you. Been drunk all that time, Juanito?"

"No," said Johnny.

"Oh boy, but you were drunk! Oh boy!" said Jose. He laughed and looked up at Johnny. The sun fell in his eyes so he laid down the inner tube and leaned back in the shade.

The boy dismounted and sat down near Jose. He looked all around but there was nobody else in sight.

"First I thought you gone crazy," said Jose. "Runnin' around out there on the highway with hardly no clothes on and yellin' and actin' loco."

"I wasn't drunk much," said Johnny.

Jose laughed.

"Oh, no, not much! You were the drunkenest man I ever see. You were falling all over the highway. It's funny some car didn't run over you and bust you up. I almost did."

"Where's that girl?" asked Johnny.

"Say, I thought you was gonna grab hold of her," said Jose. "You like to get yourself locked up in jail?"

"No," said Johnny, "I want her."

"That's my wife's sister. We were drivin' her up here from El Centro."

"She live here?" asked Johnny.

"Sure, she's workin' for Mrs. Mack in the kitchen. She's my wife's sister."

"Nice girl," said Johnny. "I want her."

"She's lookin' for a husband only she don't know it," said Jose. "She got a father and a mother and four brothers and four sisters. They all gone broke in El Centro because not enough work in lettuce fields. She youngest so my wife and I get her and let her stay here for workin' for Mrs. Mack."

"I like to have her," said Johnny. "You got one."

"Say, we like to get her married, but she wouldn't marry you. No sense to that."

Johnny was disappointed.

"Why?" he asked.

"Dinero," said Jose, laconically. "No dinero."

Johnny thought for a moment.

"You got a wife," he said.

"Sure, but I got a job. I make damn good money. Got a Ford. Got money in the bank. I got a right to have a wife. You ain't got nothing. I got a education. You don't know nothing. Ain't no girl gonna live with you less maybe some Indian girl."

Jose reached for the inner tube and examined it. Then he placed a tire pump on the valve and inflated the tube until it was round.

"He ought to stay fix now," said Jose.

He got up and walked to the tool shed where he dipped the tube in a tub of water to see if he could find any escaping air bubbles.

Johnny went with him and watched the work. His mind, however, was thinking of other things than repairing inner tubes. Why couldn't he have a job, and money, and a Ford car, and a wife?

"Say, what was the idea you had gettin' drunk and

goin' around without clothes and paintin' up your skin?" asked Jose. "We all thought you gone loco in the head. My wife and Maria were scared of you. What's the idea, huh?"

"No idea," said Johnny. "That's nothing."

Jose had said "my wife and Maria." So her name was Maria. He said it to himself, "Maria." Then he thought of what Jose had said about marriage. They must have a rule that nobody will marry you if you don't have a job. Then why couldn't he get a job? He would like to have a job. He had always envied Jose.

"You son of a bitch," said Jose, calmly, to the inner tube. "You damn bitch."

Johnny looked. The tube was leaking air under water and a series of small bubbles were coming to the surface.

"Now I got to fix again," said Jose.

He took the tube out of the water and tossed it aside.

"I fix him to-morrow," he said, and he took a pack of cigarettes from his pocket and lit one. Then he sat down beside the tool shed. He blew smoke, and Johnny sat down beside him. There were a lot of questions he wanted to ask Jose but he had to think them out first.

"So you like to get married," said Jose with a smile.

"Yes," said Johnny.

"You been around much?" asked Jose. "You had many muchachas?"

"No," said Johnny. "You have?"

"I been around," said Jose, knowingly. "When I lived down Imperial Valley I saw everything. I play black-jack and get drunk in Mexicali. That's a damned good place. You oughta see that. Lots of whores there. One night I lost fifty dollars all at once. Boy, I spend money like water. Gamble all night. That was before I go to work and get married. No more gambling now."

Jose's adventures were interesting, but Johnny was intent upon other things. He wanted to know more about Maria.

"How old are you?" asked Jose. "Nineteen? Twenty?"

"Twenty," said Johnny, although he was not yet seventeen.

"Maria, she's about eighteen. Maybe she like to have you for husband if you had money and a job. She got to have somebody."

"Sure," said Johnny.

"To-morrow I got to fix corral fence," said Jose. "Horses busted it."

Johnny didn't want to hear about the corral fence. He wanted to know how to get a job and how much money he had to have before any girl would live with him. He tried to formulate these questions but they were difficult to put into words. Jose didn't seem to think of offering any more information. They sat in silence.

After a while a door opened over at the main house and a bright red dress appeared on the porch. Johnny was excited at once. He watched Maria as she came down from the porch and along the sandy road. In the bright sunlight her dress was very red and her skin was very pale and her hair was very black, and Johnny thought she was wonderful. She came abreast with them and Jose spoke to her in Spanish. She stopped and answered him, but they were so used to the language and spoke so rapidly that Johnny could only catch a word now and then.

He could tell that they spoke of him for there was an occasional "Juanito." After half a dozen sentences Maria laughed and went on toward Jose's shack. Her laughter sounded beautiful and Johnny saw that she gave him a second glance as she moved away.

"Maria don't want to get married," said Jose with a grin.

"What she want?" asked Johnny.

"She say she like you but you came up here and watched her one day and she little afraid of you. She think you get drunk and go crazy again. Beside she already in love with another man."

This was bad news indeed.

"What's his name?" asked Johnny.

"Rudolph Valentino," said Jose.

Johnny had never heard of him. He wondered what this rival was like. He wondered if he had a job and money and a Ford car. A new emotion welled up from within him—a sensation he had never had before. He hated this Valentino, but it wasn't hate alone. It was a vindictive personal resentment. He was better than this Valentino. He could kill this Valentino. What right had he to be in the way? What business had he to spoil the scheme of things?

He decided that there was no time to waste and if he were going to have Maria he better find out what to do next. He made it as clear to Jose as he could that he wanted a job and he wanted it right away. At first Jose was reticent but when he saw that Johnny was serious he said he would ask Mr. Mack. Mr. Mack, however, was away and would not be back until evening. Johnny must wait.

But of course if he wanted to work now, Jose had an idea. He could start fixing the horse corral, and perhaps if he did a good job of repairing the fence Mr. Mack would give him a regular job.

Johnny got up at once. He was ready to start. Jose got some tools and they went over to the corral. He showed Johnny how to use the various tools, how to straighten the posts, and how to fasten the boards on the inside of the posts instead of the outside so that the animals could not push them loose. Johnny understood. He went to work and Jose went back to the shade and sat smoking and smiling to himself. Perhaps when Mr. Mack came he wouldn't say anything about Johnny at all, but would pretend that he had fixed the corral himself as he had been told to do twice before this. Still Johnny was a nice boy and he might try to get him a job. He'd see how he felt and what kind of humor Mr. Mack was in. Just now he didn't want to bother thinking about anything. It was nice to lie in the shade and not think at all.

Johnny fell to it with violence. He ripped a post loose and drove it down into the earth with savage blows. He yanked a bent nail out of a board and threw it to the ground. That Valentino. He'd show him. With his teeth clenched he wielded the hammer, driving the nails into the boards with two or three blows and giving them a couple of extra wallops for good measure.

Maria sat in the little house and talked to her sister, Nasaria. They spoke of Nasaria's baby and of Nasaria's new dress, and then Maria picked up a thumbed copy of a magazine called Photoplay. She turned the pages idly and glanced at the pictures even though she knew that issue so well that she could tell what was coming before she turned each page. When she had finished she went to the screen door and looked out. From time to time she could hear pounding and hammering, and when she opened the door and leaned out she could see Johnny up at the corral. He was busy and he was quite a distance away.

"That Indian is here again," she said to Nasaria.

"I don't like him," Nasaria said.

Maria didn't say anything. She stood still with her nose against the screen and looked out. He liked her. That Indian liked her. It was funny. It was ridiculous. Still it was nice in a way. It was pleasant. It was flattering to be noticed. She held the motion picture magazine in her left hand and ran the fingers of her right hand through her hair and stared out at a tamarisk tree without seeing it. After a while she took another look toward the corral. He had his clothes on now. He was dressed like an Indian but she knew what he looked like underneath.

"Neither do I," she said.

"What?" asked Nasaria.

"I don't like him either," said Maria.

Nasaria was sewing the new dress. She didn't know what Maria was talking about.

"Don't like who?" she asked.

"That Juanito," said Maria.

"Oh, is he still here?"

"He's working."

"What doing?"

"Corral."

"Have you seen my black thread? I've lost my black thread. Have you seen it?"

"No," said Maria, without looking around.

Nasaria got up and looked on the floor under her chair. Then she went to the table and looked there.

"Pablo, did you take my black thread?" she asked the baby.

Maria left the door and sat down near the table. She opened the motion picture magazine at random. Among the advertisements near the front was a full page picture of a strong man in a defiant pose, nearly nude, his arms crossed over a huge chest, and muscles bulging around his shoulders. Around his middle was a leopard skin.

"Be an athlete! Develop your body. Gain twenty pounds in thirty days. Read the amazing testimonials of my pupils. I can do as much for you! Clip the coupon and enclose ten cents to cover postage of wonderful free forty-page booklet entitled 'Your road to health and strength.' Professor Magnus Strongbow. The Strongbow method has no failures."

Maria didn't think Professor Strongbow's body was beautiful. His muscles were unattractive. His body was not as lithe and as sinewy as—as it might be.

She turned the pages to the picture she liked best, a full-page half-tone of a Latin gentleman in a toreador costume. He was looking straight at you. His head was lowered slightly and his eyes were burning up at you beneath thin dark brows. His tapering fingers held a cigarette and a wisp of smoke was disappearing into the air. There was a smile on his face, not a broad smile, not a hearty smile, but a cool, devilish, sardonic smile that told volumes. Life was no mystery to him. He was superior to it all. You knew at once that in the face of all dangers, in the midst of raucous humor, before all the sirens and vampires of the world, before kings, queens, and paupers, he stood aloof with that same knowing, sardonic smile. He was perfection. Maria held the magazine in her lap and studied the picture for a long time. She didn't notice that Nasaria had found her black thread and was sewing again.

Presently she looked up. There was the sound of an automobile approaching, and past the door on the sandy road went Mr. Mack's car with Mr. and Mrs. Mack and a strange lady in it. They were back much earlier than she expected. She must get up to the main house. They might want dinner early. She put the magazine on the table, looked at her face in a mirror, adjusted her hair, and walked out of the house.

Jose scrambled to his feet as the car came toward him. He felt foolish to be caught loafing and he nodded, and smiled, and took his hat off as the car went by.

"Look at that lazy Mexican, George," said Mrs. Mack. "I declare they are the laziest people I've ever seen."

"It's all in knowing how to make them work for you, my dear," said the other woman. "Mr. Reeves employed thirty Mexicans at Chama and we never had any trouble with them."

"This boy's all right," said George Mack, as he stopped the car at the front porch. "Jose's all right. He's got somebody working on the corral, I see. All I ask is to get the work done. I don't care if he loafs all day if he delivers the goods."

They all got out of the car, and as they did Jose came up, bowing and nodding, his hat in his hand.

"Is that all you've got to do, Jose?" asked Mrs. Mack. "I thought you were going to build an arbor for the bougainvillea?"

"Si, señora," said Jose, smiling. "Si, señora."

"Anything new, Jose?" asked George Mack.

"No, sir," said Jose.

The other woman was watching Maria as she approached. Maria intended to hurry by and go into the house without speaking. She didn't look up. But Mrs. Mack spoke to her.

"We shall have a guest for dinner, Maria," she said, impressively. Maria looked at her. "You understand?"

"Yes," said Maria, and she went on into the house. She lacked the finesse that Mrs. Mack had hoped she might have intelligence enough to assume. She made a mental note to explain to Maria how to act like a servant.

Then they all noticed another figure who had come on the scene. It was Johnny, and he had a hammer in his hand.

"What's this?" asked Mr. Mack.

"Oh, he's Juanito," said Jose, casually. "That's just Juanito."

"Want job," said Juanito, without any hesitation.

Mrs. Mack was about to say. "Won't you come in, Mrs. Reeves," but she hesitated as Mrs. Reeves seemed very much interested in the Indian.

"Looks like you got one," said George Mack.

"Does he work for you?" asked Mrs. Reeves.

"No, not that I know of," said George Mack. "Now look here, Jose, you can't hire anybody who happens to—"

Mrs. Reeves interrupted.

"I believe that's an Apache. I know Apaches whenever I see them. Mr. Reeves and I lived among them for years. Skhin Apatieh?"

The last words she addressed to Johnny. He looked at her. They sounded strange, and although he knew what she had asked he didn't answer.

"Come, come, don't play dumb with me. Skhin Apatieh?"

"Sure, damn right," said Johnny.

George Mack smothered a laugh, and Mrs. Reeves drew herself up to her full height. She stared stern disapproval at Johnny for ten seconds, but he didn't know it.

"Want job," he said again.

"Mr. Mack, I know this Indian," said Mrs. Reeves. "There's bad blood in him. He's the son of Fig Tree John, and Fig Tree is a bad Indian."

"I know about him," said George Mack.

"Hostile to the ranchers, murdered his own wife, raised the boy in ignorance in spite of the fact that I went down to his hovel and told him face to face what he ought to do. If I were you I wouldn't have him around the place. And that's the advice of one who knows Indians."

"That's right. I know all about him," said George Mack.

"Won't you come in, Mrs. Reeves?" asked Mrs. Mack.

With a final look at Johnny, Mrs. Reeves walked up

to the porch and into the house, and Mrs. Mack followed her.

"Now look here, Jose, you can't hire somebody to do your own work for you. You had no business to hire this man," said George Mack.

Jose looked down, fingered his hat, and then began to explain.

"I was fixin' the inner tube, but it didn't stay fixed so he started the corral because he wanted to work somewhere. He wants a job all the time and I told him he have to show you how good he can work."

"Good work," said Johnny.

"I don't need any help," said George Mack. "Wait'll it's time to pick dates, then I'll let you work. Go try some other ranch where they're short-handed. Go see Paul. He's looking for a hand."

Then he turned away and walked into the house.

Jose felt a little abashed. He felt that he was open to criticism and he tried to help his position by explaining it to Johnny.

"That's good—see, that's good. You go over to Paul's ranch and get a job. Tell him you worked for Mr. Mack. I got no dinero to pay you for fixin' corral but I tell you what I do. I give you some old clothes so you look like you know how to work. You wear them instead of them Indian clothes and go see Señor Paul and get a good job."

They went back to the shack and Jose gave Johnny an old pair of pants and an old shirt with the sleeves cut out. Johnny put the pants on over his own breeches and buttoned the shirt over his coyote hide jacket. That was the first time he had ever worn a white man's clothing.

Paul's ranch was smaller than Mack's and the property ran inland from the beach of the Salton Sea. It was a half mile from the highway by a sandy trail, and one mile north of Fig Tree John's water hole in the grease-wood. It was the southernmost of the ranches and was not regarded as a desirable section until Paul set out his date trees which flourished immediately. Paul's house was a one-story frame building of four or five rooms. He lived there with his wife, and his ranch help con-sisted of whatever itinerant laborers drifted in.

Johnny rode up to the ranch house late in the after-noon. He thought there was a good looking automobile standing there, which he was later to identify as "the Buick." He dismounted, and Mr. Paul came to the door and looked out.

"Hallo!" hailed Mr. Paul.

Johnny liked the sound of his voice.

"Hallo!" he answered.

Mr. Paul came out of the house and walked toward him. He met him half way, and they stood talking as the sun swung lower.

"Want job," began Johnny.

"What can you do?"

"Work."

"What kind?"

"Good work."

"Ever work on a date ranch before?"

"Sure."

"Where?"

"Over that way."

"Know how to pollenize?"

This was a hard one, and Johnny didn't know what it meant. Still, he wasn't afraid to answer questions.

"Sure," he said.

"What's your name?"

"Johnny."

"Johnny what?"

"Johnny."

"Got a last name?"

"Sure."

"What's your other name?"

"Johnny Mack?"

"Oh, did you work for Mack?"

"Sure."

"Did he fire you?"

"Sure."

Mr. Paul laughed. He had expected a denial. He liked Johnny's honesty, not knowing that it was ignorance.

"What for?"

"Want job."

"I need somebody to help me pollenize in about a week. I'll give you a job for ten dollars a week. If you make good I'll keep you on steady. What do you say to that?"

"Sure."

"You'll have to build yourself a shack unless you live around here somewhere. Do you live anywhere near here?"

"That way," said Johnny, "with Fig Tree John."

Mr. Paul frowned. That sounded bad. He had heard some nasty things about Fig Tree John. This boy, of course, was his son.

"Well, you behave yourself and we'll get along all right. If you don't, off you go." He looked at Johnny closely. The boy seemed friendly and willing, and he decided to go through with it. "All right, Mr. Johnny Mack Fig Tree, you come see me in the morning."

He went back to the house and Johnny rode down the beach of the Salton Sea. Half way home he took off the pants and the shirt and hid them in a mesquite bush. Agocho wouldn't understand them. He knew that there was going to be trouble about this and he wanted to avoid it as long as possible.

Agocho was happy that night. The corn was growing. The figs were plentiful. He had made himself a beautiful new belt. They had a lot of food stored away. What more could any one ask? He wanted to know what the boy had been doing all day, but Johnny avoided his questions. Agocho was not suspicious and he didn't mind if the boy was tired and didn't want to talk.

But the next day the boy rode away in the morning and was gone all day. And the third day he did the same. He was up to something. That night Agocho questioned the boy again. Then he suspected, but he was loath to believe the worst. He said nothing more, but he wondered. He let things go on that way for several days. Then he followed the boy's tracks as far as the southern boundary of the Paul ranch. That left no room for doubt. All hope that he could be wrong was gone now. He went back to the clearing.

Why this should be he could not understand. Was there something wrong with his son? Had he been accursed? It was incredible, especially after the great suc-

cess of the ceremony and the powers that had been
invoked thereby.

Two more days went by and still the boy continued
to go to the white people. Agocho knew that this must
stop. It had gone on long enough. Apparently it was a
situation that was not going to correct itself. In that
case he would correct it.

The boy came home that night and they had little to
say. Each knew what the other was thinking. They
had to have it out sometime. Yet they both hesitated.
Agocho's plan was simple. He would wait until morning.
When the boy was about to leave he would stop him.
He would not let him go up to that country again if
he had to beat him into insensibility in order to keep
him away. His word was law; he was the patriarch; and
it was time to exercise that authority. He slept, but his
sleep was troubled. He dreamed of battles with wild
animals in which he was alone and unarmed; he dreamed
of games and contests among the clan back at White
River in which he was pitted against great odds. He
dreamed of winning, but always after triumph he lay
spent and exhausted, the winner of a Pyrrhic victory so
weakened that he was easily overcome by the next
adversary.

In the morning all his plans went for nothing. The
boy made no effort to leave. He stayed around the clearing of his own free will, and he occupied his time by
making a necklace of animals' teeth—a necklace bearing
contributions from coyotes, sheep, mountain lions, and
jackrabbits. Agocho was relieved but wary. Perhaps
everything was going to be all right now. He didn't

know that it was Sunday and that Mr. Paul had told
Johnny not to come to work, but to rest and get ready
for Monday when they would begin pollenization and
there would be plenty to do.

Agocho was hopeful and he gave thanks to the Great
Spirits for recognizing the error and correcting it, for
doubtless this was due to their efforts. He had not had to
raise a hand. The spirits had seen to it first, and that
was right and just. But the next morning when he rose
at dawn the boy was already up and away. He had
slipped off quietly and the tracks showed the way he had
gone. Agocho was furious. He had passed the point where
he had to consider. It was time to act now and he
wouldn't delay again. He mounted a horse and rode out
of the clearing northward through the desert, not deign-
ing to use the highway or the beach, but taking a
straight line for the Paul ranch.

Chapter XV

JOHNNY had had a good week. He discovered that he
liked Mr. Paul and that he liked Mrs. Paul and that this
white man's world was a source of information all of
which was thrilling to know. For instance instead of being the month of T'a Nu-chu as Agocho supposed, it was
really April, 1924. And the next month instead of being
Shosh-ke would be May.

He learned many things about the organization and
maintenance of a date ranch that he never knew existed.
He had two more rides in an automobile that was not a
Ford car, but a Buick. Twice he had gone to town with
Mr. Paul. They had made purchases and brought back
things and he began to get some idea of what had to be
done in order to drive an automobile. Mr. Paul said he
must learn to drive so that he could go errands alone
and so that he could take Mrs. Paul places. He was
anxious to learn.

Several times during the week he went over to the
Mack ranch. The two ranches were close together, and
the west boundary of the Paul ranch really touched the
eastern tip of the Mack ranch. In between the two was a
stretch of desert, forty acres that belonged to Mack and
had never been cleared. Paul's grove of date trees stopped
abruptly at this forty acres, and Mack's trees began on
the other side. Across the middle of this uncleared land
ran a dry wash full of soft sand and smoke trees. Oc-

casionally, when there were storms in the Santa Rosas
the water ran down from the mountains, and for a day
or two the wash became a small river which ran into the
Salton Sea. Such storms were rare and the wash was dry
for two and three years at a time. It was in the bottom of
this wash that Agocho had seen the two white men when
he was on his way to Mecca to trade Kai-a's baskets, but
that was long before the Mack ranch or the Paul ranch
existed. To drive from one ranch to the other it was
necessary to drive from Paul's house to the highway, and
up the highway a quarter of a mile to the entrance to
Mack's. But on foot the two properties were really adjacent.

Johnny had walked across the desert and into Mack's
grove and then on to the houses. On each trip he saw
Jose for half an hour and he had two glimpses of Maria.
Once she passed by and when he looked at her she smiled
at him, and then went on faster.

Jose was pleased with himself for getting Johnny a
job, and he told Nasaria and Maria all about it. Nasaria
wasn't impressed but Maria listened and said nothing.

Then came the Sunday when Johnny stayed in the
clearing and made a necklace of animals' teeth, and then
Monday and the time to begin pollenization. He was at
the ranch early and presently Mr. Paul came out of the
house with a knife and a number of short pieces of string
and a basket containing blossoms heavy with pollen from
a date tree. The blossoms were cream colored on long
and slender shoots, and Mr. Paul was careful not to
shake them and disturb the pollen. He told Johnny to
get a ladder and then they walked out into the date
grove.

Mr. Paul had the ladder set against the first tree and he climbed up and did mysterious things with the knife and the pollen blossoms and the string, and then he came down and Johnny moved the ladder to the next tree. From the ground Johnny could not see what was going on, and after a while Mr. Paul made him climb up the ladder with him. Johnny saw him open the stalk by slitting it, place one of the shoots containing pollen flowers from the basket within, and then hold the stalk together and tie it with a small piece of string so that the pollen blossoms could not escape. That's all there was to it.

Then Mr. Paul explained to Johnny as simply as he could that this process would make the trees bear dates, and if the pollenization were not skillfully done the dates would not be good. These were all female trees but the blossoms were from a male tree, and if they waited for the wind to blow the pollen from the male tree they might have dates and they might not. Johnny had never heard of such a thing. He marveled at the white man's knowledge of how to insure himself a crop. Certainly Agocho never knew anything like this.

After several more lessons Mr. Paul sent Johnny up the ladder first and he followed. He gave Johnny the knife and one of the shoots containing pollen blossoms and Johnny tried to imitate what he had seen Mr. Paul do. At first he made mistakes. He put the blossoms into the stalk but he spilled much of the valuable pollen dust, and another time he tied the string too tight and once he cut the stalk in two instead of only slitting it. But after a while he got used to it and they took turns with Mr. Paul watching him and explaining when he did something wrong. Johnny wanted to please Mr. Paul

and he tried hard to do it right. He decided that he had
been lucky to get such a good job. He wondered if Jose
had learned to pollenize as quickly as he was learning.
They went on down the line, tree after tree, until they
reached the end of the grove at the edge of the desert.
Across the uncleared forty acres he could see the tops
of the date palms at the Mack ranch. Then they moved
to the next line of trees and they began to work their
way back toward the ranch house.

Agocho rode through the desert, cut across the salt
grass and followed the eastern boundary of the date grove
to the house. Nobody was in sight. He rode around to the
rear and he saw one of his horses nibbling salt grass beyond the feed shed. He dismounted and looked around.
He went over to the house and peered in a window.
Then he walked around the house and he looked in the
front door. Mrs. Paul, inside, saw him and for an instant she was frightened. Agocho was fifty-nine, almost
sixty, and he looked older. He was dressed in native
costume, his face was wrinkled and his mouth was set
and grim. He didn't look friendly. Mrs. Paul watched
him walk around the house toward the rear. She got a
glimpse of him through a side window as she went to the
back door. Then he was standing beside the pump house.
She was afraid he might interfere with the irrigating
machinery.

"What do you want?" she called.

He turned and looked at her.

"I know you," she said. "You're Fig Tree John. What
do you want, Fig Tree?"

"Want my horse," said Fig Tree.

"That's your son's horse. That's Johnny Mack's horse."

"Where white man?" asked Fig Tree.

"They're out in the grove somewhere, pollenizing. That way."

She pointed. He mounted his horse and led Johnny's horse after him, and rode into the date grove.

As he descended the ladder, Johnny turned around and saw his father riding toward him with his own horse in tow. He was startled. Agocho looked angry. He stopped his horse some twenty feet away and stared. Johnny walked slowly over to him, and Mr. Paul, who had been above Johnny on the ladder, stopped half way down and looked at the stranger. He was about to hail him, but there was something in the silent figure on horseback that stopped him. He stood on the ladder and watched while Johnny Mack went over beside Fig Tree and they spoke. Mr. Paul could not understand their words. They spoke quietly, almost softly, and every once in a while some unknown Indian words floated over toward him. Johnny Mack had his back to Mr. Paul, and he couldn't see Johnny's face. But he had a good view of Fig Tree who was looking down. He especially noticed Fig Tree's eyes. They were maniacal, with a small staring eye ball and a great deal of white showing. He wondered why the scene held him and why he didn't get down and move the ladder on to the next tree, and just as he started to do so there was a sudden shriek, a wild animal yell, and he couldn't tell whether it came from Johnny Mack or from Fig Tree.

In the flash of a second Johnny was dodging to one side, and Fig Tree, in a frenzy, was trying to beat him over the head with his fist. And Fig Tree's horse, startled by the sudden activity, was rearing and plunging, and the other animal was trying to bolt. Johnny slipped and fell on one knee and for an instant Paul thought the horse had reared and driven its hoofs down on him, but apparently the animal missed him, for Johnny rolled to one side and leaped to his feet.

"Hey! Hey! What's going on here!" yelled Paul. He brandished the date knife, but he was afraid to get near the plunging horse. Johnny was on his feet, standing between him and Fig Tree, watching Fig Tree every instant.

Fig Tree quieted the horse. He glared at Johnny and at Paul. The other horse had broken away in the excitement and had galloped a short distance across the grove. Paul waited, holding the knife ready for action expecting anything to happen.

"Fig Tree John, you get out of here," he commanded. "Get off my land."

Fig Tree stared at him, and Paul fully expected to be attacked.

"Go on. Get out," he said.

Fig Tree pulled his horse's head to the right and rode off across the grove. He trotted over to the other horse and retrieved it. Paul watched him go. Fig Tree didn't look back. He tied the other animal to the saddle of his own and then walked the animals toward the ranch house.

Johnny was still standing near the ladder. He was trembling and he didn't say a word. Paul was afraid Fig Tree might do something more, and he followed him at a discreet distance out of the grove, past the house, and on into the desert. Paul stopped at the desert edge and watched Fig Tree until he was out of sight in the greasewood and mesquite. He went back to the house and told Mrs. Paul that Fig Tree had been around "looking for trouble" and if she saw him again to call for help and keep out of his way.

Then he went back to the grove. Johnny was waiting for him. Paul tried to ask him about Fig Tree, if he was crazy, what he meant by his attack, and what he and Johnny had said to each other, but Johnny wouldn't answer. He simply looked serious and shook his head and once or twice mumbled "no sabe."

They went on with the pollenizing, but Johnny wasn't good for much the rest of the day. He was excited and nervous. Once up on the ladder he dropped the knife, and it just missed Paul. Another time he got the strings tangled and couldn't seem to tie a knot. So Paul, realizing that Johnny was suffering from shock, made him stop the accurate work and let him hold the ladder and move it about for the balance of the day.

Formerly Johnny had always ridden south at sunset, but this day he had no horse to ride the mile down to the clearing. He hesitated, and hung around the ranch house. Mrs. Paul offered him some supper and he ate it. She told her husband that she thought Johnny was afraid to go home. Paul went out and spoke to him.

"Look here, Johnny Mack, if you want to sleep here to-night you can have some blankets and make yourself a bed out of hay and straw in the feed shed. Do you want to do that?"

Johnny did. He was quick to accept. Paul gave him the blankets and told him to make himself comfortable. Johnny put the blankets in the feed shed. It smelled nice of corn and hay. But he wasn't ready to sleep yet. It was dark but not too dark to walk around and before long the moon would be coming up. He walked through the date trees to the end of the grove. He crossed the uncleared desert and the dry wash and entered Mack's property and followed Mack's trees to the houses. There were lights in the main house, but he detoured around it and walked toward Jose's shack. There was a light in Jose's shack, too, but before he got to it he saw the red glow of a cigarette out in the dark under a tamarisk tree.

"Quien es?" asked Jose.

"Hallo," said Johnny.

"Juanito?"

"Yes."

"What do you want?"

"Don't want nothing," said Johnny.

He sat down beside Jose and Jose gave him a cigarette. He struck a match for Johnny and Johnny smoked the cigarette and liked it. They sat still in the warm night air and said little. Jose asked about his job and Johnny answered in one or two words.

After a while Johnny was surprised by a strange voice from the interior of Jose's house. It wasn't a human voice at all but it resembled it. He couldn't understand the words. He asked Jose what it was.

"Victrola," said Jose. "Plays nice music only we ain't got many records."

Johnny didn't understand any of this. Jose smoked another cigarette and the strident inhuman voice stopped and started and stopped again. When Jose finished his cigarette he threw the butt away and stood up.

"I'm goin' in," he said. "I guess you can come in if you to if you don't act loco."

Johnny was willing to go in. He wanted to see the inside of a house. He had often wondered what they were like. He followed Jose through the door. There was an oil lamp on the table and Johnny thought it gave off a bright light. Nasaria was there, and best of all, Maria was there. They were sitting down and they looked up in surprise as he stood in the doorway.

"Juanito came to see us. He don't know much," Jose said.

Nasaria and Maria didn't say anything. Jose sat down in a chair and he told Johnny to sit down. But Johnny preferred to stand. He looked around at many curious objects—furniture, pictures, a crucifix on the wall. He wondered what they all meant. Presently Nasaria spoke to Jose in Spanish, and Jose led Johnny over to a corner where there was a closet with a small wooden door.

"My wife show you her shrine," said Jose.

Johnny watched while Nasaria opened the wooden door. Inside was a small wooden figure of the Virgin. She held a child in her arms and looked up with an innocent and beatific gaze. Nasaria had clothed her in a remnant of scarlet cloth, but the garish color gave no idea of incongruity to Johnny. He looked at the figure and the child and the candles before it and the slightly damaged Christmas tree ornaments hanging over it, and he had no idea what it all meant. It looked pretty and the red dress made him think of Maria.

"He don't know nothing," Jose said. "He's not Catholic."

"La Madre de Dios," said Nasaria to Johnny.

"That's the mother of God, the mother of our Lord," said Jose. "She's the Blessed Virgin and that's Jesus."

To Johnny it was both clarifying and confusing. He thought the mother of God was Ste-na-tlih-a, but this was another one.

"She ees Maria," said Nasaria, slowly.

Johnny thought they must have named the image in honor of the real Maria who was there in the room. He turned and looked at her. She was watching them.

"You pray to the Blessed Virgin and she answer your prayers for you," said Jose.

"La madre de Jesus Cristo," said Nasaria.

They seemed like a lot of facts that together ought to mean something, but to Johnny the idea was still muddy. Why was the mother of God like Maria, named Maria, a virgin in a red dress? The elements of a chain of reason all held together but didn't quite mean anything.

Nasaria was pleased to show her shrine to an ignorant visitor. She thought it was a good thing for Johnny to see. She looked from him to the shrine and smiled, and then she closed the little closet and felt very happy.

Jose said something in Spanish to Maria and she went to a queer looking box and did something to it. Johnny thrilled to be so close to her. He watched everything she did.

Then he was surprised to hear the same strange voice that he had heard outside. He reacted with a start and Jose and Nasaria laughed at him. The noise came out of the box and it made a curious sound that wasn't particularly pleasant. Johnny's first exposure to jazz left him neither liking nor disliking it. Jose seemed to enjoy

it, and he watched Johnny with a broad smile and white
flashing teeth. Marie looked at Johnny, too, but she
turned away when his roving gaze fell upon her. Then
the volume of the music fell away to a background and
a voice came over it. It sang "Barney Google."

> "Ba-a-arney Google,
>   With a goo, goo, googley eye.
>   Ba-a-arney Google,
>   With a goo, goo, googley eye."

Johnny couldn't understand most of the words, but
the idea of a wooden box playing music and singing
words made him laugh. He began to like it, and when
the record stopped he was sorry. Maria went to the box
again and took a black disk off and put another one on.
Johnny was delighted when it sang

> "Charley, my boy, oh Charley, my boy,
>   You thrill me,
>   You fill me,
>   With oceans of joy."

Jose joined in and sang with it and Nasaria and Maria
seemed to like it, too, and Johnny laughed. Suddenly
Jose jumped up and grabbed Nasaria around the waist
and they began to move about the room together. Johnny
was amazed. They lightly stepped and hopped and
glided about the little room, bumped into furniture, and
shouted and laughed. Johnny had never seen a man grab
a woman and hold on to her and move around in a
steady rhythm. He had danced once to the rhythm of a

drum but this was much wilder and more grotesque. It was startling. He looked at Maria and he wondered if she could do that.

The music stopped and Jose and Nasaria stopped, too, gasping and laughing, and they both sat down.

"Whew—I'm the best dancer in the valley!" said Jose, breathless, and Nasaria laughed and nodded her head.

Maria went to the box and in a moment it was singing

"Just a love nest, cozy and warm,
  Like a dove rest, down on the farm,
  A veranda with some sort of clinging vine,
  Then a kitchen where some rambler roses twine."

And after that they had several more. Then Maria played "Barney Google" and "Love Nest" over again until Jose and Nasaria were tired of them and told her to stop. Nasaria put the baby to bed in the next room and Jose began to yawn. He lost interest in Johnny and he got up and went into the other room with Nasaria. Johnny was left alone with Maria. She was embarrassed and didn't know what to say to him, but she wasn't as embarrassed as he was. He wanted to tell her about the necklace of animals' teeth he had made for her, but he didn't know how to begin. She sat still and he stood still and they didn't say a word. He wished he had that necklace with him. After this he would always carry it until he had a chance to give it to her.

It seemed like a long time. It was only a few minutes. Maria got up and abruptly walked into the other room. Johnny, alone, felt better, but he understood that the evening was over and he walked out of the house. Maria heard him go. She was listening for every sound.

"What's Juanito doing?" asked Jose.

"He's gone," said Maria.

"He go without saying anything?"

Jose looked into the front room.

"He just went out," said Maria.

"He's strange," said Nasaria.

"He's a nice fellow," said Jose.

Then they forgot Juanito and never thought of him again that night—all but Maria.

Johnny went around the Mack house, through the date grove, and out into the desert. He felt exhilarated. The moon was bright and he ran across the dry wash. It had been a grand visit. When he got into the shadow of Paul's date trees he had to go slower. He passed the spot where he had talked that morning with Agocho and he felt sorry for Agocho. He went on to the ranch house. There were no lights in the Paul house and he knew they were asleep. He wondered if they had a box that could play and sing. He went to the feed shed, spread out his blankets and then wrapped them around him. The night had been exciting and he reviewed the events in his mind. He thought mostly about Maria. As soon as he had worked enough he would have her for a wife and they would get a singing box and listen to it every night. He went to sleep.

All the next day he worked with Mr. Paul, and in the afternoon Mr. Paul let him pollenize some of the trees all by himself. He was very careful to do it exactly right and Mr. Paul was pleased. Agocho didn't come to the ranch at all, and at sunset Johnny didn't wait for supper. He went to the beach of the inland sea and he walked south, turned into the clearing, and looked around.

It was still light. Agocho wasn't there. One of the
horses was missing, also a pair of saddle-bags, a water
container, and the rifle. He guessed that Agocho was
away for the night, perhaps for a day or two. He looked
around for some food. There was some tough dried meat
and some yucca pulp. Before he ate it he searched for the
necklace he had made. It was in the kowa. Agocho hadn't
touched it. Johnny put it around his neck, and after he
had eaten he sat in the clearing for a long time and
thought about the interesting world that he was discov-
ering. Jose's life was so far removed from the clearing;
Jose only a mile away, knew nothing about this kind of
living. He almost knew more than Jose. He had always
enjoyed living but now he was enjoying it more than
ever. He had never understood before that life in the
clearing was only a part of living. He had thought it was
everything. Now he knew better and he was very wise.

The moon came up and he thought of it as kle-ga-na-ai,
and at once he knew that was wrong. It must have another name that the white men had given it and that
was its right name. Ste-na-tlih-a's right name was Maria.
He must ask what kle-ga-na-ai's right name was.

That night he slept in the kowa. Agocho did not return. In the morning Johnny awoke before the sun rose.
He ate some figs and mescal. He didn't take a horse. He
walked back up the beach and arrived at the Paul ranch
at sunrise.

Again they worked at pollenizing. Mr. Paul worked
with him only part of the time, and devoted the rest
of the day to other things. He asked about Fig Tree, but
there was nothing Johnny could tell him.

Late in the afternoon when Johnny was still in the grove but almost ready to stop work, he was surprised to look down from the ladder and see a red dress among the date trees. It was Maria and she was coming along toward the ladder. She looked up and saw him and she smiled. Johnny said "Hello," and she went right on. After she had gone he came down and watched her. She went straight through the grove toward the Paul house. Johnny didn't know that she had a note from Mrs. Mack to Mrs. Paul. All he knew was that she must come back. He moved the ladder to the next tree and climbed up. He wasted as much time as he could. He placed a shoot of pollen blossoms in the stalk and tied it carefully. He took plenty of time and he kept looking toward the house. He wanted to stay in that one spot until Maria came back again.

The sun hit the mountains and the shadows began to merge. The light began to fade and it was time to stop work. There were only a few pollen blossoms left. He had worked well and there wasn't anything he could do now until to-morrow morning. Just as he dismounted the ladder he saw Maria coming back. She was walking slowly. He waited for her to come up, and when she did he took off the necklace of animals' teeth and held it out to her.

"I make this for you," he said.

Maria stopped and looked. She held the necklace in her hands. She thought it was ugly. She thought the animals' teeth were hideous things, but she liked Johnny. She didn't like to touch the necklace but she put it over her head unable to resist anything in the nature of deco-

ration. She tried to look at it as she wore it. The string
of teeth lay on her bosom and they rose and fell with the
contour of her breasts as she breathed. The sight made
Johnny catch his breath. He took half a step toward her
and stopped when she looked up.

The gift did not please her as a gift. But she liked it
coming from Johnny. She looked at his shirt—an old
shirt that had belonged to Jose. It had no sleeves. In
the half light his brown arms looked very dark. He was
smiling and looking at her. His eyes shone. She thought
of that brown body that she had seen that day on the
highway. It was the same; it stood here now before her.
She reached out a hand and, lightly, for the fraction of a
second, she touched that brown arm.

Then she gasped and moved back a step or two. She
remembered him, naked, painted, wild. She caught her
breath, turned, and ran as fast as she could toward the
Mack ranch.

To Johnny that touch was electric. It meant everything. For an instant he was startled when she ran. The
red dress moved off in a flash, and in a flash he was after
her.

She darted out of the date grove and started across
the desert land. Johnny was close behind her. He was surprised that she could run so fast. In and out among the
desert bushes she ran and then down into the dry wash
among the smoke trees. Here it was sandy and she could
not move so fast, and in the bottom of the wash he
caught her.

She slipped and fell as he reached her. She was frightened and breathless and yet she was glad he caught her.

She did not resist him. She surrendered to him entirely. They didn't speak. They didn't need words. She wanted him and he wanted her, and now he had her. Through the fading twilight they lay in the warm sand almost unaware of the coming of night and bright moonlight.

Chapter XVI

AT the age of sixty Agocho considered himself in the prime of life. He was strong, healthy, and wise. The fact that he lived a solitary vindictive life to the point of obsession, that he mistrusted, disliked, or hated all other human beings outside the clearing, that he brooded on the injustices forced upon him and considered his son a failure and a traitor to his blood, never in any way led him to consider for an instant that life might require adjustment on his part, and that he could alleviate his sufferings by intellectualizing them and analyzing them apart from himself. That was beyond his instinct, beyond his religion, and beyond his comprehension. He lived by his own code and that code made him the center of the universe with the power to judge all issues by the mandates of his tribe and his Gods. There was no questioning such fundamentals. He knew what was right and he knew what was wrong. His judgment came directly from the divine trinity, Ste-na-tlih-a and her two sons, the God of fire and the God of water. Together they ruled and accounted for the universe and as long as he lived under their guidance error was impossible.

All his life he had been faithful and devout. The sins committed against him must be punished, and if the Gods withheld justice it was only to make its eventual execution the more complete. He would be expected to balance the scales, but only in the way that the Gods intended that balance to be expressed.

For fifteen years Kai-a had been unavenged. And now there were other complications that he did not understand. The loss of his son, the fact that the boy had gone white, and the gradual encroachment of white civilization on all sides, were things that were wrong. Some day they would have to be accounted for. All of them were personal grievances against himself which meant that he must be the agent of justice to nullify these sins.

He made many prayers to the Gods. He sat for hours before round cairns with twigs deposited upon them, mumbling sometimes aloud, or concentrating in silence upon his rights and looking within himself for the answer to injustice. On Kai-a's grave he had put many stones and sometimes he sat for days, mumbling, praying, thinking, and looking for the answer.

Sometimes he took a horse and rode for a day or two or three into the desert or into the mountains. Once he went into the remote canyon north of the inland sea where he had found the palm trees and the spring many years ago. The mound of stones as high as his knees that he had built that day so long ago was still there. That was a good sign. Nobody had disturbed it, nobody had been in the canyon. That mound of stones had been built before N'Chai Chidn was born. It was still there. It was a very good sign. It meant wait, watch, observe. The time was coming.

For many months he saw little of his son. He didn't want to see him. The boy had grown up, but he was weak and corrupt and the Apache in him was dead. The white men had ruined him. He worked on the Paul ranch and he mingled with white men and he was forgetting his own language. He was mature and a man and there was no way to stop him. He could kill him, but that wasn't the answer, certainly that wasn't the answer. No, the stones said wait and he would wait.

He rarely rode into the ranch country, but when he did he ignored all white men and went about his business. His business was helping himself to whatever he wanted. The white man was a trespasser and he had no compunction about taking anything useful that these outlanders had brought with them. From McCabe he took a hammer, pliers, and a screwdriver. From Mack he took an old tire and the radiator cap from his automobile and Mrs. Mack's nightgown from the clothes line. From Carr he stole a ham and vegetables and from Paul, whom he particularly disliked because N'Chai Chidn worked for him, he stole anything or everything that was loose. At first none of these thefts were committed surreptitiously, but in broad daylight for any one to see who cared to look. He became known as a great thief, but he wasn't really a thief, only an arbitrary collector of tithes. All things were basically his. The ranch owners and the Mexicans dreaded to see him, and more often than not he was driven off by an irate rancher who called him a dirty thief, warned him never to return, and threatened to have him arrested, something that he did not understand at all. Gradually he had to confine his raids to dark nights, but not always, for the Mexicans were afraid of him and he knew it. More than one Mexican who saw Fig Tree John prowling around a ranch looked the other way.

Much of his stolen property he took into Mecca and

traded for cartridges, tobacco, or food, until Petterman's son, who ran the store after his father's death in 1925, was forced to refuse to trade with Fig Tree because of his thieving. Then articles accumulated in the clearing.

From time to time Johnny came down into the greasewood. He lived there now and then, but most of the time he was either at the Paul ranch or the Mack ranch. Sometimes he would return articles which he knew belonged to Paul or to Mack, but Agocho invariably stole them again so he gave up.

Agocho had no idea that Johnny was planning to marry a Mexican girl and get himself a bank account and a Ford car. He had no idea Maria existed, he never heard of a bank, and he resented Ford cars. He settled into a sullen silence. He bore a grudge against Johnny; he really hated Johnny; but he seemed to have given up violence and to be resigned to Johnny's disgrace. Johnny felt that time had driven his father into a disgruntled acceptance. Outwardly it seemed so, but inwardly Agocho was belligerent. Johnny mistook an armistice for peace.

For almost a year Johnny worked for Paul. He learned many things, and in that time he passed the transitional stage of an Indian who lived like a white man and thought like an Indian, and became an Indian who lived and thought white. He could speak coherently and do a simple amount of reading and writing. Mrs. Paul taught him a vocabulary, and while spelling was always a nuisance and never made sense, he could make himself understood on paper. "Cat, rat, and watermelon," he would occasionally say aloud while working, to the perplexity of anybody who happened to hear him. It was

not idiocy, however, but practice. Cat, rat, and watermelon were the first words he conquered. He knew them
whenever he saw them and he could write them down
whenever he wanted to. It gave him a great sense of
power.

Then he learned the mysteries of Mr. Paul's Buick,
and after several abortive efforts and one slightly dented
fender he became accustomed to controlling a car. While
he never became a good driver, for like Jose he would
drive at a steady pace through or over anything, he managed to operate an automobile well enough as long as he
stayed on the highway. But it was always a bother to him
that white men hadn't invented a car that could be
driven across a field or a desert without being trapped
in sand or caught in bushes. The horse, after all, had
some superiorities.

And while Johnny was interested in working and
learning, his chief interest was Maria. He saw her as
much as possible, and often he managed to see her alone.
In reality she became his mistress, though neither he nor
Maria thought about it that way. She expected some day
to be married, and Johnny expected to marry her. That
was enough. Both Jose and Nasaria knew that Maria was
seeing more and more of Johnny, but they took life for
granted and failed to interfere.

Johnny began to accumulate money, and as he obviously didn't know what to do with it, Mr. Paul took him
into Coachella one day and tried to explain to him what
it meant to put money in a bank. Johnny was more than
willing to do with money what the white men did and
so a certain Johnny Mack became a depositor in the
First National Bank of Coachella.

Many a strange experience happened to Johnny through his acquaintance with Mr. and Mrs. Paul, and Jose, and Nasaria, and Maria, but one of the strangest took place late in 1925 when, on a holiday known in Mexico as the Fiesta of All Souls and the Dead, but unknown by any name in the United States, Jose and Nasaria and Maria and Johnny squeezed themselves into the little green Ford and drove to Indio where they celebrated by going to the movies. Jose understood it all and explained most of the scenes aloud for the edification of any one who cared to listen. Maria understood it, too, but she was too much interested to waste time explaining any parts that Johnny did not understand. Nevertheless he felt that he knew what was going on and when the pictures disappeared and intermittent bits of printing took their place he found he could read a word now and then. But what puzzled him most was the audience. They laughed for no palpable reason when a cross-eyed man stepped on a cake of soap and landed on his posterior. Johnny looked around in the dark, smelly, little theater and laughed, too, though he didn't really know why.

Later the same cross-eyed man lost his trousers and tried to hide behind a sign board only to find himself in full view of a crowd of ladies approaching from the other direction. The cross-eyed man fled trouserless down a busy street, and a number of stern serious men with clubs, whom Jose said were policemen, chased the poor man and fell all over each other and everybody else until the whole thing ran riot in a baker shop where all the characters were so angered that they indiscriminately hurled pies and cakes at each other, wrecking the shop and their respective features. Jose almost burst with laughter and the whole audience shrieked with glee, and Johnny realized that there was something about it he had not understood.

Then there was more printing and the whole tone of the audience changed at once. They were serious and they sat still and watched the unfolding of a drama that plucked at their heart strings. Both Nasaria and Maria wept and Jose clicked his tongue against his teeth and said "Ain't that too bad, pobre muchacha." Just why this reaction should be, Johnny did not know. The pictures showed a lot of men and women and a pleasant ranch house and a beautiful young girl who seemed to leave the ranch house because of the dreadful anger of her father. Later she was seen in a great big city where she worked in a paper box factory, but in tears she left this place when another man seemed to be following her around all the time. Presently there was a baby and the girl and the baby seemed to get poorer and poorer and the box factories didn't want her to work any more. There were many pictures of her walking to other factories and close pictures of her beautiful face drawn with sorrow and streaked with tears. There was a picture of the baby laughing and trying to bite its toe-nails and this made the audience laugh sympathetically. Then the sad girl walked out over a great body of water, almost as big as the inland sea, and the lights of the city were in the distance. There was a pathetic flash of her as she looked up at the stars and the printing came on and said "Oh, stars, you can see it is the only way." She stood over the water and she surely would have jumped into it if, at that moment, a handsome young man in a big

beautiful automobile with bright headlights that fell full
upon the poor sad girl had not happened to see her.
He dashed from the car and caught the girl just as she
was about to leap. Soon she was being driven beside him
at a reckless pace through city streets and finally they
were in a house such as Johnny never knew existed. It
was the ultimate in luxury and the poor sad girl revived
and smiled. Then, all of a sudden, she looked about her
and she was afraid of the handsome young man just the
way she had been afraid of the man in the box factory.
But he only smiled pleasantly and pressed a button and
immediately a large fat jolly negress appeared and took
charge of the sad young girl. The sad young girl gave a
start and the letters came on and said "My baby!" Immediately there was more rushing and driving and for some
strange reason the baby was found in a burning house
and the handsome young man had to climb up the outside to rescue it while firemen held a round circle of
white cloth for him to jump into. After this there were
several more exciting adventures and suddenly the pictures were in the country again and the handsome young
man had caught another man who had been in the first
part of the picture and he wanted to hit this man with
his fist. But the coward begged on his knees before the
handsome man and presently the cowardly man was in a
room that had bars on it. Then the sad young girl was
there again and she and the handsome man and the baby
met the girl's father who had been so angry in the early
part but who had since gone blind and was happy. He
shook hands with the handsome man and patted the
baby and kissed the sad girl and while a lot of other
happy people looked on the thing came to an end with a

wedding. It was all complex and swift moving, and full of meanings that Johnny could not interpret, but there was a thread of pictorial continuity to it that was clear even if cause and effect seemed questionable. Johnny liked watching it. It was life. It was real. He was learning.

One source of amazement was his understanding of how little Agocho really knew. Agocho who had been omniscient was, after all, actually ignorant. He knew nothing and he had not the aptitude for learning anything and whenever Johnny was in the clearing it was impossible for him to explain any of these new phenomena to him. Even if Agocho had wanted to hear, Johnny would not have known how to begin.

For instance, Johnny would like to have told Agocho all about the Ford car, but there was no way to do it. He had to let Agocho find out as best he could. One afternoon when Agocho was sitting beside the fig trees mending a broken water bottle there was a rattle and clatter out in the greasewood toward the highway. A motor was racing and spinning and small bushes were being crushed, and into the clearing drove Johnny in the light green Ford roadster, the car straining and struggling in the sand, and making its own road as it came.

Agocho stood up and looked at this spectacle. He walked over toward the spring and Johnny drove the car up close to him. He shut off the engine and jumped out, grinning and looking at the car with pride. He would have told his father about it before had there been any way to make Agocho understand. He would have explained that his job had earned money and that the money enabled him to buy Jose's Ford car when Jose bought a new one, and that now that he had a car the next thing was to build a shack, and then he would get a wife and put her in it. Everything was progressing perfectly, and yet there was no way to acquaint an antipathetic Agocho with the whole idea or any part of it.

Johnny did explain, however, that the Ford was his. He saw it; he liked it; he had it. And nobody could take it away from him. That part of it was all right. If Johnny had taken something that appealed to him, that was commendable. And while no power or persuasion could have inveigled Agocho into riding in this Ford, he was, in spite of himself, pleased with Johnny's acquisition. He was a little proud of it, for he knew that he couldn't have stolen a Ford if he wanted to. It was one of the best things he had seen Johnny do in a long time.

Johnny was delighted. The Ford car was handsome and powerful and made a great noise. He didn't need a horse any more. He could come and go at will as long as he remembered to put gasoline and oil in it. It was a great step forward.

There was another step to be made and he accomplished that in the winter of 1926. Again he was unable to explain anything to Agocho. It simply had to happen and Agocho had to analyze it as best he could or ignore it altogether.

Johnny drove the Ford into the clearing loaded to overflowing with boards and planks and odds and ends of lumber of all kinds. He dumped all of this refuse beside the kowa. Agocho thought it was firewood and he was surprised at Johnny's objections when he tried to burn it. Johnny had other ideas about this wood, and a few days later he brought in another load with an assortment of nails and a few tools. Agocho could see no good purpose in this at all, and to his disgust Johnny began the construction of a two-room shack. Agocho wouldn't lift a finger to help build an unnecessary object that was derivative of something Johnny had picked up from white men. He considered tearing it down, but he was sure that it would fall down anyway and he let Johnny go ahead.

It was a more difficult job than it looked and Johnny discovered that building a house was a harder task than chopping wood or mending a fence. He knew what Jose's shack was like and his idea of architecture was to duplicate it. Originality had no value, and he studied Jose's home and then reconstructed it as closely as possible, board for board. This took time and had Agocho known that the shack was to house a Mexican girl who would be Johnny's wife he would have destroyed it at once. That possibility never entered his head and he showed his scorn and superiority by ignoring the thing and never walking into it or looking at it. In his mind was the half-formed idea that he would break it up or burn it some day when Johnny wasn't around and that would end the shack problem.

Of the cataclysm that was about to take place he was entirely ignorant. He had no knowledge of the fact that Nasaria was making Maria a new white dress—that it was a time of great excitement, celebration, feasting, and prayer—that Johnny and Maria were going to be married by the Catholic priest of Coachella.

Johnny wasn't any too clear himself on the details of this arrangement. It had been generally conceded and decided that he and Maria would be married, and he found himself caught up in a flux of preparation which was exciting and interesting if not always elucidating. He understood, however, that he was an outsider to this white religion called Catholicism and he agreed to everything that Jose, and Nasaria, and Maria, and the priest said. He was perfectly willing to have all the children of his union with Maria brought up and educated in the Catholic faith. It was one of the least of his considerations. If they had told him that his children must be reared as Zulus he would have been glad to acquiesce.

In June they were married.

After a demonstrative scene with much emotion and a special supper of chicken and beans and peppers at Jose's shack, Mr. and Mrs. Johnny Mack drove proudly away in their green Ford to their new home in the clearing. Maria had never been to the clearing and the primitiveness of it surprised her. All her life she had lived on ranches, but here was a shack out in the desert unlike anything she had seen before. Still, it was a new shack and it had possibilities and it was hers and she was glad to be in it. They had a little furniture in the car and Johnny unloaded it. They had a dog, a gray mongrel with a thin ratty tail. They had several boxes of food. The furniture was cast-off junk from the Paul house, the dog was a present from Nasaria and so was the food, and Johnny had a black stogey that he kept in his mouth but didn't smoke—a present from Jose. They were "at home."

While Johnny was unloading his domestic possessions Agocho walked in from the greasewood. He could hardly believe what he saw. At first it didn't mean anything to him. A sudden madness seemed to have descended on the clearing, and a dog barked at him. He stood still and looked at all this strangeness. He looked at Maria and he looked at Johnny and they looked at him. Maria knew that Johnny had a father. Once or twice she had seen him from a distance when he prowled around the Mack ranch. But she had never seen him at close range and for a moment she didn't realize that here before her was her father-in-law. He was a solid man, not tall, but heavy and very brown. He wore moccasins and leggings. His trousers and his jacket were made of coyote hide decorated with Apache designs and studded with deer teeth. He wore a neckerchief of bright red cloth around his throat. His hair was long and fell down almost to his shoulders. It was black, but there were traces of gray. His face was wrinkled and the jowls were prominent. To her he gave the appearance of an old man and she would have thought he was in his seventies instead of his sixties. She noticed that he wore a bracelet on his right wrist, but she couldn't look at it because his stare was so direct and so compelling that she looked at his eyes and turned away, and then looked back at his eyes again. She didn't think that she liked him, but he was such an unexpected figure that she hesitated and continued to look. Knowing the answer she couldn't help saying, "Who is that?"

"Oh, that's Fig Tree John," said Johnny. "You know him. He's my father." And he carried a battered chair into the house and came out again. He looked from Fig Tree to Maria, and it suddenly occurred to him that he had thought of him as Fig Tree John instead of Agocho, as an impersonal figure instead of his father, and it seemed strange and inevitable at the same time. He looked from his father to his wife and he felt awkward.

Maria turned to Johnny. This old Fig Tree John staring at her was strange. She felt that she didn't belong
in his family and that Johnny didn't either. Johnny was
usually happy and smiling. He never wore Indian clothes
any more. He always had trousers and shoes and a shirt.
He never stood and stared the way this man did. She
looked at Johnny helplessly.

Johnny grinned. He wanted to tell Agocho that he
was married and that Maria was going to live here. He
wanted to make everything clear with a few words, but
when he tried to say them they wouldn't take form.
Again there was no way to talk to Agocho. Well, he had
gotten the Ford and that had come to be a fixture. He
had built the shack and Agocho was used to that now.
And here was his wife and in time Agocho would understand all that and realize that Johnny should have a wife
and that she should live here and—well, that's just the
way things were. He picked up a box of foodstuff and
took it into the house.

Agocho let the meaning of all this come to him slowly.
His son had gotten himself a woman. Yes. But by all the
Gods in heaven, she was white. A white girl. Even her
dress was white. She flaunted whiteness. She stood there
in a white dress and white legs and white shoes, and she
had a pale skin. Only her hair was black, and she was
white through and through and she was N'Chai Chidn's
woman. It was a staggering blow. It was the end for his
son. Everything was lost now, and there was no hope of
saving him. Here was one more crushing indignity thrust
upon him. Here was a final disaster.

Why—why—why?

Why, when he had tried so hard and done so much,

did everything always come out wrong? What could that mean? Why did the Gods torture him this way? Why didn't they explain; why didn't they show him what they wanted him to do?

He watched the girl with rancor and hatred welling up within him. He would like to kill her with one blow. He would like to smash the life out of her. But he gave no sign. He stood perfectly still and he heard N'Chai Chidn refer to him as Fig Tree John. His son called him by the name the white men called him. His son had become a white man. He was beneath contempt.

They were carrying their things into the shack. He turned away. He was heartbroken. He went over to the kowa and sat down. Night came and they had their supper. He didn't want any. He sat there for several hours and they stayed in the shack. They were together. His son was sleeping with a white girl. She was his wife. It was horrible. He went into the kowa but he was unable to sleep the whole night. In the morning, as soon as it was light, he saddled a horse and rode away. He took food and water and blankets and he was away for almost a week, camping and roaming in the Santa Rosas. But he couldn't get away from the thoughts that haunted him. He came back to the clearing and remained for a few days and then went away again. Probably they were glad. Probably they hoped he never would come back. That was his clearing—he'd come back any time he wanted to. This was all his country and he would do anything he felt like doing. Everything was his.

For all of July and August Johnny stayed around the clearing. Mr. Paul had no job for him, but in September and October it would be time to pick the dates, and then he would go back to work. He devoted the hot summer months to putting the finishing touches on the shack. Mr. Paul gave them a goat and a few chickens and they added them to the stock. Goat's milk was good and useful in many ways and the chickens were invaluable. Several times they went into Mecca and Coachella and once they went to Indio. They were happy and they had no worries and they enjoyed married life. Agocho was in and out. He never talked to them and most of the hot summer he was in the mountain country.

In late September Johnny began going daily to the Paul ranch and Maria stayed in the clearing and kept herself busy with her house. Agocho came and went and they never spoke a word to each other. She was afraid of him and she avoided him. When he was around the clearing she remained indoors. Once when she was picking figs he had ridden silently in from the desert and when she turned around there he was standing between the house and the fig trees, looking at her. It gave her a start. She picked a few more figs and then she walked briskly toward the house, making a slight detour so as not to pass too close to Agocho. She glanced at him a time or two and she knew he was watching her every instant. She went into the shack and he went over to the spring. He sat around the clearing in the shade of the fig trees all day, and when Johnny came banging home in the Ford, Maria felt much better; Johnny seemed to think Agocho was perfectly all right, but Maria was afraid of his eyes. Things went on that way until December. Johnny was away almost every day and sometimes Agocho would be around and sometimes he would be away for two or three days or a week. Once he killed

some animal and brought it in and skinned it and dried
the meat in front of the kowa. It made a bad smell.

In the month of December, Sos-nalh-tus, Agocho
planned to visit the canyon with the palm trees in the
mountains to the north of the inland sea. He sat around
the clearing all the day before and he saw the white girl
several times. Sometimes she wore a white dress and sometimes she wore a red dress, but that day she had on the
white dress. The few glimpses he had of her reminded
him of something but he didn't know just what. Then
she came out of the shack and went to the pool where
she filled a bucket with water. He watched. She had to
bend over and dip the bucket in the pool, and when she
walked back the bucket was heavy and she could not
move as fast. The white figure was reminiscent of something and she disappeared inside the shack before he
remembered what it was.

Many years ago he had sat in front of the fat man's
store in Mecca and a white woman in a white dress had
come by. He had sat there a long time with his rifle on
his knees waiting for the fat man to return, and that
white woman in a white dress had come down the street
and brushed past him as she went into the store. Then
she had come out and he had watched her as she walked
away until she disappeared from view. He remembered
her vividly. He would know her if he were to see her
now. Her dress had fallen about her figure and she had
looked nice. She was a pleasant recollection.

But that was all long ago and this girl was different
and he hated her. He wanted to forget that other woman
and only remember that he hated this one. He didn't see

her again, and soon after Johnny drove home he ate his supper and went to sleep in the kowa.

He was up at dawn and he rode away without seeing the couple in the shack. He rode out toward the inland sea, around the sea, and then north toward the mountains. In the afternoon he found the canyon with the hidden spring and the palm trees. He threaded his way around the rocks and clambered over boulders, and there were the palms and the water. And the mound of stones that he had built to the Gods so many years ago, that was—no. The mound was gone. The stones were scattered. He found the spot where the mound had been; there were four stones. The rest were scattered around in several directions. Some one could have been in the canyon and disturbed the mound. That was possible. But likely, far more likely, that mound had been scattered by the Gods. That was a sign. That meant something. That was a message. Those rocks had been piled together as an offering, and the Gods had let them stand there for years, meaning wait, watch, observe.

Now they were gone. The Gods had blown them away. One puff and the rocks were scattered. No longer did they mean to wait and to watch. No! That was all over now. The time had come. That was it. That's what it meant. It is here. It is time to act. At last it is time to act. They don't say wait any more. They say act now. The Gods have given a command.

He looked up at the sun. The God of fire spoke to him. He looked down at the spring. The God of water spoke to him. He gave a thankful prayer to the mother of these Gods, his divine Ste-na-tlih-a. The light began to

fade as the sun went down. All through the twilight
Agocho prayed and gave thanks to the Gods. He slept
under the palms beside the spring. At sunrise he prayed
again to both fire and water.

> "Ste-na-tlih-a, you are good.
> I pray for strength.
> I pray for life.
> I pray for justice.
> Ste-na-tlih-a, you are good."

He paused for a moment in the absolute stillness. Then
the wind blew and rustled the leaves of the palm trees.
With eagerness and excitement Agocho retrieved his
horse. He rode over and around the rocks—out of the
canyon—into the desert—straight toward the inland sea
and the clearing.

Chapter XVII

AGOCHO rode around the northern end of the inland sea and down the beach line and into the greasewood. He dismounted before he came to the clearing, left his horse to roam at will, and continued on foot. He reached the edge of the clearing and he stood still and looked around, screening himself from view by the bushes. Everything was just the same. The trees and the spring and the shack were unchanged, and the gray mongrel was stretched out asleep in the shade. Two or three scrawny chickens were foraging near the fig trees. The goat was over near the horses. The green Ford was missing which meant that Johnny was away. The white girl might be away, too. He couldn't see her.

He could have walked into the clearing and found out at once if she were in the shack or not, but he preferred to wait. It was more of a game. It was more dramatic to stalk quarry than to charge after it at once. He slowly circled around through the greasewood until he had a view of the rear of the shack. She was there. He could hear her moving around.

Suddenly she came out the rear door. He was only a few feet from her, but he was partially hidden by the bushes and she was not looking in his direction. She had some scraps and garbage which she tossed to one side and the chickens came running over to salvage it. He was glad to see that she was wearing the white dress. All

253

the way from the canyon he had thought of her in the white dress.

She turned away from the chickens and walked away from him around the outside of the shack toward the front. He came out of the bushes and followed. The chickens were busy gobbling the garbage and they did not scamper away as he walked past them. He lost sight of her for a moment but when he rounded the front of the shack she was moving slowly toward the spring. The gray mongrel looked up and saw them both. There was something in Agocho's stealth that made it watch and partially raise its ears.

Maria saw the dog's attention and she turned to look behind her. She saw Agocho and she stopped. The sight of him startled her as it always did. Now what was he up to?

Slowly he came toward her. His black eyes looked mad and his face had an eagerness coupled with a desperate, concentrated stare.

She didn't say anything, and neither did he, but she knew this was different. He came on—one more step, two, three. He was coming right up to her.

·Suddenly she whirled and dodged to one side and then ran toward the shack. He leaped for her as she whirled, and for an instant his hand clutched her shoulder. Neither one of them made a sound. Straight for the shack she ran and he turned and ran after her. The dog jumped up and raced beside them barking and snapping in excitement.

Maria reached the shack and leaped inside. There was a door and she slammed it after her. She did not expect him to follow. He had never come into the shack. She

stopped and turned, but almost at once the door was
flung open and Agocho charged in. His face was wild;
his eyes were flashing. He saw her and leaped for her.

Maria was panic-stricken. She had always been safe in
the shack, but now here he was. She rushed through the
two little rooms to the back door and he rushed after
her. She knew that he was right behind her as she paused
to push the door open. She ran out and he ran out reaching for her. She screamed, several short piercing screams,
and fled in panic through the midst of the feeding
chickens and they scattered while Agocho, without a
sound, leaped after her.

She was lost now. There was no place to run. He would
follow anywhere. She dashed aimlessly toward the fig
trees, screaming in terror, and near the kowa he caught
her from the rear. She turned in desperate panic and
struck at him. She was almost blind with fright and she
struck without touching him. He hit her with his fists.
He slapped her with his hands and beat her with his
fists, and when she fell he kicked her and then he reached
down and pulled her to her feet, tearing the white dress,
and shaking and beating her.

Insane with a frenzy of sadistic hate, he dragged her,
screaming and gasping, into the kowa and there he beat
her again and tore the white dress from her and raped
her.

Late in the afternoon Johnny drove into the clearing.
He swung the Ford around and brought it to an abrupt
stop beside the shack. Everything looked the same as
usual. The chickens were walking around, the dog came
running and jumping to greet him, Agocho was sitting
over near the fig trees, watching him, saying nothing,

just sitting. Johnny walked into the shack, found nobody, and walked out again. He looked around for Maria, but he could see only Agocho. He walked slowly toward the seated figure and as he came nearer the kowa he heard a sound. It was a quiet, almost muffled, sobbing. He stepped rapidly into the kowa entirely unprepared for any shock. Before him was Maria. She lay on the earth floor, her body bruised and beaten and her clothing torn to shreds. She was crying steadily, and when Johnny tried to pick her up she became hysterical.

Outraged, Johnny sprang from the kowa to find Agocho. He found him immediately. Agocho had gotten up and had come over to the entrance of the kowa. He was standing there, waiting for Johnny, knowing that he would come rushing out. He stood before Johnny with his arms crossed and looked at his son with mingled triumph and belligerence. Yes, he had done this, and he wasn't trying to conceal it, and who had any right to voice an opinion about it?

Johnny hadn't. He stopped in his tracks and stared at Agocho. He opened his mouth and hesitated. The black eyes were glaring at him and Johnny faltered. He wondered why he had come rushing out and what he had intended to say and do. Just what was there to say or do? He didn't know.

Had any other man in the world assaulted his wife Johnny would have fought him. He would have tried to kill him. But Agocho standing still, glaring at him, triumph written in his glare, left him completely at a loss. Why had this been? What had made his father do this and what made him react in this way—proud, victorious, and defiant. It was all confusing and wrong and yet—what? Baffled, nonplussed, Johnny turned back into the kowa. He picked up Maria and carried her to the shack.

Agocho watched him take the girl inside. Satisfied that Johnny was going to stay inside he turned and walked slowly out of the clearing to the inland sea. He stood on the shore and watched the sun sink behind the mountains. He stood still with his hands at his sides and his head up. It was all just. He knew that. It was right. It was the answer. It was an eye for an eye. The Gods of fire and water knew it and Ste-na-tlih-a knew it. They had explained it to him at last.

Why else had a white girl been sent to the clearing? For what other possible reason had the Gods connived that? None. It was the end of the old score. Everything was falling into line now. The inevitable balance was forming and justice was making its inflexible and indomitable power felt in the most logical course.

At first he had been stupid, or he would have understood at once. It had taken him a long while to wake up to the fact that, as he had always known, the Gods were settling the old injury in their own way. He hadn't thought that they would bring a white girl to him. And yet what more natural and simple justice was there? What more perfect justice could there be? He blamed himself for his mental sluggishness in not seeing the way sooner as it had slowly expressed itself before him.

Everything had a meaning now, as he had known always, but now he saw not only the pattern, the design, but the actual significance of all the details.

There had been a woman in a white dress in Mecca. That very day the Gods had sent him a sign—a white dress—but he hadn't been acute enough to recognize the meaning of it until now. They had driven his son white. He couldn't understand why, but now it was obvious. They had sent his son out into the white civilization in spite of Agocho, and they had made of his son an instrument in the progress of the scheme. Without either of them knowing it N'Chai Chidn had been an agent of justice all the time. But for him there would be no white girl here now.

The boy could never have had an Apache girl after all. He was destined to find this white girl and bring her back. They would keep her here together for a while, and perhaps they would even take her back to the White River country. She really wouldn't be N'Chai Chidn's wife, or anybody's wife, but she would be their property to work for them and cook for them and sleep with them. That's all she was good for and she was only a white girl. And when N'Chai Chidn got back to the White River he could have an Apache wife for himself. The ways of the Gods were always plain to see if you had the perspicacity to look.

N'Chai Chidn, of course, would not understand now. But he would some day. Agocho would explain to the boy as simply as he could, and though he knew that the explanation would be challenged, it would help in the eventual clarification of the meaning of the whole pattern in the boy's mind. Some day he would understand that his father had been right.

Johnny remained in the shack and tried to reconcile himself to the problem. It wasn't actually a problem. It was something that had happened and it left no mystery to be solved. Yet the reason back of it all escaped him.

He knew that somehow Agocho's actions had been governed entirely by the fact that Maria was white. Had she been an Apache girl he was sure that his father would not have attacked her. It wasn't dishonor or lust on the part of his father. He was positive of that. It was something beyond mere desire. It was something that went much deeper into the scheme of things and had been prompted by impulses more spiritual than physical. Vaguely Johnny sensed these values, but the why and wherefore he could not grasp. The way his father had waited there near the kowa—and the way he had looked —there must be something beyond the mere superficial understanding of the actual event. He hated Agocho for abusing Maria and yet, somehow, there was an ultimate reason, a final provocation, over which none of them had any control. That unknown element of which he **was** cognizant but not comprehending prevented him from doing anything except enduring the situation and rather vaguely accepting it as an act over which he had no power—a storm, a draught, an illness—a manifestation of some further jurisdiction that was beyond criticism.

He took Maria to the Mack ranch in the morning. She had little to say and he was almost afraid to talk to her. She kept insisting that she must go back and live with Nasaria, and while Johnny disliked that, he had no alternative. He left her in Jose's shack and he drove over to the Paul ranch and worked the rest of the day. In the evening he returned to Jose's but Maria refused to go back to the clearing with him. He went alone. It was all very disappointing. It was a phase that he had not anticipated and he didn't know how to deal with it.

Agocho was there and they had supper together.

Agocho was happy. He was a changed man. All of his morbidity, drawn into himself and introverted for years, was miraculously turned inside out. He was liberated and vindicated. Everything was right and justified and at last he understood it all. He tried to impart to Johnny the reason for his ecstasy and his optimism toward life. Johnny could make nothing of it—and yet, there was something there that he had to respect and admit its rightful existence. He wasn't enough of a white man to be able to deny a codified and idealistic Apache behaviorism which he dimly recognized in Agocho, and he wasn't enough of an Apache to be caught up in the circular philosophy of cause and effect as determined by a supreme fatalism. He never clearly understood either side.

Agocho asked about Maria, a person whose existence he had refused to acknowledge until yesterday. Johnny told him that Maria was going to stay with her sister Nasaria for a few days. Agocho was satisfied with that, but Johnny instinctively knew that Maria might never return to the clearing again—at least not as long as Agocho remained.

Through December and the holiday season Johnny continued to work at the Paul ranch and live in the clearing. He saw Maria every day but he never lived with her and he began to miss her and to be terribly dissatisfied with this awkward domestic arrangement.

Jose and Nasaria were dissatisfied, too, for Maria was an expense to them and she earned nothing by working for Mrs. Mack as she used to do before she had married Johnny. The Macks had a servant now, and she was a Swedish girl whom they had brought down from Los

Angeles. She did all the housework and lived in the house as well, so there was no place for Maria. Jose **was** annoyed. Mr. Mack hadn't increased his salary and he had his new Ford car to pay for, and Maria was an expense and a nuisance. She had a husband, why didn't she live with him? Nasaria was more tolerant, but she wished, none the less, to make some other arrangement about Maria. She thought of their sister Rosa who had a husband and who lived in Banning and she wondered if it wouldn't be possible for Maria to go to Banning for a while and perhaps find some way of staying there.

Maria wasn't anxious to go to Banning, but she refused to go back to the clearing, and both she and Johnny became very unhappy.

Mr. Paul noticed that Johnny looked glum and he also noticed that he didn't work as efficiently as he used to. He asked Johnny what was the matter. At first Johnny was evasive, but as he really liked Mr. Paul he told him a little of his domestic difficulties.

"Got some trouble down there," Johnny said.

"What kind of trouble?"

"My wife she don't like it."

"Why doesn't she like it, Johnny?"

"Fig Tree," said Johnny.

"Doesn't she get along with Fig Tree?"

"Nope," said Johnny.

"What's the matter?"

"He act like she's his wife 'stead of mine."

"Why, the old he-coon," said Mr. Paul. "Why don't you tell him where to head in? Tell him to leave your wife alone."

"Can't," said Johnny.

"Why not? She's your wife."

"Yeah, but he's Fig Tree," said Johnny.

Mr. Paul laughed.

"I guess there's a lot to that," he said. "Well, listen to me, Johnny Mack. He can't get away with anything like that. You got to have some guts. Tell him a thing or two. Tell him she's your wife and hands off or there'll be some hell a-popping. Let him see you mean it. Make him understand that you mean business. Why, the old varmint—at his age. You got to be boss, Johnny, you got to wear the pants. Do you see?"

But Johnny slowly walked away. He looked very sad. There was no use talking any more. Mr. Paul didn't know how it was. There was nothing Johnny could do. He knew it because Fig Tree knew it. And Fig Tree knew it because there was nothing anybody could ever do to conquer him again. Life was at its zenith for him. Almost twenty years of waiting and then—vindication. Only Maria must not stay away from the clearing too long. Johnny must make her come back. She belonged to them now and there was no point in having her stay at the Mack ranch. He wanted her in the clearing where the Gods had decreed that she belonged.

Gradually taking form in Fig Tree's mind was a complete satisfaction, a recognition that in the ego was everything, and that he had battled and defeated the external world by the sheer power of being himself. This megalomania reached a climax of self-exaltation. The world was his. He was absolute. He had solved the riddle of existence. He had never given up; he had never compromised. Now he was almost a God. He really didn't hate anybody any more. He was beyond hating. He was superior to all things. Perhaps he was a God. Perhaps that was his destiny, to be one of the hierarchy of heaven, one with Ste-na-tlih-a.

He roamed the country more than ever. He loved to ride over his domain, knowing that it was his and that all things and all people in it were ultimately subject to his will.

Once he rode up to the Carr ranch. There was no one around. He dismounted and walked to the house. He knew Mr. Carr and he knew Mrs. Carr, but he had never had any friendly dealings with them. He walked into the house as if it were the most commonplace thing for him to do. Mrs. Carr was in the kitchen and she was astounded to see this strange figure.

"Got any sugar? Got any coffee?" he demanded.

He didn't really want either one, but he wanted to get some for the sake of getting it. He hadn't drunk coffee or used sugar for years, but there was no reason why he couldn't demand it if the whim happened to strike him. Mrs. Carr, alarmed, but anxious to placate him, gave him a little coffee and a little sugar.

"Now be on your way, Fig Tree," she said.

He walked out with a bag of sugar in one hand and a bag of coffee in the other. He placed both bags in the saddle-bag around his horse's neck and rode away.

It was dark before he neared the clearing and to save a little time he cut across Paul's property. The moon was rising and its light fell upon a strange instrument that he had never seen before. He stopped his horse and looked at it. The thing was in a patch of cactus that the white men had gone to all the trouble to dig up in the desert and transplant so that there were half a dozen or

more varieties of cactus growing right in front of the
house. And in the middle of this cactus garden was a
shiny piece of metal on a post standing about three feet
high. The metal had an upright arm, placed at a curious
angle, and there were strange notches and markings on
the smooth surface. It was about the most useless thing
he had ever seen, but as a piece of decoration it shone
nicely in the moonlight. More out of curiosity to examine
it than an actual desire to possess it, he dismounted and
tried to move it. It was surprisingly heavy and was
securely fastened to the upright post that supported it.
So he shoved the post back and forth until he had it
loose and then he pulled the whole thing out of the
ground. Still it didn't make any sense, so he took sun-
dial, post, and all, and rode on south to the clearing.

It was late in January before Johnny was able to get
Maria to come back to the clearing. And then she
wouldn't have come if Jose hadn't been insistent that a
wife's place was with her husband and not with her
sister's family. She was afraid of Fig Tree and she refused
to stay in the clearing during the day unless Johnny
stayed there, too. So she went to the Mack ranch and
spent the days with Nasaria and rode back to the clearing
with Johnny in the late afternoon. This was not a satisfactory arrangement, but it was the only thing that she
would agree to do. And even then she wouldn't let
Johnny touch her until he began to wonder if she were
ever going to be his wife again or if this frigidity on her
part were going to last indefinitely. He remained passive
toward the whole business, and slowly Maria began to
be more like herself. He made no effort to hurry the
situation and eventually Maria lost some of her fear of

Agocho and her reticence toward Johnny and began to be more at ease and more natural. Agocho let her entirely alone, and one day when he had ridden away in the morning, she remained in the clearing staying in or near the shack and ready to barricade herself in if necessary. Agocho came home before Johnny but he made no attempt to get in the shack. He wasn't interested and he ignored her altogether. Johnny came home in the Ford at dusk and he was pleased to find life back to normal. He was sure that everything would be all right now. He was glad that he had not added to the difficulty by getting angry and fighting, but had let it run its course until everything was just the way it should be again. He decided that was a pretty good plan, not only for this instance, but for life in general.

February and March went by and in April Johnny began to have less to do at the Paul ranch. It was almost time for the long hot desert summer and there was little to do but let the date trees thrive in the heat so that they would bear dates in the fall. It was a lazy time of the year, and Johnny worked only two days a week. This cut down his salary, but he didn't care. He had everything he wanted and about thirty dollars in the bank and he was pretty well off.

In May, however, things reached another crisis, and Johnny, faced with another difficulty, counted on non-interference as the best way of handling the situation. Agocho spoke to him as they stood beside the spring. It was evening and Johnny could not see Agocho's face. But his voice was calm and deliberate and he seemed to expect Johnny to understand. He spoke casually as if he were discussing the weather.

"To-night, I shall have the girl," he said. "You have had her most of the time, and that is right, but to-night she stays with me."

He spoke in Apache and Johnny had difficulty in framing his answer.

"She may not want you. What should you do then?"

"That doesn't matter. It's I who want her. Tell her she comes to the kowa or I come get her. The Gods have sent her here for both of us and she has nothing to do with it."

"She is afraid of you," said Johnny, and then he added in English, "she thinks maybe you wanta kill her."

"She is useful," said Agocho, in Apache. "I won't kill her because she is useful."

Johnny didn't say a word. He looked down at the spring. The water was black. The bushes around the clearing were black. In the sky were thousands of stars and in the shack was the light from an oil lamp. He could hear Agocho breathing as they stood side by side. He was glad it was dark. He didn't want to have to look at his father. He waited a long time before saying anything more, but he knew Agocho was waiting for him to speak. In the sky a shooting star burned through space, a white flashing arc alive for a second as it passed through the earth's atmosphere. Johnny wanted to speak of it. He wanted to change the subject from Maria to a shooting star—to anything. Agocho must have seen the star, too, but he didn't comment. Johnny took a long breath. Agocho could be right. He wasn't, of course, but he could be. Ste-na-tlih-a could be the chief Goddess instead of the woman they called the Virgin Mary. If Ste-na-tlih-a were the real one, then Agocho was right. But even if she weren't, Agocho didn't know it, and perhaps if you don't know something, it doesn't exist. Perhaps if you think something is right, it is. How else can you tell except by thinking it? And he didn't know—he wasn't sure—Ste-na-tlih-a or Virgin Mary?

Virgin Mary said Maria belonged to him and to no one else. Ste-na-tlih-a said Maria belonged to Agocho if he wanted her. Who was the real Goddess? Who knew more? Why were there two? How could there be two if only one were right? There couldn't be two rights. There was only one. It was you who explained her to yourself and it was you who decided whether you worshiped Ste-na-tlih-a or Virgin Mary. Some people did one and some did the other, and one named Johnny Mack saw a little of both and wondered. He wasn't all Ste-na-tlih-a and he wasn't all Virgin Mary, and yet he never doubted that one Goddess was there, call her what you will. So what difference could it make and why would it matter to her if those two ideas of her were just different ideas about one Goddess whose name might be one or the other or both—or, and this was a remote and difficult thought, whose real name might be neither.

Agocho was still standing there, saying nothing.

"All right," said Johnny, quietly.

And he turned from the pool and walked to the shack. He would not interfere. He would let things take their own course and in a critical pinch he wouldn't be guilty of upholding one Goddess over the other. He would tell Maria. She might kill Agocho, and if she did, he wouldn't stop her. For that would mean that Virgin Mary was stronger than Ste-na-tlih-a. Or she might give in to Agocho, and that would mean that Ste-na-tlih-a was stronger than Virgin Mary. It would decide itself without interference.

Agocho watched the dark figure of Johnny move away. When the door of the shack opened the figure was silhouetted for a moment, and then it disappeared. He waited beside the spring for a long time. Once in a while there were voices coming from the shack. He stood in the dark and watched the door. Then Johnny came out. He walked toward the spring but he didn't come all the way. He turned to the kowa and Agocho could hear him moving about. He went inside the kowa and Agocho knew that he would stay there.

Agocho walked to the shack. He wondered if she would resist. It didn't matter. If she were difficult he would beat her until she gave in. He pushed the door. It was not fastened. He walked in, silhouetted for an instant in the light, and then the door closed after him.

Johnny determined to stay in the kowa. He vowed to himself that he would stay there until dawn. That was the only thing to do. He lay down and he tried to sleep but sleep was impossible. He sat up and listened and lay down again. When he could stand it no longer he got up and marched out of the kowa. He walked toward the shack. The lamp was still burning. It looked just the same. He paced back and forth in the dark. He walked close to the shack and he walked away again. He stood still and listened and he walked up and down and looked at the dark outline of the building and the yellow streaks showing from the windows and the door. He told himself he must not go into the shack. That was the only way. It must settle itself. Ste-na-tlih-a or Virgin Mary. It must settle itself.

He paced up and down the clearing for hours and finally he forced himself to go back to the kowa. He wouldn't let himself look toward the shack. He went into the kowa without looking back and he threw himself face down on the ground. He tried to dig his fingers into the soft earth. He wanted to root himself to that spot. He must stay there until dawn. It was the only way. Over and over again he told himself it was the only way.

Chapter XVIII

SOMETHING had happened and time was standing still and the night was never going to end. Something had happened to the sun and it was never going to come up again. Johnny knew that no night could be that long. Everything was standing still and it might be the end of everything. He didn't care much. Let it all end.

He lay on his face and he squirmed around so that he could look out the front of the kowa. It was pitch dark. It was going to stay that way. It didn't matter any more. Then the rooster began to crow. It was lighter, but Johnny couldn't believe it. He closed his eyes and tried to keep them closed for a long time, and when he opened them again he could see the other side of the clearing. It was cool before the sun rose. He could see the gray mongrel trotting across the clearing. It walked up to the spring and drank out of it and then it disappeared from his sight, back around the fig trees.

Johnny hadn't slept at all, and now that it was morning, and it was over, he didn't care any more. He wanted to sleep. He lay still and watched the sky get brighter. He didn't look at the shack any more. He would find out in due time. He would know sooner or later. It was nothing to stay awake about. It was cool out there. He would stay where he was until the sun came up.

Then Agocho appeared, coming not from the shack as Johnny had expected, but walking into the clearing

from the greasewood. He had been out in the brush and
Johnny was surprised. Some time in the night Agocho
must have left the shack and walked out into the desert.
And what of Maria?

Agocho stood still. He wasn't looking at anything in
particular. He stood still and he seemed to be thinking.
Johnny lay on his stomach with his head at the entrance
of the kowa and stared out at Agocho. The sun came up
and the rays cleared the top of the greasewood and fell
upon Agocho's face. Johnny had always thought his
father had black hair, but in the morning sun it was
almost as gray as it was black. Agocho pulled the red
neckerchief closer around his throat and walked slowly,
very slowly, toward the kowa.

He saw Johnny, lying there, watching him. He looked
at Johnny and then he looked away from him. He came
on toward the kowa and when he was close beside it he
sat down.

Johnny first thought that Agocho had won, but in a
moment he thought differently. Agocho was defeated.
He looked sad; his mouth was drawn; his eyes had the
look of a man who has lost hope. He sighed. He sat and
looked at the ground and ignored Johnny.

Johnny didn't say anything. He tried to imagine what
it meant and what Agocho was thinking and what was
going to happen now.

Maria came out of the shack. Johnny got up and
stepped out of the kowa. He stood beside Agocho and
looked from Maria down to Agocho and back to Maria.
Agocho sat quietly and mumbled something to himself.
He ignored both Maria and Johnny.

Maria was wearing the red dress. In the clear morning

sun the red dress and her black hair and her pale skin made her look beautiful. She tossed her head back and shook her hair and walked over to the spring. She moved easily and freely and her attitude was one of confidence and assurance. She looked at Johnny and he saw her smile as he came toward her. But as he watched he didn't like the smile. It wasn't a pleasant smile. It was bitter.

He thought she meant it for him but when he came closer he saw that she was looking beyond him at Agocho. Her lips curled into a sneer and she sniffed derisively.

"Him," she said to Johnny. Then she looked at Johnny and said, "and you," and she gave that same disgusted sniff again. Johnny had never seen her act like that before. He didn't understand.

She picked up a tin cup, dipped it in the pool, and drank. She flung the dregs away, tossed the cup to the ground, and began to run her fingers through her hair. She breathed deeply and she smoothed her dress over her hips and her breasts.

"Why are you looking at me?" she asked Johnny. "Que quiere usted?"

"I want to know—" began Johnny, but he stopped and wondered what he really wanted to know.

Maria turned and looked at Agocho as he got up and slowly moved over to the fig trees, walked through them to the trail to the inland sea, and disappeared. Maria laughed softly. She was well satisfied with herself and what she knew. She turned to a bewildered Johnny and said, "Let's have breakfast."

"All right," said Johnny.

He couldn't understand her at all.

"You can go up and see Mr. Paul," she said to him

while they sat in the shack and ate. "You go up there and get a job doing something because we need money and I don't want to live here all the time."

"Agocho," said Johnny.

Maria laughed.

"He won't hurt me," she said.

"Can't tell," said Johnny.

Maria laughed again. She had a joke that Johnny didn't understand.

"You go get a job," she said. "I'll stay here and cook up some figs to-day. If Mr. Paul hasn't any work maybe he'll get you a job with somebody else until he wants you again. You don't have to stay here. I don't need you."

"Why?" asked Johnny.

"Because he's an old man," said Maria. "He can't do anything any more. He's an old man and he didn't know it. He couldn't do anything."

She laughed again, and she laughed so much she couldn't eat. Johnny was surprised, but he didn't think it was funny. It wasn't pleasant laughter. That sound she was making was harsh. He hadn't expected anything like this.

"He's mad now," said Maria. "He's mad at himself." Then she spoke softly and rapidly. "He can't touch me again and he knows it, and if he comes near me I'll spit on him and laugh at him and throw things at him. I hate him; I hate him; I hate him; and if he ever comes in here again I'll kick him and bite him and stab him in the belly with a carving knife, that's what I'll do to him. I'm not scared of him any more and he knows it and he better be careful what he does around my house."

She jumped up and went to the door and looked out. Johnny had never seen her as belligerent as this. He never knew that she had a temper. It excited him and he looked at her as she stood in the doorway. So Agocho hadn't been able to have her last night. And she was disgusted with Agocho, was she? She laughed at his senility, did she? Well she couldn't laugh at Johnny.

She turned from the door as he leaped up from his chair. He grinned at her. She stood with her hands on her hips and she laughed at him—that same harsh laugh. That Indian. That's all he was, that Indian. She hated Fig Tree John and now she hated Johnny. Johnny wasn't any good to her; he hadn't protected her. But it didn't make any difference. She was triumphant anyway. She was better than these Indians. That's all they were, Indians. They didn't know anything, and she was better than they were.

Johnny was standing there, grinning at her. He came toward her. His black eyes were shining and he was breathing rapidly. He loved her spirit and her temper. But they weren't going to laugh at him—not at Johnny. He grabbed her.

She pushed him away, carelessly. He thought he could take her, did he? Well, she would show him. He wasn't so much. She'd show him. She'd take *him,* that's what she'd do. He advanced toward her again. She allowed him to grab her again. Then she laughed at him, and with a ferocity that startled him she pulled him into the second little room of the shack where they had a mattress on an old bed spring.

Agocho walked to the beach of the inland sea and stood at the water's edge in the soft black mud. Behind him was the greasewood and before him was the dreary body of dead water. He saw none of it. His search was for the voices of the Gods that they might tell him why the curse of impotence had been put upon him and why all the egoistic world that he had built up had collapsed in an instant. He could find no answer. He asked, begged, and pleaded for it; he demanded it, and he defied the Gods to keep him in ignorance of their ways when he was an acknowledged supermortal and God-like person himself. This thing couldn't be. He refused to have it that way. But the Gods gave no answer. Though he stayed there all day they were deaf to his questions. At sunset he returned to the clearing. He ate his own supper and he stayed in the kowa. He heard Johnny come home in the Ford and he heard Maria's voice with Johnny's and once or twice he heard Maria laugh. He knew that she was laughing at him and it burned the core of his soul. He believed that he hated her more than any other person who had ever lived.

He was going to kill her. There was no further question about that. She had to die, but before he slit her throat he wanted to make one more attempt to revitalize his body. He let several days go by and he avoided any signs of violence. Maria stayed in the clearing and Johnny went to the Paul ranch and Mr. Paul managed to find a day's work for him.

Agocho prepared corn for tizwin, and after the proper amount of fermentation he filled a sumac bottle with the liquor. Once or twice a day he would get a glimpse of Maria. She never avoided him any more and he was sure that she wore few clothes and displayed her body just to taunt him and drive him crazy. She wouldn't have much longer to do that. When he was ready he would act and this time was going to settle everything. He would love killing her.

Johnny was liable to be around any time, but he wouldn't care about Johnny. He was going right through with this now regardless of anything or anybody.

Tizwin, he knew, had always been a cure, or part of a cure, for senility. For three days, before the liquor was ready, Agocho fasted, and on the morning of the fourth day he began to drink.

Johnny had noticed his preparations and so had Maria. She wanted to know what it meant.

"He's gonna get drunk," said Johnny.

"I hope he stays drunk," said Maria.

"He won't," said Johnny.

"I hope it kills him," said Maria.

"It won't," said Johnny.

"Huh," said Maria.

Johnny got in the Ford and drove north to see Mr. Carr. If Mr. Paul didn't have any work, Mr. Carr might have something for him to do. He told Maria to look out for Fig Tree. He might go a little crazy if he drank a lot of tizwin at once. She wasn't afraid. She was defiant. She was sure she could handle him. She was twenty-one and she thought Fig Tree must be eighty. He was really about sixty-five.

He sat beside the kowa and he filled a bowl with the grayish, rancid liquor and drank it. And in a few minutes he drank another bowl of it. His body had had no food for three days, and the tizwin felt warm and pleasant and he reacted to it at once.

It cheered him. He felt better and he wondered why he didn't make tizwin more often. For over an hour he sat still and drank. The gray mongrel came over toward him, sniffing and looking for garbage. He hated the dog. It sat down and scratched its flea bites, and Agocho let out a sudden, blood-curdling yell. The dog leaped to its feet and ran toward the shack. Maria came out and stood in front of the shack and looked across at Agocho. She stared at him and stood with her hands on her hips. Was he drunk already?

Agocho looked at her. He wasn't drunk, but he was feeling the tizwin and he was ready for a challenge. That red dress, standing there, staring across at him— how he despised that. He wondered if she would just stand there a few moments longer. If she would he had a clever idea. He reached into the kowa behind him with one hand and felt for the rifle. He found it, and still watching Maria, he slowly pulled the rifle to his side. He was afraid she would turn and go back into the shack, but she didn't. She stood there with her hands on her hips, an irritating figure, deserving to be shot. Quickly he sprang to one knee and threw the rifle to his shoulder and pulled the trigger.

She jumped as he did so, but there was no report. Agocho looked at the rifle and Maria went to the door of the shack. Just before going in she paused and stared at him again. He was examining the rifle. There were no cartridges in it. Somebody had sneaked in when he was away and emptied the magazine. Johnny. He threw the rifle back into the kowa and as he did so he heard Maria laugh. She went into the shack.

Agocho sat down again. Another humiliation. More
laughter. All his life he had hated to be laughed at.
He drank more tizwin. His head was light. He felt perfectly well, but just a little dizzy. He drank more tizwin
until he knew he was getting drunk. The world had been
his and the world was going to be his again. There was
no reason to wait. There was no reason for assaulting
that red dress. He didn't want satisfaction from her body
any more. He wanted satisfaction from killing her. To
see her die, that's what he wanted. It was just as well
that the rifle hadn't been loaded. That wasn't the way
to kill her. That was the way to kill an enemy in a fair
fight. This was different. This was killing for the pure
pleasure of doing it. A rifle would be too quick. A knife
was the thing. He drank more tizwin. He felt for the
knife, and he rose to his feet. Yes, the tizwin was good.
He was unsteady, but he was determined. His next act
would be to kill that girl and he would never stop until
he had done it. He was starting out to do that and nothing could prevent him. She couldn't. Johnny couldn't.
Time couldn't. He was going to win. He walked toward
the shack.

She saw him coming. She was almost glad.

"I hate him," she said aloud. "I hate him."

She had no plan. She had no preparations to combat
him. All she knew was that he was a senile old man and
she wasn't afraid of him. He better look out.

Agocho had no plan. He didn't need any. All he
wanted was to kill her, and kill her he would, and he
would never stop until he had cut her to pieces with the
knife that he held in his hand. He walked up to the
shack. She wasn't in sight. He stood before the door for

a moment and then he pushed it open. Still nothing happened. He walked into the shack and he stopped and looked around. There she was. She stood in the doorway between the two rooms. She was waiting there for him. She had a knife in her left hand and a wooden club in her right. She wasn't panic-stricken this time. She wasn't afraid of him any more. She didn't intend to run screaming from him again. This was different.

She watched him. He dared to come in, did he? He'd be sorry for that. She wouldn't back up—not an inch. She took a step forward. She held the knife close to her side and she raised the club.

"Get out," she said. "Get out of my house!"

He didn't answer; he didn't move; he watched her and he hesitated. Suddenly, without warning he gave that blood-curdling yell again, and he leaped toward her, the knife flashing in the air as he came. The suddenness surprised her and she dropped her knife and wielded the club with both hands. It struck him a glancing blow on the shoulder as he ducked under it. He tried to dodge below the blow and get in under her guard and drive the knife into her belly and rip it upward to her breast. The blow of the club staggered him and he went to his knees. She refused to retreat into the other room, but skipped around him as he slipped and raised the club again. Before he could get up she struck him over the head and he fell to the floor. She raised the club again and as she did he reached for her ankles. He grabbed her right foot and yanked her toward him. She partially fell, but swung the club and hit him on the side of the head. The blow forced him to let go of her foot and she leaped across the room.

They both paused. Agocho crawled to his knees. The right side of his head was bleeding. He still held on to his knife. He picked up the knife that she had dropped and he stuck it upright in the floor. They were both breathing heavily. They didn't make a sound. They watched each other every instant. She wasn't going to leave that room. She was better than he was and she knew it and she was going to beat him. He didn't hurry; he got to his feet slowly. There was all the time in the world. He had nothing to do but to kill her and it didn't matter whether it was this instant or an hour from now or when. All he knew was the fact that he was going to kill her.

He took a step toward her. She still had that club and she knew how to use it. He had to break through that guard somehow, and he would. He advanced—one step—two—and she clenched her teeth and raised the club. Then, instead of trying to rush in under her guard, he grabbed a chair and hurled it straight at her and immediately leaped after it, the knife held close to his side so that he could stab her low and rip it upwards. He wanted it to cut her as much as possible.

The chair struck her at the waist and fell to the floor. It hurt her, and in the fraction of a second that her attention was focused on it, he was in the air, leaping toward her. She held the club useless at her side and she dodged to the right as he thrust the knife at her. Then she kicked him in the groin with her left knee, driving it up as swiftly and as viciously as she could.

There was a sharp burning sensation on her left leg but she leaped away and swung the club again before she realized it. She drove the club down on his back and he seemed to slip under the force of the blow. She was afraid to stay and hit him again because of his knife, and she backed across the room. He got to his feet and leaned against the wall. He had almost gotten her that time. He would get her, if not now, later.

She stood on the other side of the room and watched him as he leaned against the wall. While they waited she realized that her leg hurt, and for the first time she understood that he had cut her with the knife and ripped the skirt of her dress and drawn blood.

That infuriated her. This loathsome, hated thing had dared to strike her, had actually cut her with a knife. She threw caution away. She swung the club and leaped toward him. She shrieked with fury and she wanted to kill him as much as he wanted to kill her.

He was glad to see her charge at him. That meant she was foolish; she had lost whatever good sense she had. He waited for her, but as she came she beat him over the arm with the club, knocking his knife to the floor. The blow stunned his arm and he struck at her with his other arm, hitting her in the mouth with his fist. She tried to hit him with the club again but he grappled with her. She tried to kick him again but he grabbed her around the throat with both hands and choked her. Slowly he bent her backwards and he choked her with an insane delight, for he was sure that he had her now. Her feet slipped out from under her, she dropped the club, and slipped to the floor. He didn't care whether he lost his balance or not. All he wanted was to keep that death grip on her throat. He fell over with her and they lay struggling on the floor. He exerted every bit of his strength to tighten that clutch on her throat. She couldn't breathe. She writhed and struggled but she couldn't break that grip. She grabbed his hair and pulled out a handful of it but still he wouldn't break it. Her face got black; her eyes couldn't see; she felt all her senses going numb. Then, vaguely, she remembered to kick. She even took time to wonder why she hadn't thought of it right away. She drew her right leg away from him, and then, swiftly, with all the strength she had left, she drove her knee into the pit of his stomach.

He grunted. It hurt him, and without knowing it he bent double as he lay on the floor, releasing the grip on her throat. It hurt him so much that he put both hands on his stomach. He thought he was going to vomit tizwin, but he lay there gasping for a moment instead.

Slowly Maria crawled away. She could hardly breathe. It hurt her to catch her breath. She knew she must get away from him quickly, but the best she could do was a crawl. She crawled half way across the room, and then slowly she pulled herself to her feet. She thought of his knife. It was lying on the floor beside him. If she had been smart she would have reached for it, she would have stabbed him with it. Now it was too late. He was reaching for it. It was going to start all over again. She looked at her dress. It was torn in several places. Her hands were smeared with blood. His blood. It was sickening. And there he was, struggling to his feet, the knife in his hand, advancing toward her again.

Suddenly she was afraid. She was panic-stricken and hysterical. All her courage born of hatred disappeared before fear. She couldn't fight him again. No—she was

afraid, afraid, afraid. He was terrible. And here he came,
blood running down his face, his eyes staring at her, the
knife in his hand. She couldn't bear it. She screamed and
turned and tried to run. She fell headlong over the chair
that he had thrown at her. He rushed at her, but he fell
over the chair, too. He was insane. He was crazy. She
couldn't fight a crazy man.

Screaming, and thrashing at him with her arms, she
crawled and clawed her way to the door. She managed
to pull it open and she half fell and half rolled out into
the clearing. He was coming. He had the knife. He was
on his hands and knees and he was crawling toward the
door. He was going to catch her again. She shrieked and
tried to scramble to her feet as he crawled out of the
door. He was coming. He would come anywhere. No
matter where—she couldn't escape him. She screamed
in terror and struggled to her feet. She was running.
That was all she knew—she was running. He was chasing
her and she was running. . . .

Johnny turned the Ford off the pavement and drove
over the sandy trail he had made through the greasewood. He drove into the clearing and at once he was
shocked to see Maria running and Agocho chasing her.
Instead of stopping the Ford he drove it straight across
the clearing at the two figures. Maria saw the car bounc-
ing along and she ran toward it. Johnny stopped the
Ford and jumped out as she came up. Her clothes were
torn, she was bloody, and incoherent. He stepped between her and the on-rushing Agocho but he was unprepared for the onslaught. He tried to stop Agocho by
grabbing his left arm, but Agocho, completely amuck,
struck at Johnny with the knife which he held in his

other hand, and drove it into Johnny's shoulder. It was a glancing blow and it struck below the collar bone and ran downward, and the force of the impact knocked Johnny down. Agocho held onto the knife. He didn't care about Johnny. It was Maria he must kill, and he leaped over Johnny and pursued her.

She ran around the Ford, making a circle until she came back to the spot where Johnny was getting to his feet. Blood was running down his body and staining his shirt and he was bewildered by the suddenness of the attack. Agocho was close behind Maria, and as she ran screaming past Johnny Agocho caught her. He drove the knife down at her and she shrieked with pain as it tore through her flesh and scraped the shoulder blade. She fell and Agocho fell over her, striking blindly and madly. He knew nothing but that he had her. Three times he drove the knife down at her, and twice he missed her. The third time he stabbed her in her left arm. Then he rolled over on top of her, grabbing her by the hair and pulling her head back. He wanted to hold her that way and he raised the knife intending to drive it again and again into her breast and throat when he was hit from behind and his first thrust drove the knife into the ground above Maria's head.

Johnny was on top of him and they fell over beside Maria. Johnny was trying to get the knife, and they rolled over on the ground, panting and gasping and fighting for the weapon. Agocho was completely insane and he fought with insane fury. Success, almost in his grasp, had been frustrated by another enemy, and he wanted to kill that enemy, too.

The knife was on the ground and neither Johnny nor Agocho could reach it. Maria lay beside it but she was hysterical with pain and fright and she was past reasoning. Agocho hit Johnny with his fists and they rolled apart. They both got to their feet at once. Johnny took a flying leap at Agocho and the force of the plunge carried Agocho over backwards with a crash against the running board of the car with Johnny on top of him. The blow injured Agocho's back and his head bumped against the body of the car dazing him. He sagged down in a heap and Johnny stood up, looking around for some means of tying Agocho until he was sane again. He went to Maria, and watching Agocho all the time, he lifted her to her feet. She couldn't stand and he had to hold her up. Agocho was crawling to his knees. He managed to get on his feet, and with a final effort, without a sound, he rushed at the pair of them, his eyes staring and his hands clutching.

Johnny stepped to one side, dragging Maria with him, and Agocho went rushing by. He went on for another ten steps and then crashed headlong to the ground, face down, and lay still. Johnny watched the panting body for an instant and then he dragged Maria toward the Ford. He had to lift her into it and then he ran around to the other side and climbed in behind the wheel. Maria was bleeding and the whole back of her bright red dress was stained dark red. She couldn't sit up in the car, but slumped over on Johnny. He was covered with blood, too, and his hands were sticky. He started the engine and drove the car around in a circle. It jolted and rattled and bumped across the rough ground.

Agocho lay almost in the center of the clearing and Johnny could see him as he swung the car around. Agocho hadn't moved. Johnny raced the car toward the sandy trail to the highway, drove into the greasewood, and disappeared.

Chapter XIX

NASARIA screamed as the green Ford bounced up to her shack. She thought that Johnny and Maria had been in an automobile accident. She thought they were both dying. Her screams brought Jose and Mr. Mack and Mrs. Mack and the Swedish servant woman. There was great excitement and everybody crowded around the Ford and crowded into the house and in a few minutes every one knew that Fig Tree John had done it.

They put Maria in Jose's and Nasaria's bed and George Mack went to the main house and telephoned to Coachella for a doctor while his wife and the Swedish woman tried to administer first aid. Johnny had a nasty cut but it didn't appear dangerous. Maria had been hurt badly. The knife wound in her back was deep and she suffered from shock and loss of blood. She was also wounded in the left leg and left arm and her body was badly bruised.

In an hour the doctor drove down from Coachella and dressed the wounds. He said that none of them would be fatal but he told them to keep Maria quiet and he said he would return the next day. By late afternoon the excitement began to calm down. The Swedish woman and Mrs. Mack went back to the main house, and George Mack tried to find out from Johnny just what it was all about. Johnny didn't seem to know, and

287

George Mack attributed it to one of the aberrations of "that Goddam bastard of a Fig Tree."

Maria's recuperation took longer than they had expected. She was in bed almost two weeks, which was a great inconvenience to Jose and Nasaria and again disrupted the schedule of their lives. During that time Johnny hung around the Mack ranch and slept part of the time in the tool shed or wherever he could find a place. He drove the car a few times for Mrs. Mack, but there was little for him to do. He went down to the clearing three days after the fight, driving very slowly and taking care not to aggravate his wound. He drove into the clearing and up to the shack.

Agocho was there. He was sitting before the kowa and he looked up and watched Johnny slowly climb out of the Ford.

Johnny came over toward him, but Agocho kept looking at the Ford. He wanted to be sure that Maria wasn't in it. Had she been he would surely have begun the battle all over again. But she wasn't, and he sat still and looked up at Johnny.

Johnny saw that the tizwin was all gone and that Agocho showed signs of the fight. There was dried blood on one side of his head and there were bruises and abrasions on his face and arms. He looked at Johnny with eyes that challenged.

"Where is the girl?" he asked.

"She's not here. She's in Mecca," said Johnny.

He was afraid that Agocho might go to the Mack ranch and start more trouble if he knew Maria was there.

"You nearly killed her," said Johnny.

"I will kill her," said Agocho.

"She's my wife," said Johnny.

Agocho didn't say anything. Johnny sat down beside him. The dog came over to him and sniffed him and dozens of flies circled in the air and buzzed around his head. Johnny sat for a little while and made a few casual remarks but either Agocho was getting deaf or he had nothing to say. Presently Johnny got up and went to the shack. He collected a few articles of clothing that belonged to Maria and then he got in the Ford and drove away. Agocho was still sitting before the kowa as Johnny turned the car and rode out of the clearing.

As the two weeks went by and Maria began to get better it was decided that she must go to Banning. Nasaria wrote to her sister Rosa and Rosa, who had a husband and four children, wrote back that Maria could come stay with her for a while. One day Jose called Johnny into the shack. Maria was still in bed and Nasaria was sitting beside her. Maria saw Johnny, but she looked away, and Johnny felt sorry. He didn't know what to say.

"Maria's going to Banning," said Jose.

Johnny didn't know much about Banning. It was somewhere to the north because the highway went there, but it was a strange place, a prohibitive name, a city that was bigger than any he had ever seen.

"All right," said Johnny.

They didn't have to tell him that he wasn't going to Banning. He knew that. The clearing was his home and it was the only place in which he had ever thought of living. There was no place for him in Banning and no reason for him to go there. He looked at Maria again but she wasn't looking at him. He felt a lump in his throat and he walked out of the room and out of the shack.

Her few possessions he brought up from the clearing, and two days later she said adios to Nasaria and Jose, and Johnny drove her to Coachella. There he took all the money he had out of the bank. It was more than he thought and it came to thirty-four dollars and twenty-seven cents. He bought her a bus ticket which left thirty-one dollars and two cents in cash and he gave all of it to her. He didn't need any money, but she was going to a strange place and she ought to have it.

They stood beside each other waiting patiently for the bus to arrive. It was a difficult moment. There was so much that might have been said and yet there were no words with which to say it. She was going away and he wouldn't see her again. While they waited a large, new, highly polished sedan drove by. It was one of the handsomest cars they had ever seen, and they both watched it out of sight.

"That's a pretty car," said Maria.

"Nice car, all right," said Johnny.

"Very pretty," said Maria.

Then there was a roaring, and the large gray bus swung off the highway and drew up beside the café and bus station. The driver got out and went into the café, but he left the motor purring and all the passengers kept their seats. Maria got in the bus and found an empty seat. She looked out at Johnny standing below her. There were strange words on the outside of the bus, and long afterwards Johnny remembered them. They were something like "El Paso, Phoenix, Yuma, El Centro, Los Angeles"—magic names, like Banning, full of a significance that Johnny did not understand.

The driver came out of the café. He hopped into the bus and closed the door. The engine roared, the bus moved away, and Johnny stood watching it gain speed on the highway while he stood in the stench of its burnt gasoline. When it had disappeared he went back to his little green Ford car and drove south to the clearing.

Through the hot summer Johnny lived in the clearing. He rarely went to the Mack ranch or the Paul ranch. There was no work and he missed Maria and he disliked being around the Mack ranch where he had been used to seeing her. He thought of her every day, thought of how she had looked, how she had felt, how her voice had sounded. He loved her very much.

He and Agocho had little to do with each other. Often they ate together, but Johnny lived in the shack and Agocho lived in the kowa and sometimes they would say but a few words to each other all day.

Agocho lived only for himself. Though he had not killed the girl he had driven her away and if she ever came back or if he could find her he would complete the attempt. He roamed very little. His vision was not as good as it had been and he found that he could not hear as well. He rode up to the ranch country a few times and he reconnoitered about the Mack ranch and the Paul ranch. He had an idea that Maria might be there, though probably she wasn't because Johnny seemed to have no interest in going there any more. At times Agocho thought that Johnny was swinging back to his race. He was less like a white man than he had been for several years. He had even given up using the automobile. It stood in the clearing all summer and Johnny never touched it. Pretty soon it would fall apart. Agocho thought of trying to smash it but that would have been a lot of work.

The fall months came and Johnny continued to let the days slide by with no variation. He was lethargic and he avoided the ranches. There was no point in working. There was no incentive. He had a Ford—no reason to work for that. Maria was gone—no reason to work for her. And as for money—that wasn't worth working for at all. He did nothing.

Once or twice he went up to see Jose and Nasaria, but they had heard nothing of Maria and it made Johnny homesick for her. Nasaria said she would write to Maria and Rosa sometime when she got around to it, but when Maria had been gone six months she hadn't yet gotten around to it. Mr. Paul saw Johnny and offered him a job but Johnny wouldn't take it. Mr. Paul wondered if Johnny were reverting to type, and Agocho was certain that his son was gradually becoming an Apache again. And that was the way everything should be.

December became January, and Johnny almost forgot the months in those terms and mentioned them as Sos-nalh-tus and Itsa Bi-zhazh. One day in January when the desert was pleasant he had been away from the clearing all day. He had no gasoline or oil for the Ford and no money with which to buy it, so the Ford had stood still for a long time and Johnny traveled by horse again. He had pushed the Ford close to the rear of the shack and the chickens lived in it and under it and Johnny had no desire to drive it any more. Let the chickens use it for a roost.

He rode back into the clearing in the afternoon. Agocho was sitting, squatting, in the sun before the kowa. He was muttering and mumbling to himself. The gray mongrel greeted Johnny, but Agocho did not. Either he was not aware of him or preferred to ignore him and to concentrate on his thoughts. Johnny left the horse near the shack and walked over toward Agocho. He stood looking down at his father, a decrepit brown figure in a loosely fitting jacket of coyote hide, a wrinkled skin getting flabby over a shrinking body, gray hair becoming a dirty white, a great mind that once knew everything becoming queer and misunderstanding and distorting all it saw—bitter, vindictive, religious—squatting and waiting and mumbling, nothing any more but something for flies to buzz around. Presently Agocho looked at Johnny's feet and slowly raised his eyes to stare at Johnny's face. His son might have been a stranger. Agocho seemed not to recognize him. They looked at each other for a moment, and then Johnny sat down. After some time Agocho spoke.

"He was here," he said.

Agocho was given more and more to making meaningless remarks. His speech was often difficult to follow. Johnny didn't pay much attention to it. He didn't care. Agocho didn't say anything more for a while. Then he talked about Ste-na-tlih-a and prayers and offerings. And after that he said again, "He was here."

"Who?" said Johnny, not expecting an answer.

"Paul," said Agocho.

"What for?" asked Johnny.

"Wants you work for him. He wrote it down on paper for you and left it."

This was strange—Mr. Paul taking the trouble to come down to the clearing and writing a message for Johnny.

"Where is it?" asked Johnny.

Agocho pulled a letter out from under a blanket and handed it to Johnny. Johnny took it. He knew that Agocho was wrong. He hadn't understood. This was a regular letter. This wasn't a note from Mr. Paul. He read the address.

> MR. JOHNNY MACK
> CARE FIG TREE JOHN
> CARE MR. PAUL
> MECCA, CALIFORNIA
> PLEAS FORRWARD

It was stamped and sealed and it wasn't from Mr. Paul at all. It had come in his care and that was why he had brought it.

Never in his life had Johnny received a letter. It was a new and strange experience. Agocho watched him. Johnny tore the envelope and slowly and carefully he extracted the letter. It had to be unfolded and then it had to be turned right side up.

Agocho was disgusted with this performance and he felt superior to it. He couldn't read or write and he couldn't see the need of it. By the way Johnny was staring at it he could tell that Johnny wasn't very good at it. He watched Johnny closely as his eyes moved from one word to the next. After a while he came to the end of it, but he turned the sheet over and there was more on the other side. Johnny read it without reacting, and what it all might mean Agocho could not imagine.

When Johnny finished it, he began all over again. He read it through three consecutive times, and as he did so he sat up straight, his features brightened, and he read with more and more interest. He grinned. He smiled. He muttered and ejaculated to himself.

Suddenly Agocho knew. It came to him in a flash and he wondered why he had not known it all the time. He was not used to letters and writing or he would have known sooner.

Her—it was from her. She was saying something on that piece of paper and Johnny was understanding it. She was outwitting him. She was being clever. They thought that he would never know. He knew. A ruse like this couldn't fool him. Surely she wasn't coming back here again. That couldn't be it. And if she were trying to get Johnny to leave. . . .

Johnny won't leave. He can't leave now. He's not white. He is Apache again. Nothing can take Johnny away again. She can't take him away. Johnny would be better dead than white. He would rather kill Johnny than see him slip away again. He would kill Johnny first.

Suddenly Johnny was on his feet. He took a deep breath. "Ee-yah!" he said. He held the letter in his hand and he looked down at Agocho. Their gaze met and they stared at each other. Johnny's smile disappeared. He looked at Agocho and Agocho looked defiance back at him. Johnny couldn't tell how much Agocho knew. It didn't make any difference. Nothing could stop this. Nothing could stop him now. Nothing. Nobody.

He turned and ran toward the shack. Agocho got to his feet. Whatever was going on must stop. Johnny must never leave the clearing for a white girl. Slowly and deliberately he walked after Johnny.

Before he got to the shack Johnny turned. He wasn't going in. He ran around to the rear, to the Ford. He rushed up to it and the chickens clucked and scattered in several directions. He pulled and tugged at the Ford. He turned the steering wheel and he got behind the car and pushed. There was no gasoline in it; the battery was dead; two of its tires were flat and the other two were soft. No matter. It would run. He could get gasoline. Jose would give him some. Mr. Paul would give him some. The thing to do was to get the Ford ready. He could put anything he wanted in it. He could leave any time; he could leave to-night. He pushed the car around to the front of the shack. It stood facing the sandy trail that led to the highway.

Agocho came up behind him. He grabbed Johnny by the arm and looked him in the face.

"No," he said with conviction.

Johnny hesitated. How could he explain this? He couldn't. There was no use trying. His father had better let go of him. He'd better not try to understand this.

"No," said Agocho.

Johnny couldn't answer. He was excited. He was thrilled. He was breathing rapidly and he could feel his heart beating. It wasn't from the effort of pushing the Ford. It wasn't that. It was happiness, and nothing could stop it and nothing was going to.

He took Agocho's arm and he shook it loose. He had to yank it loose for Agocho's grip was tight. He stepped back from Agocho and he smiled. He caught his breath and the smile became a laugh. "Yes!" he wanted to yell at Agocho. Yes—yes—yes. But that was useless. That would do no good. He turned and ran into the shack.

There were some things he could take with him—another pair of pants and another shirt. He could put them in the Ford. There were some blankets and a few kitchen utensils. She might like to have those. He had to get some gasoline first, but still he could load the car now. He wanted to pack it up right away.

He stopped. There was a crash outside. Immediately there was another. Johnny rushed to the door and leaped out. Agocho had picked up an ax and he was smashing the hood of the Ford. He gritted his teeth and smashed the ax down on the hood again, swung it up immediately and brought it down again. He had broken the hood, bent it in two and cracked it. So far he hadn't hit any of the machinery beneath it. He was going to wreck the car. He was going to smash it to pieces.

He looked up at Johnny and he smashed the hood again. Johnny rushed at him. He must *not* smash it. He must let that Ford alone.

Agocho turned. He stood still, watching Johnny, ready to swing the ax again. Johnny stopped. They glared at each other. It was the finish. It was going to be one or the other. There was no reconciliation now. This was the end. Slowly Johnny came toward Agocho and slowly Agocho raised the ax. . . .

PART III
1928

1928

MRS. PAUL wanted to know if her husband had found Johnny Mack. She thought he was foolish to waste his time and go all the way down to the Indian camp just to take Johnny a letter that couldn't be of any importance. Johnny was usually around the ranch every once in a while, not as much, of course, as when he had worked for them, but nevertheless he was around every now and then. He was a nice Indian boy, was Johnny, but that father of his was an old devil and you never knew what he might take it into his head to do next; and while she wasn't nervous, she kept looking out of the house to see if there were any signs of Mr. Paul returning.

When she had looked out a dozen times in the last fifteen minutes she finally saw him come in from the salt grass near the inland sea, turn into the grove of date palms and walk toward the ranch house. She breathed easier.

He went to the pump house and he was busy for almost an hour before he came into the kitchen and walked through to the living room. He sat down and glanced at a newspaper and put it aside without reading it. He was getting accustomed to his glasses and it was a strain to read without them. He wondered where he had left them—probably in the bedroom.

"Did you see Johnny?" asked Mrs. Paul.

"No. He wasn't there. I saw Fig Tree, though, and I guess he'll give Johnny the letter."

"Did he say anything?"

"Not much. You know it was that old bastard after all who stole the sun-dial?"

"It was!"

"Yeah—he ruined it so I left it there."

"That Fig Tree!" said Mrs. Paul, clicking her tongue against her teeth. "I'd like to take a rolling pin to him. He's a good-for-nothing thief. Isn't there something that can be done about him?"

"No—not now. He's about done for. Fig Tree's pretty old now."

"How old do you suppose he is?"

"Oh, he looks a hundred, but you can't tell. He might not be over seventy. He might hang on for a long time. They're pretty tough, I guess."

"Well, I don't want him coming around here, and I don't want Johnny Mack around here either. Johnny's all right, but if he comes here Fig Tree will come, and that means trouble."

"Well, I need a hand and Johnny is cheap and willing —or he used to be. I don't know what's got into him lately. Doesn't seem to want to work. I told Fig Tree I had a job for Johnny and I tried to drive the idea into his head but whether he'll tell Johnny or not I don't know. If he doesn't show up in a few days I'll get a Mexican."

"You better get a Mexican to-morrow and forget it."

"Maybe I will," said Mr. Paul. Then he found his glasses case in his hip pocket, and the glasses were in it, so he put them on and began to read the paper.

The next day came and went and there was no Johnny. The second day went by and on the third Paul hired a Mexican to work by the day. Then he forgot Johnny, but on the fifth day after he had delivered the letter to the clearing, Johnny appeared.

He rode up to the ranch on horseback early in the morning, and Paul, who had just finished breakfast, walked out of the kitchen door as Johnny dismounted.

"Want job," said Johnny, before Paul could speak.

"Hello there," said Paul. "You're a little late. I didn't think you wanted to work very much."

"Sure," said Johnny. "Want job."

"Well, I got a little work you can do; not much now because I thought you weren't going to show up and I hired a man."

"Don't want much," said Johnny. "Only about three days, maybe."

"Say, what happened? Did you fall off your horse?" Paul pointed to a cut on the side of Johnny's head. "Horse throw you?"

"No," said Johnny.

"What did you do to your head?"

"Ax," said Johnny.

"Christ sake," said Paul, "that was a nasty wallop."

"Want money to get gas," said Johnny. "Want to get gas for Ford car."

"If you're out of gas I'll let you take a gallon home with you to-night."

"All right," said Johnny. "Work three days."

"Is that all you want to work—three days?"

Johnny hesitated. He could see no point in working any longer than that.

"How much you give me?" he asked.

"Well, you can keep busy around here, Johnny, if you want to, off and on now, up until—oh, March, I guess."

"No. Gonna go away," said Johnny. "Three days' work."

"All right, have it your own way. I'll pay you five dollars for three days—three *full* days, understand."

"Sure," said Johnny.

"Where do you think you're going—hunting?"

"Banning," said Johnny. "Work there."

"Is your wife there?"

"Yes," said Johnny.

"Well, I'm glad to hear that, Johnny. I hope you get a good job there. That's just fine. That's what you ought to do. What did she say in her letter?"

Johnny pulled the letter out of his pocket and handed it to Mr. Paul. He had read the letter so many times that it was crumpled and soiled, but he enjoyed it and he wanted Mr. Paul to understand. Paul took it.

15 de Enero, 1928

DEAR JUANITO:

I thought you might want to know how I got up to Banning. I got here alright. It is a nice place and I am going to have a baby next month. Do you remember when? I do. You should be here when it is christened because you should be. Maybe it will be a Juanito, because it belongs to you and you should be glad. If you come up here my sister is Rosa Seguro and her husband is Francisco Seguro and he says you could work here. There are apples and cherries and almonds and you could work. Dates aren't everything. There are ranches here tambien. Come up, Juanito.

Yours truly,

MARIA.

Mr. Paul handed back the letter and smiled at Johnny.

"Well, well, well," he said. "Well, well, well. I guess it looks like you are going to Banning all right."

"Sure," said Johnny.

"Now listen here, Johnny," said Mr. Paul. "You work for me for three days and I'll give you five dollars. Then I'll fill up your Ford with gasoline and oil and you can go clear to Banning on that and have five dollars in your pocket when you get there. Now let's see: the first thing for you to do is to get out there and show that Mexican how to work. He thinks he's building a new roof on the pump house so you go see it's done right."

"Sure!" said Johnny, with a grin.

He started to turn away, but Mr. Paul stopped him.

"And Johnny—one more thing. You've got to keep Fig Tree John off this ranch or you can't work here at all."

"All right," said Johnny.

"Understand? No Fig Tree. He can't come here."

"Sure," said Johnny.

"Does he know you're going away? Does he want to go to Banning?"

"No," said Johnny.

"He's going to raise some hell."

"No, he won't," said Johnny, and his smile faded and he looked down at the ground. He hadn't intended to talk about Fig Tree at all, but now Mr. Paul had started it.

"Yes he will," said Mr. Paul.

"Can't now," said Johnny.

"Why not?"

Johnny hesitated. All this kind of thing was what white men always did and was so unnecessary. Why talk about it?

"He's dead," said Johnny.

"What! Fig Tree dead? How did it happen?"

Johnny hesitated again. He put the crumpled letter in his pocket. Then he looked up at Mt. Paul.

"He just died," he said, slowly. Then he turned away toward the pump house. "Got to fix new roof," he said, and he walked away.

Mr. Paul watched him go and then he went back into the kitchen to tell it all to Mrs. Paul.

Johnny was sorry that Agocho had to be discussed. He never wanted to mention him again. That would be much better than going over it all. He could have explained it all to Mr. Paul but it was something he didn't want to explain.

Why recount that battle for the ax and that final violence when Agocho tried to kill him and that last bloody scene over the Ford? What was the good of talking about that? Why should he want to remember fighting for the ax, and getting it, and swinging it, and that look on his father's face as the ax came down—no, no use in telling all that.

And then Mr. Paul wasn't an Apache and he would never understand what had to be done next. He might understand burying the body out in the greasewood where that other grave had been, where Johnny had sat for days when he was a little boy. He might think that was all right. But he would never understand why Johnny couldn't come to work right away, why Johnny

had to sit for four days beside his father's grave while
the spirit went to heaven on the Milky Way. And he
would never know that only a few rocks could be placed
on the grave at first because the spirit has to rise through
the grave, and if there were a lot of rocks put on it at
once the spirit might have trouble in rising from the
ground; especially as this spirit was not that of a strong
warrior, but only that of an old man. He would never
understand those things. They were Apache. Johnny
wasn't Apache, but Agocho had been, and that ceremony
had to be right.

Johnny was white now. He had thought it all out very
carefully as he sat out there in the greasewood. The
Apache Gods would hate him. He had defied them; he
had killed his father. That was unpardonable, but what
made it a heinous crime was that he had killed his
father when his father had been fighting for what was
right. The Gods knew that; and Agocho knew that.
Neither the Gods nor Agocho's spirit would ever forgive
him. He was forever a pariah. He was white. He would
never dare think of Ste-na-tlih-a again. But he could
pray to Virgin Mary. He had her. He had something.
Yes, but he had more than that. He had himself. He
had Johnny Mack. That's what he had. He had himself,
who was himself, and would be true to himself in the
face of any God—all Gods—Ste-na-tlih-a, Virgin Mary,
what names you please, he was Johnny Mack and he
was going to be loyal to Johnny Mack.

And if some final God had created him, he had created
him with that reasoning power potential in his mind,
and as long as he was true to the very essence of him-

self, true to that power to know, how could he be wrong? What God can defy his own work?

What God would create something imperfect? None. That wouldn't be the work of God at all. He knew he was right. He knew it here by this grave in the grease-wood. For he was a creator himself. And in creation is Godliness. That's what Godliness is—power. Here were the graves of his father and his mother. They had created him. They had been Gods then. They had made him. And then he had found Maria, and now he and Maria had made life. They were creators, all of them; Gods, all of them. And then when this little God that he and Maria had made grew up, he would create, too; and he would create in his own way, and no other God must interfere. Even he and Maria who had made him, must forego their superiority then, for that would be his moment, not theirs, and they must recognize that.

Perhaps that wasn't Apache; perhaps that wasn't white. Ste-na-tlih-a and Virgin Mary might both disapprove of that. But that was Johnny Mack, and Johnny Mack was a God, too.

At the end of three days' work on the Paul ranch Johnny was ready to go. Mr. and Mrs. Paul had been very kind. Mr. Paul gave him ten dollars instead of five but he said that the second five was a present for the baby. Mrs. Paul gave him several packages of clothing for Maria, and Nasaria and Jose were delighted. Nasaria sent the baby a crucifix, and they promised to drive to Banning as soon as the baby was born.

To Jose Johnny gave the horses and to Nasaria he gave the goat. Everything else of any value he could take with him. The broken hood of the engine he threw away; the tires were fixed; and Mr. Paul filled the car with gasoline and oil.

With everything ready he drove down to the clearing for the final loading. The clothes and packages he stowed away on the seat. The bed spring and mattress he lashed to the side of the car. Clothes, cooking utensils, a shovel, a lamp, and a heterogeneous collection of possessions he put on the floor and in the rear. The chickens he rounded up and stowed in the rear, too. The gray mongrel he put beside him on the seat. With the little green Ford car loaded to the gills he raced the noisy engine and backed it around until it faced the sandy trail to the highway. He stopped the car beside the spring, and with the motor still running, he got out and walked into the greasewood.

He went to his father's grave. The spirit had risen long since. He found more rocks and he placed them on the mound of sand, four of them in a row. Then he went back to the Ford and drove out of the clearing for the last time, bumped over the sandy road, and onto the highway.

He passed the road into the Mack ranch and he waved to Nasaria and Jose standing before their shack and they waved back. Up the desert road he drove, through Coachella, Indio, and on into a country he had never seen before.

Every motorist on the highway looked at his ridiculous outfit and he was pleased. He was stared at and he liked it. Occasionally as they sped by they tooted their horns at him and smiled, and when they did he waved at them in reply for the horn on his car wouldn't work. But he never waved unless another car saluted him first. He drove on in the desert sun and the warm wind blew in his face and he was happy.

THE END